EDEN

Jamie McGuire

Published by
Jamie McGuire, LLC
Enid, OK 73707

ISBN-10: 1475145578
ISBN-13: 978-1475145571

Cover by JustinMcClure.tv
Edited by Jim Thomsen

Second Edition

For Mimi.

Thank you for being there for us in every way you knew how.
For your support, love, and your smiles.

For Beth.

You said I could, and you always have.

Chapter One
Tomorrow

Happily Ever After. That was The End, right? The hard part was over. It was smooth sailing now. I lay in bed next to my handsome, celestial Prince Charming, the tropical breeze blowing through the window screens of our little Caribbean hut, waiting for the sun to rise so I could begin my wedding day.

Funny how Happily Ever After isn't the end after all…at least, not when Hell is trying to kill you.

That trivial little fact was easy to ignore with the light rain tapping the tin roof, and the palm fronds brushing against our casita as the wind gently pushed its way through the trees. The first glimmers of sunlight danced along the ceiling as translucent dashes of warmth. Those shuddering, glowing dots above me were the first thing I saw when I opened my eyes. Jared Ryel was the second. He smiled, waiting for my eyes to focus.

"It's tomorrow," he whispered.

Splatters of pinks and purples had just breached the windows, and the rain had all but left us for the bigger island, reduced to droplets. The fading purple splotches on Jared's forehead, cheek and chin stood out in the early light, and they brought back a flood of memories from the days before.

He and I had already survived the impossible—coming face to face with one of the most frightening beings in Hell and a few hundred of his minions, human and demon alike. Simply celebrating another day would have sufficed. That was the moment realization hit, and Jared's eyes brightened with amusement as my sleepy expression perked.

"It's today?" I said softly. I reached up to touch his skin, and the residual marks from his skirmish with Shax.

Jared pushed himself onto his elbows, and then leaned his head closer to my stomach. "Good morning, little Bean."

"Bean?" I said, one eyebrow shooting up.

"Yes, she's no bigger than a bean. That's what the book says, anyway."

"The book."

Jared reached to the floor, pulling up a thick book, its cover dripping in hideous pastel colors and childish writing.

"I thought I should be prepared for anything that might come up." Jared flipped through the pages, and then peered up at me, waiting for approval.

"Is there a chapter on balance-disrupting angel babies?" I said, grinning when Jared's eyebrows pushed together.

He tossed the book to the floor and then playfully situated himself over me, nuzzling my neck.

"Jared!" I squealed, making a poor attempt to push him away. "Stop!"

"I'll stop if you say it," he said, his voice muffled against my skin.

"Say what?" I laughed, wiggling in vain.

Jared lifted his head to look me in the eyes. "Bean," he said, his eyes a soft blue-gray.

I pressed my lips together, forming a hard line, but when he tickled me again, I caved. "Okay!" I pleaded. "Bean!"

A wide grin spread across his face. "I wish I'd known how well this tactic of persuasion works on you three years ago. Life would have been somewhat easier."

I swatted at him, knowing he would duck. "Not fair."

Jared kissed my lips, his warmth soaking into my skin. It didn't seem as warm as usual, but I attributed it to the tropical heat raising my own temperature.

"You know what's not fair? I don't get to see you until this afternoon." He left me alone on the bed, pulling a white T-shirt over his head.

"What do you mean?" I said, pushing up on my elbows.

"You'd better get dressed, sweetheart. We're expecting company in five minutes."

"Company?"

Jared tossed a tan summer dress to the bed, and I scrambled to put it on, knowing better than anyone that Jared wasn't mistaken about things like time. I pulled my hair into a messy ponytail, and then stood awkwardly while Jared opened the tin door. A line of villagers made their way to our casita, led by a frazzled-looking Beth. She held a white garment bag, and when her eyes met mine, her smile widened to its limit.

"Beth!" I said, rushing down the steps. Mud squished between my bare toes as I ran to her, enveloping her in my arms. Her auburn hair was damp, plastered to her forehead and cheeks. She was sweaty and red-faced, trying to catch her breath as Chad pulled the garment bag from her fingers.

"She wouldn't let anyone else carry it," he said, shaking his head. He held the bag out for Jared, but Beth quickly grabbed it back, smacking his hand away.

"Jared can't see it!" she said. She held the long bag up, away from the mud, but behind her to protect it from Jared's hands.

Jared was amused. "I won't look, Beth. I'm going to take Chad to the chapel now. You two have the whole day."

I shouldn't have been surprised—Jared could arrange anything—but I was speechless. Beth and Chad had arrived just eight hours after us.

"How did you…?" I began.

Jared's smile widened. "We've taken care of everything. I didn't want you stressed."

"We…?" I frowned, more confused.

"Mom is waiting for me at the chapel. See you there." He grinned from ear to ear. I'd never seen him so happy. He leaned down to kiss my cheek, and then gestured for Chad to follow.

"You've maneuvered a motorcycle before?"

Chad paused. "Yeah. Why?"

"It's a bit of a drive." Jared patted Chad on the shoulder, encouraging him along. Poor Chad seemed totally out of his element. Even though the men weren't that close, I had full confidence in my husband-to-be to make Chad feel at ease. That responsibility would serve as double duty to soothe Jared's nerves.

"Wait 'til you see this dress!" Beth squealed, pulling me inside. She hooked the bag onto a wooden lip above the closet, and then rubbed her sore shoulder. "It was a long, muddy walk."

"It is," I nodded. "Would you like me to get some ice for your shoulder?"

Beth's eyes lit up again. She pulled down the zipper of the garment bag, turning to me.

I blinked in disbelief. "That's the…um…"

Beth's eyes were wild with excitement. "The dress from the magazine that you picked out two years ago? Yes!"

"But...how is it here? How did he…."

Beth couldn't wait for me to spit out the words. "I have been hanging on to this thing forever! Can you believe it?

Lillian brought it to the apartment. She said you had picked it out, and Jared bought it, and they made me bottle this up for two years! It was awful! Why do you think I hounded you about a wedding date all those times?"

"But…why?"

Beth nodded. "I know, right? That's what I said. His mom said he was excited; he wanted to surprise you, blah, blah, blah. I personally think he just wanted to torture me because it's been hell."

I couldn't stop staring at the flowing, silky whiteness in front of me. I remembered sitting on our couch in the loft while I healed, thumbing through magazines with Lillian and pausing on a picture, unable to turn the page. It was just days after I was discharged from the hospital, the day Claire left to eliminate all the humans that threatened us. A dress identical to the one I showed a partisan interest in almost two years earlier dangled from a hanger just feet from me.

"Beth?" I said, still staring at the dress.

"Yes?"

"You're going to have to take it down a few notches. I'm feeling a little overwhelmed."

Beth's head bobbed quickly, and then she took a seat in the corner. After a deep breath, she began again, "It's beautiful."

I almost asked Beth if she knew why Lillian didn't keep the dress at her house, but it was a foolish question. Beth was safe. No one would blow up her apartment, or bust through her windows in the middle of the night—and it would give Jared an extra ally in vying for a wedding date.

"He's brilliant," I said, in awe.

"What?"

"Nothing."

Beth gripped her knees and bit her lip, struggling with every passing second. "Are you still overwhelmed?"

"I'm feeling better."

She leaned forward in her seat, quickly losing the fight to remain composed. "I brought two bags overflowing with makeup, hairspray and curling irons. I think I have every size known to man. I can make big barrel curls, or little spiral curls. If you don't want curls I brought a flat iron…."

"Beth?"

"Sorry."

"You take a Valium. I'll take a shower...wait. Is it ridiculous that I don't know what time my wedding starts?"

"One o'clock. We have plenty of time."

I nodded, grabbing my robe and a towel. I couldn't imagine how difficult the wait must have been for her. It was endearing and disturbing at the same time.

Under the warm stream of the casita's humble shower, it wasn't difficult to let go of any anxiety. Birds sang to each other from the branches of the palm trees, and the sounds of the ocean gave away its close proximity. Feeling stressed in paradise was wonderfully impossible.

"Did you want an up-do? I brought bobby pins just in case!" Beth called.

"Not listening!" I said, massaging shampoo into my hair. I wondered if she was curious about Jared's fading bruises, or if she'd even noticed. Surely Chad would. If they spent the morning together, eventually he would see them. Jared would explain them away, but if Beth asked me about them and I told a different story, it would complicate things. It was easy to convince her that I needed a bodyguard—she'd witnessed my run-in with Mr. Dawson, after all. Unless it was due to training, Jared's bruises were a telltale sign that I had been in danger. Two years of experience told me that

Beth was too preoccupied with wedding details, so I put that worry to the back of the line.

Thinking of Jared's bruises made the rest of his face form in my mind, and suddenly I couldn't get out of the shower fast enough. It made me feel anxious to wait so long before I was allowed to see him again.

I rushed into the casita in my towel, my hair dripping wet, and slipped on the sleeves of my robe.

"What are you doing?"

"I'm just going for a walk," I said, slipping on a pair of sandals.

"Oh, no, you're not. We have a day's worth of primping to do in just a few hours! Get your backside in this chair, young lady!" Beth said.

"I'll just be a minute," I said, waving her away. I swung open the door of the casita to find Bex standing in my way.

"Morning," he smiled. "Going somewhere?"

"Just for a walk," I shrugged.

"Don't you have some girly things to do? You're getting married in a few hours."

I frowned. "Are you here to keep me captive?"

Bex mirrored my expression. "No, Paranoid Schizo. Your guardian-slash-almost husband is across the island, and you and your unborn baby are two of Hell's Most Wanted. I'm here to keep you safe. If you wanna leave, leave. I have to walk with you, though."

"Oh," I said, feeling silly. "Okay, then. I want to leave."

Beth grabbed my wrist, a hair dryer in her other hand. "I jumped on a plane at a moment's notice. I rode a boat across an unknown body of water—in the pouring rain. There is mud caked under my newly painted toenails, and I'm pretty sure a bird crapped in my hair on the walk here. I've endured all this to come here and help you get ready for a wedding that I've kept a secret for two years. You can give me a few hours!"

"Okay! You're right, I'm sorry," I said. I followed Beth back into the casita, sitting in the chair she'd placed in front of a makeshift salon counter.

"Whoa," Bex said, sitting on the bed. "Girls are crazy."

The counter was covered in wires that led to various hot irons, makeup, brushes, curlers, combs and hair products. The black wires were hooked into an orange extension cord that led outside to the solar-powered generator Jared had rigged outside. The mess of wires were an eyesore, but at least we had power without the annoying drone of a gas-powered generator. Beth brought several lamps to make up for the limited natural light filtering through the windows, and a manicure and pedicure kit. A large camera also sat among the clutter, beside two packages of fresh memory cards for her camera.

"Thank you, Beth," I said. The planning alone had to have been time-consuming.

"That's what best friends do."

After hours of combing, scrubbing, powdering and polishing, I was finally ready to slip on my wedding dress.

"I'll step outside," Bex said. "I need some fresh air, anyway."

"Good idea," I smiled. "No telling what that much hairspray will do to a young man's lungs."

Beth waited for Bex to leave, and then sighed. "We have to wait to put on your dress," she said, fidgeting.

"You're joking," I said. I took a step toward my dress, but Beth ran around me, holding her arms up and out, shielding the dress from my hands.

"I'm not! I'm not joking. We're waiting."

I frowned. "You're losing it, Beth," I said, sitting in the chair in a huff.

"You look beautiful," she smiled.

"I'm used to being in the dark for the most part, but on my wedding day, I would like to be in the know."

"I understand," Beth said, thick with regret. "It's just that…."

A small knock at the door immediately changed Beth's demeanor. "Coming!" she said, relieved.

Cynthia stood in the doorway. As usual, her face was devoid of emotion. "Well?" she called behind her. "Put my things in the adjacent building. Thank you." Her tone was opposite her words—also her usual.

"Mother," I said, surprised.

She wore a champagne-colored sheath dress. Even after marching through a tropical rain shower and the mud in six-inch heels, her dress and matching shoes were immaculate. Her hair was pulled back into its usual tight French bun, making her eyes even more severe when she pulled of her sunglasses and huffed.

"I apologize for my lateness, Nina dear. I had several functions to reschedule, since my presence was demanded at such late notice."

"Sorry," Beth and I said at the same time.

"Well," she sighed. "You are my only daughter. We do what we must." I smiled, and Cynthia took the few steps to offer a cold embrace. The awkward gesture was the most she could offer; knowing that made me appreciate it more than others might have. She quickly let go, and offered a polite smile. "You look wonderful, dear."

"Thank you. I was just about to step into my dress…."

"Oh. Well, then, I'll just step out," Cynthia said.

I fidgeted. "Would you mind helping?"

Cynthia hesitated. "Er…Isn't that why Beth is here?"

"No," Beth smiled. "We've been waiting for you."

Cynthia's eyes scanned my dress and its yards of white silk, and clouded with tears. "Oh, my," she whispered, pulling a tissue from her purse.

I was taken aback. Cynthia rarely cried. In fact, she'd only found two occasions in my lifetime for it, and both had more to do with my father.

"It's okay, Mother," I said, hesitating to find an appropriate place to comfort her. I settled on her shoulder, patting awkwardly a few times.

She sniffed once, lifting her chin to ward off the uninvited emotion. "It's just that Silk Charmeuse wrinkles so easily."

I nodded. "I know."

After one last dab at her eyes with the tissue, she turned. "Beth best assist you, darling. Call for me when you're dressed." She closed the door behind her, and I turned to Beth.

"I'm so sorry," Beth whispered. "I thought…I waited for her because I thought she'd like to be involved. I should have known better. Now you both just feel awkward."

"It was worth a try. One never knows with Cynthia. She might have been insulted if I hadn't asked, so you did the right thing."

"Did I?"

I smiled. "You did. Now help me get this thing on, and let's not let it wrinkle. I don't want to upset my mother."

Beth nodded, and carefully pulled the dress from its hanger. "Neither do I."

Chapter Two
Promises

"She was right," Beth said, tears in her eyes. "It does wrinkle easy."

I nodded, staring at my reflection in the full-length mirror Beth had brought for the occasion. The woman staring back at me was soft and mature, draped in the muted sheen of silk and chiffon. Beth wasn't human after all; only magic could have transformed me into the elegant, graceful creature in the mirror.

Soft, blonde curls caressed my shoulders, and just a hint of blush and pink lip gloss reminded me that I had makeup on at all. Beth had spent hours making sure that I appeared timeless and natural.

Beth clapped her hands together and held them tight to her chest, as impressed at her work as I. "Jared is going to crap!"

I laughed. "I knew eventually Oklahoma would break free from the professional East Coast stylist role you've played today!"

Beth gathered the tools she used to transform me, rolling wires and putting the various bags of makeup into the different tubs the villagers had carried to the casita. I stood in place, afraid to move. The realization hit that the church was miles away, across a muddy jungle, and I was wearing white.

I blanched. "Oh, God. Cynthia will stroke out if this dress is soiled before the wedding."

"If she can get here without a speck, I'm sure she can get you to the church mud-free."

"You're probably right," I nodded, trying to relax.

"I wish Kim could be here," Beth said, shaking her head. "I called her, but she's out of town."

"I understand. This was very sudden." I hated lying to Beth, especially while she was being the poster child for a best friend, but I already knew Kim wouldn't be at my wedding. She was two hospital rooms down from Ryan, nursing wounds she'd sustained when Isaac had sent her flying across the cathedral of St. Anne's. It wasn't right that she had saved my life, and that instead of being at her side, I was primping in a tropical paradise.

"She did say to tell you to not worry about her. She said she's fine and she wants you to enjoy your day...why would you worry?" Beth said. Her question was a second thought, as if it hadn't crossed her mind until that moment.

"When do I not worry about her?" I said, fidgeting with my dress.

Beth thought for a moment. "True," she agreed, carrying on with tidying up the room. "Okay, I'm going to grab your mom, and then I'm going to get ready. If you need anything, I'm just a casita away."

"Beth?" I called.

"Yes?" she said, spinning around.

"Thank you," I smiled. "For everything."

Beth returned my smile. "Of course."

"And Beth?"

"Yes?" she said. She was clearly impatient about getting to her casita.

"Think I could sit for a while?"

"Oh!" Beth said, rushing to fetch me a chair. "Here. This one has a back on it so you can relax. Thirsty?"

"Not at the moment. You are the best maid of honor, ever."

"I know," she beamed. She backed out of my room, shutting the door on her wide and excessively proud smile.

With Beth's absence the room became uncomfortably quiet, but I didn't feel alone. I looked down to my stomach. Bean was invisible, nestled under the fabric of the dress I would wear to marry her father. I placed both of my hands above my bump, and smiled. Would Bean know he or she was a guest at our wedding? The thought of a tiny body inside of me with a fancy dress or tux on made me giggle.

"What's funny?" Cynthia said as she entered the room. "Certainly not the sight of you. You're a vision." I smiled and stood so that she might get a better look. "I've arranged for a car. Well, not so much a car as a beat-up truck, but it will get us to the chapel."

"I wondered how I would get there and keep my dress white."

Cynthia frowned. "I didn't say it wouldn't be difficult. I've considered wrapping you in plastic. It will take all of us along with a concentrated effort, but it can be done."

"Thank you," I smiled. "I'm so glad you're here."

Again, a deluge of emotion caught Cynthia off-guard, and she furiously searched through her purse for a tissue. Before the first tear could pour over her lashes, she dabbed it away. "I've never," she said, annoyed. "I hope this doesn't continue throughout the day."

I rested in the chair and Cynthia sat on the bed, seeming uncomfortable and out of place, yet she remained cordial and poised. She brought up appropriate subjects such as the weather, and stayed far away from anything that might induce another onslaught of tears. We shared a few polite laughs, and I silently prayed that Beth would return sooner rather than later.

"Ding dong!" Bex said, opening the door. "The truck is less than a mile away. You ready?"

"Something like that," I sighed.

Beth popped in behind Bex. Her smile lit up the room. She was stunning in her French blue cocktail dress, and for the first time since I'd met her, she actually looked like the former beauty queen that she was. Her lips were stained a wine color, and her short auburn hair was wavy and soft instead of sticking out in every direction. "Oh, good!" Beth squealed as the engine grew louder upon the truck's approach. "It's like a Bronco! It has a back seat!"

"That's nice," I said, minding my mother's expression as I gathered my skirt.

The trip from my chair to the door was uneventful, but the preparations for me to step outside into the murky jungle were firmly coordinated by my mother. Cynthia barked orders at Bex, Beth, and the driver. Bex lifted me and held me away from his body—at Cynthia's request—to keep from wrinkling the dress further. Beth and Cynthia held any protruding pieces out and away as Bex made his way to the truck, and then help spread the fabric while he lowered me to the backseat. Cynthia's tactic worked. I was seated atop a clean blanket, and my dress remained untouched by the jungle.

Bex led us to the chapel on a dirt bike, while Cynthia commandeered the passenger seat. Beth squeezed against the door to my right to give the dress plenty of room.

"You are all being a little ridiculous about this dress. Once I get out of the truck, the wrinkles will fall," I said.

"It's possible. What will you do if mud is splattered on it? Have you found a dry cleaner on the island?" Cynthia asked.

"Good point."

Within half an hour, the truck was bouncing over familiar cobblestone streets. My heart pounded against my chest when the chapel's steeple appeared above the palm trees, and I could barely restrain myself from bursting from the truck and running inside when the fountain, and then the wooden double doors came into view. Jared was inside, and the wait had already been an awful test of my patience.

Beth lightly touched the top of my hand, and only then did I realize I was tapping her knee.

"We're here," she said, pulling at the door handle.

Bex stood on the walkway with a wide grin on his face. "You look good."

"Thanks," I said, touched by his sentiment.

"All right, enough chitchat. We're not in the church, yet," Cynthia said, orchestrating another transfer. She lifted the hem of one side of my dress while directing Beth to lift the other, and together we climbed the steps.

Inside, Lillian waited. Once recognition hit, her eyes lit up, and she clapped her hands together, quickly bringing them to her mouth. "Oh. Oh my goodness," she said, tears glossing her eyes. "You're even more beautiful than I imagined." She looked to Cynthia. "It's so good to see you," she said, hugging her old friend.

"As it is you," Cynthia said with a warm but demure smile.

Lillian blotted her eyes with a tissue and shook her head. She looked upon me with pure love and adoration. She had always regarded me with an adulation that I never quite understood, but the look in her eyes was new to me.

"May I seat you?" Bex said to Cynthia, offering his arm.

"Yes, thank you," she said, walking with Bex into the church.

Lillian watched them disappear behind the door, and then leaned into my ear. "You don't know how long I've waited for this moment. You've always been family, Nina. I can't explain it," she whispered. A sweet, innocent laugh escaped her throat. "Some nights, after Jack and Cynthia took you home after I'd make you all dinner, I would cry."

My eyebrows popped up. Lillian was always so candid about her feelings for me. Even so, her words surprised me.

"Gabe used to shake his head. He always thought me to be irrational when it came to you. But each time you left my home, I felt I was letting my daughter go away to live with someone else. I must sound crazy. It sounds silly to say out loud. I…I just wanted to tell you how happy it makes me that after today…I can call you my daughter."

I hugged her to me. The intensity of emotion in the room was overwhelming. I didn't hear crazy. Lillian's words sounded like love.

"No, no, no, no…," Beth said, pulling a tissue from her purse. "Don't cry. Your mascara is waterproof, but it's not magic. It could smudge." She carefully dabbed under my eyes. "You're only marrying the man of your dreams soon. What's to cry about?"

I smiled. "Touché."

The music sounded. Beth handed me an exquisite bouquet of pink and white tulips, winked at me, and then slid out of the double doors to take her walk. I stood alone in the vestibule, in my dress, holding my favorite flowers—the same Jared presented me on our first date. I was amazed, then, at the coincidence. Now it just made me smile. Why he was ever nervous about whether I would fall in love with him was a mystery. Not only was he the most thoughtful, most selfless and loving person I knew, he was also armed with the knowledge of all my likes and dislikes.

He was more armed to win me over more than any man could any woman. The tulips were perfect. Jared had sent me this very bouquet many times over the course of our relationship. It just occurred to me that these flowers had also been sent to me before our relationship; on birthdays, my high school graduation, and I remember feeling comforted by a wreath at my father's funeral bearing the same flowers. Jared had never mentioned it before, but I knew they were from him. That thought made me smile. He had loved me for a long time, and now I was about to walk down the aisle of our chapel, on our island, to pledge my eternal love to him. Life had never felt so right.

I thought about my father, and wished he were next to me. I imagined him in a smart tuxedo with teary eyes, fawning over my dress and how beautiful and grown up I looked. As a little girl, I imagined him giving me away at my wedding, and now he would have to do it from Heaven.

"I know you can see me, Daddy," I whispered, closing my eyes.

Suddenly, I was no longer alone. Someone was beside me, with an arm hooked around my elbow.

"Hope you don't mind a wedding crasher. Jack sent me," Eli winked and tightened his grip.

"N-No," I said, shaking my head. "Of course not."

"I've always wanted to do this." He stretched his neck and shoulders. "Looked like fun."

"Thank you," I said, as the wedding march began to play in the chapel.

"Ready, kiddo?"

I smiled, and took a deep breath. "Ready."

Both doors swept open, held by two young local boys, and our small audience stood.

Eli leaned into my ear. "You are breathtaking, by the way." He took a step, and I followed his lead. Together we walked slowly down the aisle.

The sanctuary was a bit dim, with beams of sun breaking through the windows and spotlighting the different faces of our friends and family. The dust motes slowly floated in and out of the sunshine, delicate and graceful. I saw Jared's Uncle Luke, first. I was surprised to see him, and it must have showed, because he and his wife Maryse chuckled softly at my expression. I was glad to see Chad sitting next to my mother, although it wouldn't have occurred to her to feel…well, anything...I didn't want her to be alone. Lillian, Luke and Maryse sat together in the first of the heavy, wooden pews, parallel to Cynthia and Chad. Luke whispered something into his sister's ear, and Lillian nodded, taking a deep, satisfied breath.

And then, I saw him. Jared stood next to Bex at the head of the chapel, at the top of a few steps that lead to the pulpit and the rest of the stage. Eli waited before he took a step, sensing that I had stopped in my tracks. Jared was dressed in a khaki suit with a white-button-up shirt. The top button was undone, and he skipped the tie. He looked perfect, and his bright blue-gray eyes were locked on me, over a slightly nervous, beaming smile.

Without thinking, I took a step, now anxious more than ever to be next to him. Eli picked up his pace as my feet insisted on placing the rest of me next to the man I loved more than life itself. My love for Jared surpassed needing normal, enough to conquer fate and beat death. In that moment I couldn't fathom why I had waited so long, and I wanted to be nowhere else but in that chapel, making the easy promise to love him forever.

The reverend was short, swallowed by his officiant's gown. His brown skin was dull and wrinkled, but his kind smile brightened his face. He spoke in a thick accent. "Hello, Nina. I'm Father Julian."

I nodded, my gaze returning to Jared.

"We gather here, in the presence of God and this company, that Jared and Nina be united in holy matrimony. We here to celebrate and share in glorious act that God is about to perform—the act by which He converts their love for one another into holy and sacred state of marriage.

"This relationship is honorable and sacred, established by our Creator for welfare and happiness of humanity, and approved by Apostle Paul as honorable among all men. It is designed to unite two sympathies and hopes into one; and rests upon mutual confidence and devotion of husband and wife. May it be in extreme thoughtfulness and reverence, and in dependence upon divine guidance, that you enter now into this holy relationship."

Jared didn't take his eyes from mine. Just a few feet away from him, Father Julian stepped down to meet me. He looked to Eli, and spoke with a thick accent, "Being assured that your love and your choice of each other as lifelong companions are in God's will and that you have your families' blessings. I now ask. Who gives this woman to be married to this man?"

"We do," Eli said with confidence. He spoke for my father, for Cynthia. He might have even spoken for Gabe, but I felt Heaven was smiling on the moment.

Eli lifted my hand to his lips and kissed my knuckles, and then took Jared's hand, placing his gently under mine. With a small, tender squeeze, Eli left us alone at the bottom of the steps, disappearing behind the double doors he had just helped me through.

Jared raised an eyebrow, a permanent smile etched on his face. "That was unexpected."

"Jack sent him," I said, feeling my eyes gloss over.

Jared touched my face once, and then the reverend spoke again. This time his voice blurred into the background as I watched the blues and grays of Jared's eyes shine in ways I'd never seen them. His expression was relaxed and nervous; happy and concerned; every emotion he'd ever felt collided inside of him in a beautiful display of the barely noticeable shifts in the skin around his eyes and mouth. No one could have noticed it but me, and I read each one as he struggled with a lifetime of duty, and the relief of hearing me promise myself to him.

"Jared Ryel?" Father Julian said. "Are you ready to enter into this marriage with Nina Grey, believing the love you share and your faith in each other will endure all things?"

"I am," Jared said simply.

"Nina Grey?"

"I am!"

Our small audience laughed at my haste. Jared chuckled as well.

Father Julian regrouped, and then finished his part. "Are you ready to enter into this marriage with Nina Grey, believing the love you share and your faith in each other will endure all things?"

I waited for the minister to correct his mixup, but he never did.

I nodded quickly. "To Jared Ryel. Yes. I'm ready."

Father Julian didn't skip a beat. "Nina, do you take Jared to be your wedded husband? Promise to love him, to honor and cherish him, in joy and in sorrow, in sickness and in health, and to be to him in all things a good and faithful wife as long as you both shall live?"

"Yes."

Father Julian repeated Jared's vows. The closer he came to the end, the tighter Jared's fingers were around mine. Finally, when it came time for Jared to speak, he didn't hesitate.

"Yes, and after that," Jared said. "For a thousand years, and then a thousand more...I will love you."

A smile stretched across my face. His hands were cupped around mine a bit too tight, and his body leaned into mine eagerly. This was the moment he had waited for, and he seemed to want to take it all in and rush it at the same time so nothing could keep him from it. That moment in time was the light switch in a dark room, the doorway at the end of a scary hallway. It was anything and everything that had ever saved anyone.

Father Julian closed his eyes. "Father in heaven, You ordained marriage for your children, and You gave us love. We present to You Jared and Nina, who come this day to be married. May the covenant of love they make be blessed with true devotion and spiritual commitment. We ask that You, God, will give them the ability to keep the covenant they have made. When selfishness shows itself, grant generosity; when mistrust is a temptation, give moral strength; when there is misunderstanding, give patience and gentleness; if suffering becomes a part of their lives, give them a strong faith and an abiding love. Amen."

I opened my eyes to see Jared looking at me with total love and devotion, more so than I ever saw in the proud eyes of my father.

"What token do you give to perform your vows?"

Bex opened his hand, and Jared plucked a white gold band from his brother's palm.

"Nina," Jared said softly. He closed his eyes, thought for a moment, and then looked into my eyes. "What can I say to you that I haven't already said? What can I give you that I haven't already given? Is there anything of me that isn't yours already? My body, my mind, my heart, even my soul. Everything that is me belonged to you long before this, and it shall be yours long after this. I will follow you anywhere and everywhere you lead. I will keep you and anyone created with our love safe from all harm. From this day on, I choose you, my beloved, to be my wife. To live with you and laugh with you; to stand by your side, and sleep in your arms; to bring out the best in you always, and, for you, to be the most that I can. I promise to laugh with you in good times, to struggle with you in bad; to wipe your tears with my hands; to comfort you with my words; to mirror you with my soul; and savor every moment, happy or sad, until the end of our lives and beyond."

A long pause followed Jared's words. No one moved; an awe-inspired silence swept the chapel as everyone took in his breathtaking promise. He took my hand, and slipped the ring onto my finger. It glided over my skin, and rested next to my diamond engagement ring, as if it were returning home.

"D-do you," Father Julian stuttered, "Nina, have a token to perform your vows?"

I turned to Beth, whose mascara streaked her cheeks. She opened her hand to reveal Jared's simple wedding band. I took it from her, and turned to face him.

He grinned, waiting on my promise. I had thought about my vows many times after we decided to write our own. Our relationship had never been traditional, so we chose to make our promise to each other unique to us. I took a deep breath. Nothing I would say would be nearly as articulate and beautiful as what he had said, but I knew well enough by now that he would love every syllable.

"Jared," I whispered. I held his hand, and then placed the ring around the tip of his finger. "I choose you as my best friend, and my love for life. I promise you my deepest love, my fullest devotion, my most tender care...through the pressures of the present and the uncertainties of the future, I promise to be faithful to you. It wasn't until just now that I recognize that this wasn't coincidence, or a battle. We were always meant for each other. Our love is heaven sent, and I promise to honor that forever and always. From this day forward, you won't walk alone. My heart will be your shelter and my arms will be your home."

The mixed emotions scrolling across Jared's face disappeared; the only one left was happiness. I pushed his ring over his knuckle, and he squeezed my hand.

Father Julian put his hand over ours. "What God has joined together, let no man put asunder. Jared and Nina have consented together in holy matrimony, and witnessed the same before God and this company, have pledged their love and loyalty to each other, and have declared the same by the joining and the giving of rings. By the authority of the state, I pronounce that they are husband and wife."

A small sigh emanated throughout the chapel, and Jared let out a breath of relief, followed by a small smile.

"Kiss your wife," Father Julian said with a smile.

Jared cupped my cheeks, looked into my eyes, and then pulled me to him, touching his soft lips to mine. He kissed me gently at first, and then wrapped his arms around me, his lips forgetting everyone and everything around us. We were married. He was my husband, and I was his wife.

He pulled away. His eyes brimmed with tears, and he looked as overwhelmed with happiness as I felt. I pulled him to me by his shirt to kiss him one last time.

"I now present to you, Mr. and Mrs. Jared Ryel," the minister said loudly.

Jared's smile faded, and he gritted his teeth.

"Not today," he said, closing his eyes.

Chapter Three
Trial

The inside of the chapel darkened. The sunlight coming through the windows dimmed, but it was early afternoon. The air around grew cold and stale. The hairs on the back of my neck stood on end. Fearing the worst, I was desperate for a mundane explanation. “A storm?”

Jared's eyes darkened. “I’m sorry.”

The sound of the tropical winds that regularly blew against the building was noticeably absent, and soon the only light was the dim flickering of a few sconces along the walls of the church. I shot a nervous glance over my shoulder at our friends and family below. They were frozen in time.

I quickly walked down the stairs, with Jared just behind. My movement didn’t faze the small crowd, and I gasped, falling to my knees. “Lillian?” I said, reaching out.

Her hands were folded daintily in her lap, a small smile suspended on her face. I stood and took a step to the next pew, realizing in horror that the living statues' eyes were all still fastened to the space where Jared and I once occupied.

“Beth?” I whispered, reaching out to touch her cheek. Her skin was still warm. “She’s not breathing,” I said, looking back to my new husband. Bex stood at Jared’s side. He frowned before looking to his brother. Only the humans were affected.

“He must have claimed a grievance,” Bex said.

“Shax?” I asked.

Jared shook his head. “Michael...for murdering his son.” He closed his eyes and took my hand, holding it against his chest. “No matter what happens, Nina, stay with Bex,” he said.

“What do you mean? Where are you going?” I said. He took a step toward the double doors of the chapel. With my free hand, I grabbed at the fabric of his jacket. “Jared,” I whispered. His demeanor terrified me.

The double doors opened, and Eli stood in the entrance, his expression blank. “I’m sorry, Jared. This can’t wait.”

Jared nodded, and then tilted his head to the side, speaking under his breath. “Don't speak, Nina. Let me handle this.”

I agreed without words. Jared led me through the doors, to the top of the chapel steps. The sky was black, the darkness filtering down to surround our chapel. Several dark forms stood in formation at the bottom of the stairs. Jared continued. With each step closer to the unknown, my heart seemed to be punching through my chest. Finally, I was face to face with Jared’s accusers, but they remained a mystery. Their faces were obscured by the hoods of black cloaks. If they were angels, they were much more frightening than any I’d encountered.

Eli stood on the other side of Jared, waiting patiently for something, but I knew better than to ask. After a few moments the black forms parted, and two figures, differing dramatically in size, walked forward. Eli made a subtle motion with his hand, and the air around the small assemblage created its own light, leaving a muted glow. I glanced at him from the corner of my eye, and he winked at me. I was the only one unable to see clearly through the darkness. Eli lit the surroundings solely for my human eyes.

His consideration set me somewhat at ease. He won’t let anything happen to us, I thought.

Any feeling of comfort offered by Eli's small gesture didn't last long. The two forms were now recognizable, and a lump formed in my throat at Claire's nervous expression as she walked alongside Samuel.

"What are you doing here? Where's Ryan?" I asked.

Jared squeezed my hand, and I remembered too late his rule of silence. A man at the front of the opposing group ripped away his hood, revealing his enraged eyes. "You are not allowed to speak here!" he said. His body shook as he spoke.

Samuel and Claire took a defensive stance in front of Jared and me. Jared squeezed my hand again, this time in comfort. He brought my fingers to his lips and kissed them. An overwhelming urge to cry overcame me, and although I begged myself not to, my eyes filled with salty tears and dribbled down my cheeks.

Eli casually pushed Samuel and Claire to the side to approach me. "Look what you've done," Eli said, lifting my chin. He used his thumbs to wipe the twin lines of tears. "Upsetting the bride on her wedding day." He turned to the man. "Apologize, Michael, and then mind your manners for the remainder of our time here."

Michael stood tall. "Forgive me," he said, his body rigid with subdued rage.

I nodded once, cowering against Jared.

Samuel took a spot next to Jared, and Claire stood next to me. Eli returned to his position, but this time he stood more central between the two groups. He lowered his head and closed his eyes. The Ryel siblings, along with Samuel and the cloaked men, did the same. I followed suit, wondering if I looked ridiculous, or if it was expected. Jared didn't offer a suggestion either way, so the safe option was to imitate the others.

After a short time, Eli began to speak in his usual soft, matter-of-fact tone. "All praise to the Most High, as this is His court and His kingdom. I will use the common tongue for our Nina, so that she may understand. I, Eliath, angel of the Divine Plan, will act on the Lord Almighty's behalf. My decision is final." He glanced at both Jared and Michael. "Aggression will not be tolerated."

Jared and Michael nodded.

Eli looked to me, and his eyes softened. "Michael has made a claim against Jared for the death of his earthen son, Isaac."

My first inclination was to open my mouth, but after my public reprimand from Michael, I was hesitant.

Eli sensed my fear, and smiled. "Don't be afraid, Nina. You may speak."

"Um…." I looked to Jared, who'd told me just the opposite just a few minutes before. Any caution was absent from his face. "Jared didn't kill Isaac," I said. My voice was soft, but firm. Even if I incriminated myself, I couldn't let Jared take the blame for my actions.

Eli nodded, knowingly and patiently. "The actions leading to Isaac's death are why we're here, Nina. You may enter your argument in a moment. I assure you this will be a fair proceeding."

"Then why do Jared and Claire seem so nervous?" I said, deliberately leaving Bex's name out. "This doesn't feel like a casual inquiry."

"You're right. It's not. The charges against Jared are very serious. A life was lost. Archs are not allowed to kill humans to protect their Taleh. Half-Breeds are exempt from our rules, as they are half human and allowed free will. However, because Half-Breeds are privy to those rules, it is important that they not take advantage. Do you understand?"

"Y-yes," I said, afraid to say my next words. Eli seemed to have unending patience, but I didn't want to test it. "But…Jared didn't kill Isaac."

Michael's body twitched, and he began to speak in a language so beautiful, I knew it was of Heaven. Eli interrupted.

"English, Michael. It's polite."

Michael sighed with frustration. "Why do you waste your time?" he said to Eli. "We don't explain ourselves to them."

"Patience," Eli said simply. He looked to me, then. "All actions leading to Isaac's death are in review. In this case, Jared revealing himself to you plays a part. Typically, we would trace to the beginning, and hold the individual responsible. In this case, the individual would be Jared's father, Gabriel, for revealing himself to Lillian Van Buren. That action ultimately resulted in Isaac's death. But, because Gabriel has already been judged for that action, the responsibility falls on Jared."

I frowned, still confused.

Eli smiled in understanding. "Think of the Garden of Eden. Our Lord judges wrongs based on chain reactions. It is the way of things."

"You mean he holds grudges," I said.

"No," Eli said with a small chuckle. "No, that is not what I mean. He considers the root of the problem when He makes a decision."

"'The sins of the father' type of thing?"

"It's difficult to explain in human terms, Nina. The short answer is yes."

Jared had made his choices, but being blamed for being the product of his parents' love, and for me for the death of

Donovan was unacceptable to me. He was my husband, after all. It was now my duty to protect him, as well. I stood tall. "What about me?"

Jared tensed. "Nina," he chided.

I glanced at Jared, but didn't heed his warning. "On grounds that my father made choices that could have been the cause of everything that's happened, and the fact that I am the one who killed Isaac's Taleh…shouldn't I be the one on trial?"

"Yes," Michael growled, low and frightening, through his teeth.

Eli touched my shoulder. "You are, Nina. Every choice you make. His decision for you will be later. Jared is held to a different standard, set apart from Heaven and Earth; rules for his kind that he is aware of. Now," he smiled with kindness and maybe a bit of amusement, "if you are satisfied, we will continue."

Knowing that even if I did come to understand, I would never agree, I nodded. The expression on Eli's face told me that he was aware of my feelings, and he appreciated that I was willing to let him move forward.

A new level of intensity weighed on everyone—everyone but Eli, who seemed impervious. Michael's chest heaved as he readied himself to make his case and avenge Isaac's death. As Michael took a step forward, his small army lifted the cloaks from their faces. I shouldn't have been, but I was surprised. I expected them all to look like Michael: Dark eyes and hair. Instead they more closely resembled Claire. A few of them looked upon me with curiosity, others with disdain, but mostly they seemed to be there out of duty and not personal reasons. That logic went against why Claire and Samuel appeared so uneasy.

Eli spoke. "Michael…."

"Isaac had no choice!" he said. "He was important. He was given gifts unlike any Half-Breed. The choices of his Taleh do not justify his death!"

Eli nodded. "Jared…."

Jared showed no emotion. "The choices of our Talehs never justify our deaths, but it is the duty and curse that we must accept to be obedient."

Michael shifted his weight. "What do you know about duty, Half-Breed?"

Blood rushed to my cheeks. "How dare you," I seethed.

"Nina," Jared warned.

"Your son—the one with such gifts—was also half human. I suppose since Jared doesn't support his Taleh living a life of crime and serving a demon, he doesn't take his duty seriously?" I said, my temper temporarily removing any thoughts of my own safety.

A deep line formed between Michael's brow, and his eyes glistened with anger. "My son was not as fortunate as Gabe's. He accepted his fate and made the best of it. We cannot interfere with the free will of humans. It is against His will."

"So is serving the other side," I grumbled.

"Nina!" Jared growled.

Michael jerked forward, and arms burst from the long, black sleeves of cloaks behind him as hands held him at bay. Simultaneously, Samuel angled his body toward Jared in a protective stance. He didn't crouch, as I had seen Claire do so many times before when she protected me. Samuel would not fight his brothers, but he wouldn't allow them to harm us.

Claire leaned against my arm, and whispered in my ear. "Shut up, stupid. You're not helping."

"She should not speak here!" Michael said, jerking away from his allies.

"Enough," Eli said, his voice calm and even. "Nina's fate is affected. She is allowed an argument," he said, looking to me. "Your thoughts have been considered. That will be all."

For the first time, I didn't feel Eli's bias. I nodded quickly, showing my obedience with a small step back.

"Claire…." Eli said, moving the trial forward.

"The truth is, Isaac and Donovan were working with Shax, and they were there to kill Nina, in effect to kill Jared," she said in her no-nonsense way. "Eli, it was going to be Donovan or Nina. Isaac or Jared. If you ask me, the best man won."

Her words stung Michael, but he didn't argue.

Eli's eyes scanned the looming angels behind Michael. "Do any of your supporters wish to enter opinion?"

Michael shook his head. "It is my claim."

"And what exactly is your claim?" Bex asked.

Michael's eyes narrowed, staring directly at Jared's younger brother. "That he murdered my son."

Claire took a step forward. "Your son murdered Nina's father."

When recognition hit that Claire was speaking of my father, my knees buckled, and Jared tightened his grip to keep me on my feet.

"W-What?" I said, my voice barely a whisper.

Jared leaned into my cheek, his nose grazing my ear. "Donovan shot your father. Isaac was with him."

My eyes widened, focusing on Michael. "You want to blame Gabe and Jared? You come here, interrupt our wedding day, yell at me, accuse us of murder, and your son was an accessory to the cause of all of this?"

Michael's dark eyes darted from me to Eli.

Eli shrugged. "She has a point."

Michael's jaw dropped. "Isaac did not to deserve to die. He was a good son. He accepted the curse and honored his duties."

"Michael," Samuel said in his deep, firm voice.

Michael stepped toward Eli. "Gabriel's son should be punished! He allowed his Taleh to kill my son! Rebecca's son!"

Eli looked to the ground in thought. "Rebecca was unhappy with Isaac's choices, was she not?"

Michael's eyes flickered to each of us. "I demand Jared be punished for taking Isaac's life."

Samuel spoke again. "Michael…."

"Jared should be killed, and leave his Taleh to the savages," Michael said, pointing to Jared.

"Michael…" Samuel repeated, this time with a low growl.

"An eye for an eye, Eli! I demand it!" Michael said, his fists balled at his sides.

"MICHAEL!" Samuel boomed. The earth trembled when he spoke, and my hands flew to my ears.

Eli watched the interaction between Samuel and Michael for a moment, and then spoke. "Okay. All right. I've heard enough from each side. Only one argument remains."

We all looked to one another, wondering who was left.

"My apologies," a warm voice spoke. It was a voice I hadn't heard in a long time. A voice from my childhood.

Jared's hand was still in mine, and the moment the voice could be heard, his hand went limp. "Dad?" he said.

I turned, seeing Gabe Ryel at the top of the chapel's rock steps. He looked exactly as I remembered him: tall, his blond hair and piercing, ice-blue eyes glowing even from several feet away. A flash broke from the crowd and up the steps, and in the next moment, Claire was in her father's arms, sobbing uncontrollably. She pressed her cheek against his chest, whispering something I couldn't understand. Gabe bowed his head, spoke something back, and then he kissed his daughter's forehead. They descended the stairs together, and approached Bex.

Gabe offered a small smile to his youngest son, who fell against him with a clap.

My mouth fell open, and I immediately searched Jared's face for a reaction. There was none.

Gabe's expression turned remorseful. "I'm sorry for your son, Michael. You and I are in unique positions…to know love for a child. You and I agree that if we could change the outcome, we would make it so."

Eli reached out to Gabe. "It's important to remember that it is in the height of adversary that we must come together. Michael, you've lost your son. Your widow has now lost her husband and her son. It is unfortunate."

Michael bowed his head.

Gabe approached Michael, pulling him into his arms. "We need you on our side, Brother."

Michael shrugged out of his grasp.

"Eli?" Michael pleaded.

Eli offered a small, comforting smile. "You already know the answer."

Michael shot an accusing glare at Jared.

Jared's brows pulled in. "I didn't want Isaac to die, Michael. I swear to you, I wish it hadn't happened.

"Very well, then." He gestured to the cloaked angels, and they all disappeared into the darkness.

Eli clapped his hands together, lacing his fingers together. "Impeccable timing, as always, Gabriel."

Gabe nodded. His eyes paused on me for a moment before fixing on Jared. "This isn't your fault, Jared."

Jared didn't speak. His face tense, his dark eyes meeting the eyes of his father, he was paralyzed. The scene brought back memories of the moment I saw my father for the last time, and I ached for Jared. He would have to say goodbye a second time.

"Jared," Gabe began, "it's not your fault. You've done everything right."

Jared's head dipped slightly as he attempted a nod.

"Son…." Gabe cupped both of his hands on Jared's shoulders. "I'm proud of you."

Jared choked, and his body gave way, allowing him to fall against his father. I covered my mouth, unaccustomed to seeing Jared relinquish control of his emotions. They embraced, and Jared's knuckles turned white as he held Gabe in his arms. When Gabe released him, Jared used his thumb and index finger to make a quick swipe of his wet eyes.

"It's good to see you again, Dad," Jared said with a weak smile.

Gabe beamed. "You've done well, Son. You've done well."

"I've tried," Jared said, relieved at his father's words. He took my hand, then. "You remember Nina."

Gabe leaned down and kissed my hairline. "Of course."

Eli walked up the steps, watching with amusement as Claire and Bex crowded their father. "Gabriel…."

"I know," he said, seeming a bit sad. "One more thing," he said. He wrapped his arms around Bex and Claire again, and then followed Eli through the double wooden doors, down the aisle of the chapel. Lillian was still frozen. The same sweet, small smile on her face hadn't moved a centimeter.

Gabriel kneeled before her. He noticed her folded hands in her lap, and tenderly covered hers with his. "She is as beautiful as the day I first saw her," he smiled. With two fingers, he brushed her cheekbone, and then leaned in to kiss her lips. His mouth lingered on hers for a few moments, and he closed his eyes, taking in his last moment with his wife.

Claire wiped a stray tear from her cheek. "Eli…"

"I'm sorry, no," Eli said.

"We're already pushing the rules allowing Nina to be animated, not to mention allowing me to be here at all," Gabriel said. His eyes didn't stray from Lillian's delicate face.

"Not unlike hacking into dreams to get your point across…." Eli said, looking away in dramatic fashion.

"The dreams," I said. The moment I spoke, I wished I hadn't. Bothering Gabe while he spent his last moments with his wife was ridiculously selfish. Regardless, Gabe touched Lillian's lips to his once more, and then stood to face me.

"Yes, the dreams," Gabe sighed.

I hesitated, and then decided to ask, anyway. "Why did you come to me in the dream if there was nothing in the book to help us?"

Gabe looked to the floor, and then to Jared. "At first, we were hoping you wouldn't go right along with the prophecy and get pregnant the first chance that presented itself."

A flush of red lit my cheeks, and Jared cleared his throat. "That's not exactly how it happened, Dad."

Gabe gave a quick nod. "You have the book?"

"Yes," Jared said.

"Now that you have it, it's safe to say that it would behoove you to help the Pollocks replace it. One less thing to worry about, wouldn't you agree?"

Jared frowned. "But…if it puts us in danger, why did you take it from the Pollocks to begin with?"

"Answers. Jack knew the moment she was born she was in danger of being the woman in the prophecy. When you fell in love with her, Son, we knew it was a matter of when, not if. We were fighting time and fate…an impossible task. Still, Jack loved his daughter, and he wanted to do everything in his power to try to keep her from that path. We knew there was a chance the book could help us find a loophole, so we took it."

In frustration, Jared shifted his weight. "But…by the time you came to Nina in the dreams, you knew there was no loophole. Why did you put her through that? Why the theatrics? Do you have any idea what she's been through? What I went through?"

"To get your attention. We were desperate to find a way to stop you from commencing the prophecy."

"By then it was too late," Bex inserted.

"Obviously," Claire grumbled.

Gabe shook his head. "Not quite. She still had time."

I looked around the room. "Where is Samuel?"

Claire shoved her hands into her jacket pockets. She wore sweats, her gathered gray pants pushed up to just below her knees, and a matching hooded jacket over a ratty white tank top. She had been summoned unexpectedly. "Babysitting Ryan until I get back. Now that the trial is over, he's vulnerable."

"Is he okay?" I asked.

She nodded. "Kim goes home tomorrow. Father Francis is in stable condition, but he will be in traction for a while."

Bex frowned. "That should have never happened. Clergy should have more protection than that."

"Father Francis' guardian is an Arch, Bex. His hands were tied when Donovan attacked him," Claire explained.

"So what now?" Jared asked Gabe.

"Shax still wants his book. Hell doesn't want the child to be born. Things are stacking against you, Jared," Gabe said. "One thing at a time."

"One thing at a time," Jared repeated, letting his father's advice sink in.

Gabe hugged his children one more time, and then made his way toward the door. "It's a long time between now and the time she delivers the baby, Jared. We'll keep an ear to the ground, but be on alert. Heaven won't step in until you give them a reason."

"You mean start a war," Jared said.

"Figure out a reason, Son." In that instant, Gabriel was gone.

"Huh," Bex puffed. "Weird."

Claire's shoulders dropped. "He's never coming back, is he?"

"Probably not," Jared said with a small, apologetic smile on his face.

Claire sat on the closest pew, beside her mother. She leaned against Lillian's shoulder and closed her eyes, pushing the remaining tears down her face. "I'm so sorry you couldn't see him," Claire whispered.

"She'll know," Bex said. "She always knows."

The windows began to brighten, and light danced down the walls as if the sun were rising.

Eli smiled, kissing me lightly on the cheek. "Congratulations, kiddo. On both counts. See you soon."

"How soon?"

He smiled. “It’s as I said before. When there is only one question left to ask.”

“But...what does that mean? What is the question?” I asked, but I was talking to empty space. He was gone.

Claire stood, taking a deep breath. “I have to get back,” she said, looking behind her. Samuel stood at the door with an outstretched hand reaching in her direction. “You look beautiful,” she said to me with a small smile. In no hurry, Claire ambled down the aisle. Once her hand touched Samuel’s, she was gone as well.

Bex laughed once and shook his head. “That’s so cool.”

Chapter Four
Little Heaven

Jared took my hand and led me to our former spots at the front of the church. Bex took a position beside his brother. We watched each other as the sun grew brighter, slowly brightening the faces of our audience. From the corner of my eye, I saw movement, and Father Julian shifted his weight, signaling their awakening.

The minister smiled, gesturing for us to turn. We faced our friends and family, and Father Julian placed his hands on each of our shoulders. "I present to you, Mr. and Mrs. Jared Ryel."

Every face in the room beamed, and applause filled the room. Even with the frightening events just moments before, joy consumed me. Jared's hand enveloped mine, and we walked the few steps to the aisle, and then made our way outside. It was surreal to return to the scene of Jared's trial, this time in the sunshine where birds sang, happily riding the bobbing branches that swayed with the breeze. The plaza at the bottom of the chapel's steps where Michael and his small army had stood not ten minutes before now bathed in the warmth of the sun, waiting for our friends to occupy its smooth, rocked surface. The fountain gushing, the road peppered with townspeople—I felt a bit sick at the sight of it.

"You okay?" Jared said, stopping to smile as Beth took our picture.

"Yeah...yeah, I just feel...confused."

"Changing planes is unnatural and unsettling for humans, which is why they typically don't allow it."

"That explains a lot," I said, stopping to pose for more pictures as Lillian, Cynthia, Chad, and Jared's Uncle Luke and Aunt Maryse filed out of the chapel. "Does it...," I smiled again, "affect the baby?"

"No," Jared answered, kissing my forehead.

"How do you know?" I said, leaning into his kiss.

He looked down to me and touched my cheek. "Otherwise Eli wouldn't have done it."

"Oh," I said, my eyes wandering until I found Lillian. "Of course."

Lillian hugged her son, and then me. Her sweet, energetic smile lit up the island. I watched and waited, wondering if she realized she'd been in Gabriel's presence just moments before.

"What is it?" she said, half curious, half amused.

"Nothing," I smiled. "I'm just glad you're here."

"Not as much as I," she winked.

Jared and I traded glances, wondering if she'd just given us a clue.

"Cynthia!" Beth called. "Stand beside Nina and I'll take a picture of the couple with their mothers."

Cynthia fidgeted with her hair, and then took her place beside me, poised and proper. I hooked my arm around her waist, and she stiffened when I pulled her closer.

"Smile!" Beth said, snapping a picture.

A few of the locals gathered on the street, their warm, smiling faces interlacing with the familiar faces of our friends and family. They began clapping and singing, and then one of the grandmothers waved us with her hands, encouraging us to walk. Jared tugged on my hand, and we walked to the street. I laughed with surprise and excitement when I realized they were following us, their hands clapping to the beat of their happy song. Our guests' white faces were littered among the brown, sun-kissed skin of the townspeople. They followed us to a makeshift downtown, where a small group of men played music.

"You did this?" I asked Jared.

He smiled, amazed. "No. This one I didn't do."

We laughed together, amazed at the random celebration that grew around us. Jared pulled me to the center of the street, where we danced to the strumming guitars and hand-tapped percussion. Chad and Beth joined us, as did Luke and Maryse. Bex pulled his mother into the dirt street as well. If I didn't know better, I would have felt badly for Cynthia, but I knew she preferred to stand away from the nonsense. Perfectly still.

The afternoon sun was warm, and my wedding dress wasn't built to breathe in the Caribbean humidity. Jared sensed my dilemma and nodded, providing me a seat in the shade. An elderly woman brought me a fan with a smile of understanding. The band played on, and the townsfolk and our guests danced into the evening, long after the makeshift street lamps and hanging lights turned on to flicker and twinkle against the night.

"How do you feel?" Jared asked, handing me another glass of water.

"Good," I smiled, taking a sip. "I feel good."

"Feel like dancing?" he said. Jared gestured to the band, and it slowed the beat.

I eagerly let my husband take me by the hand to the middle of the celebration. I wrapped my arms around his neck and pressed my cheek against his chest. His heavenly scent took me away from trials and the war we would create to stay alive. It was then that I realized his skin wasn't the feverish temperature it usually was.

"What is it?" Jared asked.

"You don't feel as hot."

"It's probably because you're overheating in that dress. I should have arranged for something you could change into."

"I'm fine." I smiled. "Quit fussing."

Jared rested his jaw against my hair, and we moved slowly to the music. A slight breeze moved through the trees that lined the small cobblestone street in the center of the town. I sunk into Jared's chest and let his arms totally engulf me. I had never been in more danger, and yet I had never felt so safe. The tribulations that we would face upon our return to Providence suddenly seemed so small in comparison to that moment.

I looked up to Jared, and noticed his content smile. "Was it exactly what you hoped it would be?"

"Something like that," he cooed. "Everything and more."

My head felt heavy, and I rested it against my husband's shoulder. My eyes swept across the landscape, seeing Beth and Chad dancing. They weren't talking, but smiling as they shared a sweet moment. It reminded me of the first time Jared and I had experienced Little Corn, and it was heartwarming to see the island make Beth and Chad feel the same way.

As the sun set, the villagers lit the primitive lamps that bordered the sidewalk. Jared and I stood with Bex, listening to Cynthia and Lillian discuss how beautiful the ceremony had been. I waited to hear some indication that Lillian knew of Gabe's presence, but if she knew, she wasn't letting on.

"Well, daughter," Cynthia said, dabbing her forehead with a handkerchief, "I have an early appointment that Jared promised I would make. I best be off."

“Thank you for coming, Mother,” I said, leaning in to hug her. Her embrace was more than the usual awkward squeeze. She held me to her, and whispered in my ear.

“Be safe, dearest. I love you.”

Cynthia turned on her heels and walked quickly to a waiting pickup truck. She didn’t look back as the truck slowly faded into the dark jungle. I waited until I could no longer hear the engine, and then turned to Jared.

He offered a half smile. “She loves you.”

“I heard,” I said, stunned. “I mean, of course she does. She’s just never…she’ll make her appointment?”

“I’ve made sure of it,” Jared said. “Bex is at the boat dock, now. He’s going to ride with her to the mainland and get her on the plane on time.”

“Good. Remind me to thank Bex later.”

“Oh,” Lillian put a thin arm around me and pulled me to her side, “he’s happy to do it. I’m going to catch a ride with Chad and Beth. She’s a sweet girl.”

“Yes, she is,” I smiled.

“See you at home. Come over for dinner soon, okay?”

“Promise,” Jared said, kissing her forehead.

“I love you both!” she waved, following Beth and Chad to another waiting vehicle.

“Where is our car?” I asked.

“I have the bike I drove over.”

I looked down to my dress. “You’re kidding.”

Jared laughed once. “No. Not at all.” He crouched and then brought up a bunched wad of my dress in his hands. “It’s a nice night. It’ll be fun.”

I shook my head and shrugged. “Why not? Cynthia’s not here to freak out about it.” I took the bunched tulle and silk under my arm and then took Jared’s hand. He led us past the band to a small dirt bike. We took several back roads that led us through a village or two—it was so dark I wasn't sure if it was tin buildings passing by or just shadows cast by the trees. Before long, the trees thinned, and Jared slowed to a stop. Sounds of waves caressing the shoreline weren't far away.

Jared took my hand, and we walked beyond the trail until I could feel wet sand breaching the borders of my sandals. The half-moon stubbornly glowed behind a thin, broken layer of clouds. We ambled to where the ocean met the sand, and walked along the beach. We didn't talk, just walked hand in hand, listening to Little Corn.

The moon finally broke free of the clouds, and its silver light danced on the water. We came upon a large rock, and Jared motioned for me to sit.

"You must be exhausted," he said, sitting next to me.

"I'm tired, but you only get one wedding day. I can feel a second wind coming on."

Jared's eyes turned soft, and they lingered on my lips. "I just wanted to be alone with you and the island for a little while."

His eyes seemed to glow in the silver light, and suddenly I was nervous. It was silly to feel that way—I was pregnant, after all—but the pressure of our wedding night made it new again. We had no constraints; no worries about a pregnancy, or being walked in on, or nightmares. It was just us, and the knowledge that we were about to consummate our marriage. For whatever reason, that made me incredibly anxious.

"What is it?" Jared asked.

Knowing I couldn't comfortably explain my feelings without some embarrassment, I pulled him to me and touched my lips to his.

He pulled away, laughing once. "I'm a bit nervous about tonight, isn't that ridiculous?"

"No," I said, tugging on his shirt. "I'm right there with you."

"Yeah?" he said, relieved.

I nodded, and then looked behind us. I returned to him, biting my lip. "How far are we from the casita?"

"It's right there," he said, nodding behind me.

"Maybe we should…I don't know, get it over with isn't the right word."

Jared cleared his throat, and then offered an ornery smile. "Get naked and get the nerves out of the way?"

My mouth fell open and I laughed out loud. "Jared!"

He laughed and lifted me into his arms, walking in the direction of the casita. "I didn't say it was a bad idea."

He carried me a few yards, past the trees, to the familiar surroundings of our casita. He opened the screen, and then brought me inside, softly leaning me against the mattress. The moonlight faded away, and the wind picked up. With a hand on each side of my shoulders, Jared hovered over my body. Distant thunder rolled somewhere over the ocean. He leaned down and touched his lips to mine just as the first raindrops began to spatter against the tin roof.

Jared's lips traveled in a line down my neck, and he anchored himself with a knee as he lifted me with one hand, and unzipped the back of my wedding dress with the other. With both hands, I pushed back his jacket and slid the sleeves off of his arms, and then unbuttoned the first two buttons of his white dress shirt. Impatient, I grabbed the hem and pulled it over his head.

Watching his bulging muscles tense and move under his smooth skin did nothing for my nerves. Determined to enjoy the comfort I usually enjoyed when we made love, I focused on undressing him. I worked on the button of his slacks, and then ripped down the zipper.

"I said it was a good idea, but I didn't promise not to take my time," Jared said, kicking off his pants. He bent his elbows, letting his body press against mine.

"You can take your time," I said. "We have all night. I think if I just get past this part I can relax," I said, pressing my fingers into his back.

He reached under the skirt of my dress, and pulled the thin, lacy fabric of my panties down my thighs, over my knees, and then past my ankles, letting them fall to the floor.

His hand traveled back up my leg, disappearing under the layers of silk. My legs tensed, and I sucked in a quick bit of air. A few moments later, I couldn't help but close my eyes and let myself sink into the mattress.

"I'm glad you said that," he said against my lips. "I fully intend to take all night."

Chapter Five
The End.

I sat on the beach, listening to the waves. The last time I had come to this island, I pretended to be Mrs. Ryel. Now it was reality. I sighed, and placed my hand on my belly. I wished things could be different; that I was like any other new bride, enjoying the beauty surrounding me on my first day as a wife. Wishing wouldn't help, and I knew that. Another life would mean the absence of Jared. If we had never met, most of the chaos wouldn't have happened, and the worst-case scenario would have been to find out my father was a different person than I believed him to be. Apart from that disappointment, life would have continued on—mundane and mediocre. I would have married Ryan, and worked at Titan. Bore a child or three. We would have lived day in and day out with a respect and love, facing day to day challenges of ordinary life.

My nose wrinkled. A life without Jared was unimaginable. Coupled with that stipulation, I didn't want it. Chaos, a constant state of being on alert and uncertain was a respectable tradeoff for a love like his. He didn't ask for this, either, after all. The danger was what we went through to be together, and it was worth it for him. He never questioned it, and I grudgingly accepted it. It might not make sense to everyone, but then again, they could never understand. Most hadn't experienced what I had. I'd been waited for, longed after for years. The safety, security, and calm I felt with Jared were unmatched; no one else on earth made me feel that way. No one was held as sacred by their husband as I was, so they couldn't fathom what one might endure to protect it. Our love, in all its imperfection, was perfect.

It was then that a moment of clarity came over me. From the moment I'd learned the truth, I had fought with the feeling of loss for a normal life, but without Jared, that life wouldn't have as much meaning. Sure, I was an individual. I was a strong person. I didn't need someone else to complete me, but I was happier with Jared than without him. More than happy. Why settle to prove that I was free? I was, with and without him. Being with him was a choice —a choice to love and be loved and exist in an affirmative state with someone. Even with the chaos going on around us, it was more than I could have hoped for. More than most hoped for. His love was the purest example of anything a human could feel for another. The more I weighed the options in my head, the less appealing normal became. It was downright insulting to compare the two. Suddenly I couldn't remember why I had missed it in the first place, and scolded myself for ever letting Jared feel that I was anything but grateful for every moment he was in my life.

"How are you feeling, love?" Jared said from behind, bringing a tall glass of ice water.

"As if you have to ask. I feel really good. It seems like every day I feel better and better. Is that normal? Aren't I supposed to feel sick, or tired, or both?"

"Not necessarily. What is normal when you're carrying our child?" Jared said, taking a seat beside me.

We watched the surf together. The storm from the night before had raged until the early hours of the morning...and there was a good reason that I knew that for a fact. Jared had kept his promise to take his time. I slept for an hour, maybe two, after the sun breached the horizon before venturing to the beach. The ocean was endless, stretching out until it met the sky. The only way to tell one from the other was the slight difference in shade. I took in a deep breath and leaned against my husband.

"What is it?" Jared said, grazing his lips across a small patch of skin on my forehead.

"It doesn't matter," I said closing my eyes. I wanted to focus on the sounds of the waves rushing the beach, and the way the breeze blew my hair forward. If it were possible to block the frightening thoughts from my head, I would have. I wanted to pretend that the truths I had come across in recent years weren't real. But they were, and inconceivable, nightmarish things waited for us at home. Those thoughts made it difficult to relax and enjoy my honeymoon, even with Jared's tireless reassurance. I had finally accepted my life for what it was, but that didn't make it less frightening.

"Look," Jared said, nodding to a spot up the beach.

Samuel stood at least two hundred yards away, too far away for my human eyes to tell if he was watching us or the ocean.

Jared nuzzled the hair just above my ear. "He has been granted a temporary new post."

"To babysit us?" I asked. "He must be thrilled."

Jared chuckled. "Something like that. Hybrids don't have Archs. Have I ever told you that?"

"No, you didn't."

"We don't. Our job to protect humans, that along with our knowledge and abilities makes having our own guardian angel redundant. Not to mention the curse…."

"But you still need protection, don't you?" I asked.

Jared thought for a moment. "We are born to protect. I think He sees it as an infinite waste of resources."

I nodded. "I see."

Jared's brows pulled in and he cocked his head a bit. "You seem different today."

"I do? What's wrong with me?"

Jared laughed. "Not your general well-being, I mean you. Your behavior. You seem less on edge. Why is that?"

My brows shot up, and I shrugged. "It's not because I'm not worried, I can promise you that. I have one more year of college, I'll be taking over Titan soon after…and I'm pregnant. The best part—my personal favorite—I have to be on guard for the next nine months just to stay alive long enough to deliver our baby, and hope the Creator of the Universe decides against his own rules to help us do that."

"Ten."

"What?"

"It's actually ten months. Forty weeks is ten months."

I frowned. "That doesn't help."

Jared stifled a grin. "I was proud of you at the hearing." When I didn't reply, Jared explained further, "With Michael. You made a great case. It might have been what kept me out of serious trouble."

"What might have happened? If Eli had decided against you?"

"The worst punishment would be death."

"But…," I began, thinking as I spoke, "you can't die unless I do."

"Or if I'm found guilty of disturbing The Balance. Heaven has zero tolerance for both of those things."

"The baby supposedly disturbs The Balance," I said, touching my belly.

Jared put his hand on mine. "God didn't create the baby, Nina, we did. Free will and The Law are on opposite ends of the universe. I could explain it for the rest of your life, and you still wouldn't understand. Even I don't fully understand it all. Just know that The Law is a constant, and The Balance is a variable. In our case, it depended on Free Will, and that makes The Balance a whole new beast."

"My head hurts," I said.

"I'm sorry. More water?"

I looked down to my glass. It was empty. "I hadn't even realized I'd touched it."

Jared moved his hand up my arm, his fingers pressuring different spots. "Your temperature is elevated, but I believe it's due to the pregnancy."

I nodded, staring out into the ocean. "Will it ever be over, Jared? Once the baby is born, will we have to keep fighting for every day?"

"No. Heaven will have to decide at some point that enough is enough. They will either save us or let us die. Once that decision is made, we are protected."

I looked up to the sky. "Why doesn't He just make it now?" Jared didn't answer, and it was just as well. I didn't expect him to. "Jared...," I hesitated. I didn't want to ruin our perfect morning. "I think I should continue my training."

He sighed. "You're pregnant, Nina."

"Yes, I know. But, can we both agree that there may come a time when I might have to defend myself...or the baby? I'm not asking you to beat the crap out of me; I'd just like to spend more time with the firearms, and for you to teach me some more complex moves."

"Okay."

"Okay?"

Jared wrapped his arms around me, resting his chin on my head. "You're right. We have to be prepared for anything. We'll start when we get back."

I smiled. "Thank you."

He leaned back, and lowered his chin so that I would meet his gaze. "You have to take it easy, though. I mean it."

"I will. I promise."

Satisfied, Jared took my glass and returned moments later with a fresh batch of ice floating in the water. I took a sip and sighed, trying my best to relax.

We sat in the morning sun, waiting as it crawled across the sky, hiding every so often behind the errant cloud. Jared and I were wrapped in each other's arms, enjoying a small moment of peace. Eventually, my stomach began to protest.

I looked down, and then to Jared. "I guess we better find something to eat."

"I'm surprised you didn't say anything sooner. You haven't eaten since yesterday."

"I'm surprised the baby didn't say something sooner," I said, extending my hand to Jared when he stood.

He tugged on my hand. "I can see I'm going to have to take better care of you."

We made our way to the eating lodge, where just a few other patrons sat at a table across the room. I dove into the fresh fruit bowl on the table, and then eagerly waited for the waiter to arrive.

An hour later, empty or nearly empty plates of grouper, callaloo, conch fritters and other Caribbean cuisine lay all over our table. For someone that didn't feel hungry, I couldn't seem to stop eating.

I mashed the leftover crumbs from the banana bread we requested for dessert with my finger and then licked them off.

"Wow," Jared said.

"What?" I said.

"You've always had a healthy appetite, but this is impressive." He grinned.

"I suppose so," I smiled. We both knew finishing the ridiculous amount of food I'd ordered was above and beyond anything I'd accomplished meal-wise before. Our table looked like we'd had a dinner party with ravenous wolves.

"Ready for a nap?" Jared said, laying a large bill on the table.

"Let's go exploring," I smiled. "Or snorkeling."

"Snorkeling? Still not tired?"

"No. I feel amazing," I grinned. Jared frowned. "What? I'm not supposed to feel amazing?"

"No. To me, you feel tired. You were hungry an hour before your stomach growled. I can't decide if I'm losing my senses or that your body isn't responding normally because of Bean. If it's the latter, I don't want you overdoing it."

"Okay, so I'll take a nap. Or at least rest a while if I can't fall asleep."

"Really?"

"Really. Why?"

Jared fidgeted. "It's just that...you're rarely this agreeable. I'm beginning to wonder if I'm in an alternate reality."

"Wow. I'm sorry I've been such a pain in the ass. I thought couples are supposed to get along on their honeymoon?"

Jared's brow rose. "So that's it? You're just being affable?"

"No, I trust you. You know my body better than I do, and I don't want to do anything that could hurt the baby."

Jared took a deep breath, and blew it out. "It's good to hear you say that." When I frowned, he shook his head. "No, I'm serious. Sometimes I wonder."

"You think I would do something to hurt our baby?"

"No!" Jared said, hugging me and chuckling at the same time. "No, that you trust me."

"Of course I do," I said against his chest. "Let's go to the casita and lay down for a while."

Jared nodded, and then took my hand. He strolled down the dirt path, and we laughed and joked as we made our way to our whimsically painted tin hut. His eyes were brighter than I'd ever seen them, free of any clouds. When we reached the door, Jared lifted me in his arms and carried me to the bed, carefully lowering me onto my back.

"You know," he said, brushing my hair away from my face. "I've always thought you extraordinarily beautiful, but this way," he said, touching my rounded belly. "I can't stop looking at you. You're stunning." His fingers returned to my hairline to sweep my bangs back, and then again, his fingertips gentle and soft against my skin. It felt so good, I could have melted into the bed. I was so relaxed, but I wasn't sleepy.

"You're not supposed to say that until I'm big as a house and need a little encouragement to be seen in public every day."

"I can't wait to see that. I've been all over the world, but that will be the most marvelous, beautiful thing I'm ever going to see."

"Until you see our child," I noted.

Jared beamed. "I have a lot to look forward to."

I cupped my fingers behind his ears and pulled him toward me, tasting his lips. "So do I." I tugged at Jared's shirt, and pulled it over his head. Jared pressed his warm chest against me, and I sighed. At least that part of our lives could return to normal.

"You should rest," Jared whispered against my skin.

"I will," I promised.

Just as I had closed my eyes, they were open. The sun still shined, and Jared sat on the edge of the bed, pulling his t-shirt over his head. He turned to me, puzzled.

"You promised to nap if we—"

"I did," I yawned. "I slept so good. What time is it? I feel like I've slept all day."

"Nina, it hasn't even been twenty minutes."

"You're joking."

Jared frowned. "This is disconcerting."

"Why? I've never really been a nap-taker."

"Yes, but when you do, you're out for three hours." Jared leaned down, pressing his ear gently to my stomach. He stayed there for a moment, and then sighed. "Something's different. I can't put my finger on it. You're different."

"I'm not. I told you I wasn't sleepy. Let's go snorkeling. I'm bored." I stood and picked a bathing suit from the suitcase, and hurried Jared to do the same. I prodded him to the beach, eager to have some fun. We snorkeled, we swam, we splashed each other and explored the farthest corners of the island. At night, we spent time together in the outside shower, and then snuggled in bed. If I hadn't already been pregnant, by the end of our honeymoon I surely would have been. Jared was insatiable, and it seemed that with every quiet moment, I whispered suggestive things in his ear.

Just like our last visit to Little Corn, the week went by too quickly. Jared noted the familiar sadness in my eyes as I packed.

"We can come back. When you graduate, after the baby is born, we can come back and stay as long as you'd like."

"I have a company to run, you forget."

"That will run just fine if you decide to take a leave of absence."

I shrugged, repeating the tedious cycle of stuffing my wedding dress into the garment bag and then smoothing it out. "Maybe."

Jared seemed to be out of sorts as well. We didn't speak much as the hired help stacked our belongings in the truck, and then again in the boat. Jared held me as the boat bounced across the waves to the main island, and relied on small talk as we waited for the plane to depart from Nicaragua. It was like saying goodbye for the last time to an old friend. It felt like loss. This time, there would be no ring to cheer me up, only the ominous thoughts of what might be waiting for us at home.

The fairy tale was over.

Once we were in U.S. airspace, I immediately dialed Beth to see what the situation was at Titan. Sasha worked to make life difficult for everyone, and Grant was more than ready for me to return so he could leave for his own vacation. Just a few weeks of school left, and then summer hours would be enforced.

Ryan was still recovering in the hospital. Beth noted that Claire never left him alone for a moment. Her comment made me think about the times I visited Ryan in the hospital after he was attacked, and I wondered if he had taught her the Logo game. I couldn't imagine Claire sitting beside his bed giggling and being silly. She was more likely to pout in the corner, trying to ignore his vies for attention and incessant questions. I hoped that I was wrong.

The pilot announced on the overhead speaker that we would make out descent soon. Jared tightened my seat belt and kissed the tender skin in front of my ear, whispering that it would be okay. I didn't feel particularly nervous about the landing, but I assumed he meant life in Providence. With everything that had happened in Little Corn, it was easy to get lost in that other world, and pretend real life in Rhode Island was just a bad dream. But the bad dream was real, and we were about to live it.

Descending the stairs of the jet, and then walking across the tarmac to the waiting car was eerily similar. The ground was wet from a late-spring thunderstorm; the air was so thick it seemed palpable. Samuel stood a hundred yards away, staying in the background, but allowing us to see him. Jared already knew he was there, so I knew his presence was for me. This time, though, Jared didn't go to him. He walked with me to the car, and nodded to our driver, Robert, as he held the door.

My cell phone buzzed and I answered. Grant wasted no time updating my schedule, hinting that I should come in right away. An important meeting was scheduled during one of my classes the next day, and he wanted to go over some key points with me to compensate for my absence.

I hung up the phone and sighed. "Maybe I should—"

"You're already looking forward to several days of makeup work and tests, and don't forget Finals coming up soon. Grant can handle it."

I nodded. "You're right. I'll meet with him this evening. He has an hour, and then I'll hit the books."

Jared shook his head.

"What? What did I say?"

"You. Agreeing with me without a single argument. It's something I'll have to get used to."

I pressed my lips together in a hard line, trying not to smile. I must have been a true nuisance to him. I owed him a nice, long vacation from my stubbornness.

"I can't believe I've been so awful to you. I'm sorry."

Jared took my hand in his, and turned to face me. "You have not been awful. You've had an incredible amount to deal with, and doing things on your terms was important to you. Making choices was the only shred of control you had in this entire, crazy situation. I've never begrudged you that. In fact, it's one of the things I love about you."

"Regardless, consider it significantly toned down."

Jared smiled. "You don't have to apologize for coping. It's been tough for everyone. It's been a lot. However, I won't lie and say I'm not going to enjoy the new attitude."

I leaned in and kissed the corner of his mouth. "You're going to see a lot of new from me. I don't want to be a victim, anymore. I am now an active participant in what happens to me and my family. We're going to get through this together or not at all."

Jared beamed. "You amaze me every day."

"Well, if you're quite finished being amazed, I need to go into work for a bit. Robert? We'll need the Escalade."

Robert glanced at me in the rearview mirror with his wrinkled, kind eyes. "Yes, ma'am." He made a turn, taking us to our home. That was one thing very different from our last trip to Little Corn. Home was no longer the loft.

The tires crunched across the gravel drive, and Robert slowed the car to a stop next to Jared's SUV. The door opened, and Robert lent me a hand. "It's good to have you back, Miss…," Robert seemed flustered for a moment before speaking again, "I deeply apologize. Mrs. Ryel."

I smiled. "Just for that, you get a raise, Robert."

He nodded to Jared, and then popped the trunk, pulling our bags from the back. "I'll have your things laundered and returned to your room."

"Thank you, Robert," Jared said. He grabbed my hand and led me to the Escalade, pulling open the door. He lifted me into his arms and placed me gently in the passenger seat. "Since I don't have time to carry you across the threshold, I suppose this will have to do."

I laughed. "It'll do," I said, placing each of my hands on his cheeks for a quick kiss.

Providence seemed different. Remnant rain dripped from the trees, the beautiful buildings still loomed over the streets, and the traffic still made walking across the post-storm street a challenge for pedestrians who wished to remain dry. But it was foreign somehow. Providence would always be home, but for now it was a battleground—a place to stand off with those who would harm my child. For the next months until I gave birth, I would walk the streets on guard, in constant suspicion of everyone I came across, and cautious of every dark street. Having no idea when Hell would act, or what they had in store for us, it was important now than ever to be prepared and vigilant. All things considered, I was glad it was on my own turf. My ancestors weren't just Rhode Islanders. I was Nephilim. We survived King David, the flood, and the yellow fever epidemic of 1797. My husband was half angel. I could stand up to whatever they could throw at me. That was what I would keep telling myself, anyway. No sense in worrying myself to death about it.

"What is that?" Jared said, referring to whatever emotion he was sensing.

I shrugged. "Courage, I think," I said. "We can do this. I believe in you. I believe in us."

Jared's eyes darkened a bit, and he reached over the console to grab my hand. The muscles under his jaws twitched, and his fingers tensed as they intertwined with mine. "I definitely like the new attitude."

Chapter Six
Answer

Titan's tall, block-and-mortar façade loomed over Fleet Rink. Summer was just a few weeks away, and the rink had been transformed from its usual icy amusement to a popular hangout for local rollerbladers. Jared parked in his usual spot, kissing my lips before I stepped out onto the sidewalk and to the front entrance of the lobby.

I paused, the first few steps without Jared felt strange. Except for the few hours I spent getting ready for the wedding, Jared and I had been side by side every day for a week. An unsettling feeling came over me, as if I'd forgotten my cell phone or locked my keys inside the car.

I pushed through the front door and walked across the lobby, dismissing my unease. Jared remaining in the car meant that everything was just fine. If he sensed even the slightest bit of danger, he would be next to me.

"Get a grip, Nina," I whispered to myself. Inside the elevator, I pressed the button, and took a deep, cleansing breath as the doors slid closed. When they opened again, the relaxing breath proved to be futile.

"Well. Look what the cat dragged in," Sasha said. One hand on her hip, one hand holding a short stack of papers, her long red curls set off her sharp features. A mature person would admit that Sasha was beautiful—I, however, had accepted long ago that Sasha brought out the stubborn, angry child within.

"Oh, my. Did you get yourself a perm while I was away? I guess the eighties are coming back." I brushed past her, deciding against shoving my shoulder into her bony arm.

"Hot rollers. Grant has made a point to mention the curls today, too."

"Where is Grant?"

"In his office. He waited for half an hour in yours. You're late."

"I came straight from the airport. Why are you still here?"

Sasha shrugged. "I keep whatever hours Grant keeps."

I rolled my eyes and held out my hand. "Are those for me?"

"Yes," she said, handing them over. "I was about to make copies."

"That won't be necessary. Thanks for staying, but you should head home." I took the papers and made my way to Grant's office. His shoeless feet, in hideous tan and green argyle socks, rested on his desk.

"There she is: Mrs. Peanut."

"Don't start," I said, setting the documents on his desk. "I told you I would be right over. Why did you send Sasha to make copies of these?"

Grant covered his face with his hands. "Sasha's a sweet girl—to me—but she's an overachiever. I've been making up things for her to do."

I laughed once. "She wants the assistant job. That's why she's been in your hair."

"In my hair, in my office, in my desk, in my face, in my way. She's incorrigible. I honestly don't have enough for her to do. She refuses to help out in the other departments and won't leave until I do."

"Grant. She's an intern. She shouldn't refuse to do anything."

Grant thought about my comment for a moment and then nodded. "That's true. You can give her a new assignment in the morning."

"Oh, no. You're not pawning this off on me. Sasha is your problem."

Grant fell back against his chair. "I don't want to upset her, and you don't seem to mind. I thought you'd be happy to do it."

"How has this company lasted so long with such a weenie in charge?" I said, scanning the document. "Are these... bullet points?"

"I had Sasha type it out. I told her I didn't want to forget anything." I made a face, and Grant shrugged. "I didn't see her for an hour. She had trouble perfecting the margins."

"Grant, you know this account inside out. You didn't need to touch base with me. Just get the damn agreement signed and send them on their way." I stood, irritated he had wasted my time.

"I plan on it. The trouble is, this deal has the potential to take Titan in a different direction than what your father had envisioned."

"Jack envisioned making money. Do the deal."

Grant's shoulders fell, and his eyes lowered to his desk, despondent.

"Wait a minute...," I said, pointing my finger at him. Grant immediately tensed. He was caught. "You didn't want to talk about the meeting at all! You wanted me to take care of Sasha for you!"

Grant reached out to me. "You don't understand! She reorganizes my desk every morning! She makes lists for my to-do lists!"

"You're not married to the woman. I can't believe you pulled me away from my first night back from my honeymoon for this."

His eyebrows shot up. "How was it, by the way? Must have been somewhere tropical. You managed a decent tan. I never thought you would run off and get married. Jack wouldn't have approved."

"You can't elope when you've been engaged as long as we have. It was more last-minute planning. I'll call you tomorrow between classes for updates."

"Yes, ma'am," Grant said, staring at the information packets on his desk. Sasha had undoubtedly worked on them throughout the week. They were color-coded and alphabetized. "She…uh…thought it would personalize the packets to put their names on them. In calligraphy."

"She's a calligrapher?"

Grant slumped in his chair. "She thought we should hire one for the task."

My face flushed. Grant was now allowing Sasha to misuse company funds for one of her ridiculous whims. "I'll have a talk with Sasha tomorrow. Beth has mentioned that the filing room needs some attention."

"Break it to her gently."

I rolled my eyes. "Weenie."

My office looked exactly as I'd left it. Beth had de-cluttered a bit during the week, but other than that, it was untouched. I sat in my father's chair and let out a cleansing breath. Taking over the company wasn't supposed to happen until after graduation, and I wondered how I would juggle my last year at Brown with my pregnancy and the pressure of running Titan. I would be a mother before I'd be a college graduate. Everything was happening so fast.

A familiar pair of hands gently touched the bare skin between my shirt and neck. Jared's thumb massaged into my tense muscles. My head automatically bowed, and I sighed. Without a word, he kneeled behind me and let his lips trail from my shoulder to my neck. I tilted my head, making the passage easier for him.

"You never come in here," I said, smiling. "I must be really tense."

His hand made its way down my shoulder, my arm, and then traveled slowly down my side, resting on my stomach. His fingers pressed into my skin, palming my belly like a basketball. His firm grip took me off guard, and I felt my eyebrows move in, curious what he was up to. His lips weren't as soft as they usually were; instead they felt dry and scratchy.

"A little lip balm goes a long way, love," I whispered.

"Is this unpleasant for you?" A voice rasped.

I looked down. The hand cupping my stomach had pasty, abnormally long fingers. The nails were filthy, and came to a point at the ends.

When I turned, a pale face and black eyes were just inches from my face. The creature grinned, revealing two rows of unnatural, razor-sharp teeth.

I sat up straight and blinked my eyes. The office was dark and quiet, except for the sound of my heart thumping in my ears. My breath was quick and shallow. The frightening man was no longer behind me, but a dark figure sat in the green chair on the other side of my desk. I gasped.

Jared reached out. "It's okay. It's okay, it's just me."

"Oh," I said, touching my fingertips to my chest.

"You're shaking."

"Bad dream. I must have dozed off."

"It's been a long week," Jared said, forcing a small smile. "My dad wasn't there, was he?"

"No," I said, trying to calm myself. "No. I don't know who it was. Someone with too many teeth."

Jared nodded once. "I could sense them."

"Or it's just that I'm pregnant. I've read pregnant women notice an increase in nightmares."

Jared frowned. He was always one to imagine the worst. With good reason, granted, but it would be nice if he would admit for once that something perfectly normal could be the culprit. I stood, grabbed my briefcase from the floor, and then shoved my feet into my shoes. I didn't remember taking them off. I must have been exhausted.

"Claire called," Jared said.

"Is something wrong?"

"Ryan's fine. They were wondering if we wanted to join them for dinner."

"At the hospital?"

"They're bored."

I ran my fingers through my hair and wiped the mascara that had likely smudged under my eyes. "I am hungry. That's the best time to eat hospital food, right?"

"I thought we could bring some take-out."

"Even better," I said, opening the door. "I know just the place." Jared put his hand on the knob over mine, and leaned down to kiss my lips. Instantly, I felt better. His lips were their usual soft and smooth. Not as warm, though.

I took a deep breath and smiled. No bullets raining down, no explosions, and no men breaking into the building with automatic assault rifles. Our first day back would be without event. I dared to hope that Hell would wait until the baby came to bother with threats. Their typical pride and overconfidence would give us a little more time to plan, and to win over some key allies on the other side.

As we drove through the streets of Providence, it suddenly seemed like the home I had known in my childhood. In that moment, it wasn't harboring threats at every corner; it didn't seem dark and sinister. It was the picturesque, bustling, traffic-heavy town I remembered. Where I was born. Where my child would be born, and where I'd walked the streets with my father. Providence was the backdrop of my love story with Jared. It was still home, and this is where we would make our stand.

"You're curiously relaxed this evening," Jared said.

"I don't know," I sighed. "Everything just feels right."

"That's encouraging."

We picked up dinner and then made our way to the hospital. When the elevator doors opened, Jared grabbed my hand and led me to Ryan's room. The door was open, but it was quiet inside.

Claire sat next to the head of Ryan's bed. Her head was resting on her fist, and she was smiling at him. Ryan's fingers mindlessly twisted a section of blanket next to Claire's arm. They seemed to be engaged in a sweet conversation about nothing in particular. I remembered when I was in that chair, giggling at Ryan's nonsensical humor, and I was glad to see the light back in his eyes.

The IVs and telemetry leads were no longer streaming from different parts of his body. He seemed so relaxed with Claire next to him. I reached out for Jared's hand. His knuckles brushed against mine as our fingers interlaced, and I looked up at him. He was smiling at his baby sister, pleased to see her finally content.

Ryan's eyes wandered to the doorway where we stood. Claire slowly turned our direction and offered a small smile.

"Knock, knock," Jared said, holding up the bags of take-out. "Cheeseburgers. Nina said it's your favorite."

Ryan's smile turned into a cheesy grin, and he threw his head back. "Oh, thank God! I thought I would starve to death."

"Oh," Ryan said, chewing an oversized wad of cheeseburger. "Red Stripe has the best burgers. Seriously. You shouldn't do this to me in the hospital. I might think I've died and gone to heaven."

Claire rolled her eyes. "Could you be a little more dramatic about a cheeseburger?"

Ryan stopped chewing, and wiped the bit of ketchup off the corner of his mouth with his wrist. "You don't have to be jealous of a burger, honey."

"Oh, brother," Claire said. She pointed at Ryan. "Do you see what I have to deal with? Will one of you call OSHA?"

"I don't know," Jared said. "You looked fairly pleased when we walked in."

Ryan took another bite and then smiled. "She acts tough every time someone visits. She doesn't fool me, though."

"Who else has visited?" I asked.

"Mom. Kim. Beth. Chad. Josh…yeah. That's about it. No, wait…."

"How did that go? With your mom?" I asked.

Claire frowned, and Ryan winked at her. "It went fine. She's developed a theory. Since the last time I was in a hospital you showed up, and now Claire's here, Mom thinks I'm getting myself hurt over girls."

"Aren't you?" Jared said with a wry smile.

"Shut it, Jared," Claire warned.

I handed Ryan his cup of soda. “You know, this is becoming a habit.”

His whiskers were far beyond a five o’clock shadow, and his hair had grown downright shaggy. He looked so much older than the last time I’d seen him in that hospital, and nothing like the Marine in the photos he'd sent with his letters. “Tell me about it. I thought I said two hospitalizations ago that it was your turn?”

“I took a turn.”

“Yeah, so you almost bled out, big deal. I’m three to your one.”

“Well, I’m pregnant, so I’m due for a hospitalization this year,” I said, processing the words as I spoke them.

Ryan laughed. “Wait…what?” he said, his face morphing from amusement to concern.

I looked to Claire. “You didn’t tell him?”

She shrugged, her platinum, angled tresses bouncing when she did so. “It’s your business to tell. Way to dump it on him, stupid.”

I frowned. Ryan mirrored my expression. “Congratulations,” he said. He glanced to Jared, sent him a lightning-fast dirty look, and then returned his focus to me. He pushed up in bed, sitting taller.

“Say it,” Jared said.

Claire watched the exchange, clearly unhappy. I wasn’t sure if she was just sensing Ryan’s change in mood, or if it was her own reaction to the sudden, unpleasant turn in conversation.

“It’s not my place to say anything,” Ryan said.

“You have my permission,” Jared said. After his last word, he gestured for Ryan to continue.

Ryan rolled his eyes and looked to Claire. “Isn’t this exactly what none of you wanted to happen?”

Claire seemed uncomfortable answering for her brother, but she quickly shrugged it off. "Yes and no. Not going along with the prophecy in Shax's book would have been the safer route—in theory—but Hell would more than likely still anticipate its completion. Now that it's happened, it's a means to an end. We have a better chance at getting Heaven on our side."

Ryan was right to ask Claire. Jared was well known for lengthy explanations. Claire went right to the point.

Ryan's eyes drifted away from Claire to me. "Are you okay?"

I shrugged. "Great. Fantastic, actually. I feel like I could run a marathon."

Ryan smiled. "That's good." He turned to Claire. "That's good, right?"

Her nose wrinkled. "Why are you asking me?"

"I don't know," Ryan shrugged, "I thought you might know better than anyone else."

Claire stood, laughing once. "I'm hardly the expert. It's never been an option for me, so I didn't bother asking my mother about the details."

"Why wouldn't it be an option?"

Claire rolled her eyes. "Because I'm busy."

"With what?" he said, dubious.

Claire placed both of her palms facedown on the bed and looked at Ryan. "Keeping you alive."

Ryan's hand slid slowly across the blanket. His fingers layered hers. "Well...what if we were together? That could make it an option."

Claire straightened quickly and crossed her arms. "Dream on."

The corners of his mouth turned up. He enjoyed unsettling Claire far too much for his own good. "Am I wrong?"

"First of all," she said, shifting her weight, "it's never going to happen. Second, I'd have a hard time protecting you when I'm as round as a bowling ball."

"I bet you could," Ryan said. "I can stay out of trouble for nine months."

Claire raised an eyebrow. "You can't stay out of trouble for one month. You've been hospitalized, had major surgeries, and needed extensive rehabilitation three times in as many years."

His eyes turned soft. "I would if I had to. I'd do it for you."

She cupped her hand over his mouth. "Shut up."

Jared fidgeted, feeling out of place. "Uh…we should go."

"No!" Claire said. She pulled back her hand and wiped it on her leggings. "No, you should stay. I'll uh...I'll get more chairs."

"I'll help you," Jared said. He briefly kissed my cheek before following Claire into the hall.

"Wow," I said, taking a seat beside the bed. "You can clear a room better than I. And that's saying something."

Ryan frowned. "She's tough. Tougher than you."

"Without a doubt," I nodded.

"No…I mean yes, but not in the physical way. She's here every second while I heal. I know she has to watch over me, but she doesn't have to sit beside my bed and hold my hand."

"She holds your hand?"

Ryan offered a half-smile. "The first morning—when I woke up—she was holding my hand with both of hers. The second I opened my eyes, she let go. But yes, she did."

"Okay, but you don't have to torture her. By her actions, she must care about you. This is Claire you're dealing with. You can't force it."

Ryan turned on his side, leaning on his elbow. "Nina, you're pregnant. Some rough shit is going to go down. Maybe tomorrow. Maybe the day you give birth to Lil' Bitty Saint Ryel." He pointed to my stomach, "But I think we can all agree that taking time for granted is precarious."

"Precarious," I said. "I'm so impressed."

"Shut your face," Ryan grinned. "I love her. I want to be with her. And not just around her. It's even worse knowing she's not here, but she's still somewhere around."

"I know the feeling," I said. My eyes unfocused as I remembered a not-so-distant past in which I struggled with studying in my dorm room at Andrews Hall, knowing Jared was somewhere nearby. Talking into a microphone hanging from my wall, standing in the freezing rain. Knowing he would come.

"I think she likes me, too, she just won't admit it. I just gotta crack that shell."

Ryan's voice snapped me back to reality. "Good luck," I said.

Claire and Jared returned carrying chairs in their arms.

"I love you," Ryan said, looking straight at Claire. She stood, speechless.

"Smooth," I nodded.

"I…uh…," Claire said, looking around. She sat the chairs on the floor and then looked at her brother. "Someone else might visit…I better get more chairs."

When the door closed behind her, Ryan looked down and laughed once without humor. "So stubborn."

"Better than stupid," Jared said.

Ryan's head jerked up. "Excuse me?"

"Let her do her job," Jared said, his voice flat.

"Coming from you? That's hysterical."

The tension between them thickened the air in the room. "Come on, guys," I said.

Jared's eyes were tight, and Ryan leaned forward a bit. Any civility between them had always seemed forced. It was only a matter of time before they exchanged words.

Jared shifted. "What is that supposed to mean, exactly, Ryan?"

"You seem to forget why everyone is in this mess to begin with. If you'd done your job by the book, none of this would have happened. So how about you let us all make our own choices without judgment?"

Jared's body was rigid; his jaw tight. I waited for him to let Ryan have it—to come back with one of his undeniable and logical retorts, but he didn't. Without a word, he left the room.

"Finally…he's speechless," Ryan said, relaxing back against the bed.

"You shouldn't have done that," I said.

Ryan frowned. "Why not? Because he's Jared? He has no problem telling everyone else what they've done wrong, but he hasn't made the best choices, either. He insinuated I'm keeping Claire from doing her job when he was in the same situation not too long ago."

"I know."

"Then why defend him? Why can't you just say, 'Ryan, you're right. Jared's wrong.'"

"Because he's trying his best. Because everything he does, he tries to do what's right, and what is in everyone's best interest. He loves me, and you rubbing it in his face after the fact is just cruel."

"He should keep his opinions to himself," Ryan said, crossing his arms.

"Trying to hold on to some control in a situation where he has none is not unreasonable. Claire is his baby sister. He's loved her far longer than you have, and he has firsthand knowledge of how hard it is to be in love with your Taleh. He's just trying to save her from what we've experienced. You should think about that."

Ryan raised an eyebrow. "So you regret it?"

"What?"

"You regret falling in love with him? Knowing everything?"

"No, and no! Of course not. It's just hard, that's all."

"What isn't?"

"A normal relationship?"

"Says who?"

"Normal people."

"What would you know about normal people?"

"I know a few!" I said. Ryan was attempting to subdue a smile. He enjoyed getting under my skin. Poor Claire. She wasn't the most patient person, anyway, and the most annoying, argumentative, persistent butt nugget—as Bex had once called him—was in love with her.

"What are you smiling about?" he said.

"Oh, nothing. Feel better," I said, waving to him before opening the door.

"Wait! You're going to leave me alone?"

"We're never alone," I smiled.

Jared stood in the hallway with Claire. She was looking up at him, whispering words of comfort. He seemed to be a bit calmer, listening to her every word.

"He's all yours," I smiled to Claire.

"Huh?" Claire said.

I took Jared's hand. "He knows the exact thing to say to throw you into a rage, and you just let him."

"It's different with him. I can't explain it other than pure, unadulterated hatred."

"Once upon a time it was me he was after, and now he's being just as annoying while pursuing your baby sister."

"Exactly."

"What if he wasn't?"

"Wasn't what?" he said, clueless as to where I was going with the conversation. A rush of exhilaration swept over me. Jared being on the wrong side of enlightenment was quite satisfying.

"In love with Claire. Honey," I said, standing on my tiptoes to wrap my arms around his neck, "this is a very good thing."

"For you, maybe," Claire grumbled.

"Did you forget what it means that he loves her? They are meant to be together; not him and me. Best of all? You would've had to deal with Ryan either way, but because he loves Claire, it isn't because you're watching him annoy the crap out of me—it's because he's annoying Claire." I allowed a proud, wide smile to stretch across my face, even though Claire looked as if she wanted to shove her fist into the wall. Through my face.

Jared's face relaxed, and he chuckled. "All true," he said, leaning down to kiss me. "It could be worse. Much worse." He looked to Claire. "Sorry. Good luck."

She glared at both of us as we departed down the hall.

"Er…hey, Nina?" Claire called.

I turned, noticing again how tiny she was. Her skintight blue leggings and oversized, off-the-shoulder T-shirt made her seem even smaller. Her ankle-high boots scooted across the hospital floor as she approached.

"Yes?"

She laced her fingers on top of her head, clearly exasperated. "You really think I'm just being stubborn? You think that's why he's my Taleh? Because we're meant for each other?"

"Yes," I said. "You care about him, don't you?"

"I don't know," she shrugged. She let one hand fall to her side; the other to her mouth. "I guess so."

I looked to Jared and gestured with my eyes to Claire. Jared frowned, but when I persistently jerked my head in Claire's direction, he spoke up. "It's okay, Claire. I can't say I like the guy, but I don't see another purpose for it to happen the way it did. Do you? Because if you do, I'd love to hear—mmph," he puffed, jerking when I elbowed him in the ribs. I didn't hurt him, of course, but I still enjoyed his reaction.

"No," Claire whispered. "I don't see another purpose." She walked slowly to Ryan's door, deep in thought. She turned the knob, and then shook her head. "Doesn't mean I should muddy the waters."

We followed her in, noticing her pulling her chair farther away from Ryan's bed. She ate her burger quietly, and Ryan watched her for a moment, and then looked down when he realized he wouldn't get the reaction he'd hoped for.

I felt bad for him. I knew all too well how awful it felt to love someone who insisted on keeping a distance. "So you're feeling better? When do you report back for duty?"

"They gave me a week off. Too bad I wasn't on duty when this happened. Could have saved me a chunk of change."

"Don't worry about the bill, Ryan," I said. "It's taken care of."

Ryan opened his mouth to argue, but he knew it was futile. He had no way to pay for what the little insurance he had wouldn't cover. He managed a humble nod. "This is my last time. Next time it's someone else's turn. I'm not playin' around. I mean it."

Claire's frown softened, the corners of her mouth turned up an infinitesimal amount. Her expression reminded me of the way Jared used to try to hide his emotions when he was fighting tooth and nail to stay away from me. Claire definitely had an uphill battle. Ryan was far more persistent than me.

We enjoyed our late-night dinner, teasing one another about our last few days together before Jared and I left for Little Corn. Ryan recounted his recovery, and Claire halfheartedly complained about being his nursemaid. Mentions of demons, Shax, and Isaac sprung in and out of our conversation. Discussing the paranormal elements of my life outside of the Ryels felt both a relief and strange. But, there we were: sitting around a room, discussing the sickening odor of the hundreds of misshapen creatures scaling the walls of St. Ann's.

"Have you heard about Father Francis?" I asked.

Claire nodded. "He's home. The first night was touch and go, and then he came right out of it. His doctors were amazed."

Jared touched my hand. Ryan's eyes zeroed in on the movement.

"So," Ryan said. "I hear you two skipped town for a while. You're…tanner."

"Yes," I said, nodding once. "We went to Little Corn."

"Again?" Ryan said.

Claire's eyes didn't leave Ryan's face. She watched warily for an expression she didn't want to see.

Jared squeezed my hand. "We decided to get married in the chapel there."

Ryan nodded. It was obvious an inner monologue was monopolizing his thoughts. Claire didn't move. She waited silently, but I couldn't decide what she was waiting for.

"What's the rush?" Ryan said.

"Didn't you hear her say that she's pregnant?" Claire said with disgust.

Ryan's head jerked in her direction. "Yeah? So?"

I shrugged. "We were engaged, anyway, Ryan. It didn't make sense to wait."

"You're married. To Jared." Ryan's eyes were wide with shock, his eyebrows as high as he could push them. Claire's body was tense, her eyes fixed on Ryan. In the next moment, a wide grin plastered across his face.

"Congratulations, Nigh! That's wicked awesome!"

Claire's blank stare melted away, and she took a deep breath. She managed a small smile, and then looked to me. Had I not seen the same pleading expression on Jared's face the year before, I might have missed it. She was worried that Ryan was still in love with me.

"Thanks," I said, looking down.

Thinking back on the past year, the dynamic between the four of us couldn't have been more different. Even so, it seemed every word uttered, every decision each of us made, led us to this very moment. Ryan looked at Claire with nothing less than adoration, and Jared reached over, resting his palm on my stomach.

A knock on the door abruptly disturbed our sweet little moment.

"Kim!" Ryan said.

Her clothes were dirty, her hair a mess. A small brown satchel hung from her shoulder, secured under her arm. I assumed it was the book. She was forced to keep it with her at all times. Kim was the only one who could keep the Naissance de Demoniac safe from Shax and his demons.

She didn't look like herself at all. "You!" She pointed to Jared. "You made me a promise, Half Breed, and you're going to keep it."

Chapter Seven
Broken Promise(s)

Kim breathed hard; her arm outstretched with a pointed finger just shy of Jared's nose. The air in the room was immediately heavy, the hairs on my neck stood on end. The Others were following her more closely, now, just waiting for her to make a mistake. Shax was back in Hell where he belonged, but his failure only made him more determined to have his property returned to him before Kim and Jared hand it over to the safety of the Holy Sepulchre Church in Jerusalem.

The constant presence of the enemy had taken a toll on Kim. The skin under her eyes was a deep shade of purple. Kim's typically flippant and impervious nature had slowly slipped away over the last two years. Her possession as a teenager had left her with the ability to take power from demons that Hell didn't understand, making her the perfect guardian of the book—until it could be returned to the one place Shax couldn't reach. She was just as desperate to free her family from the Naissance de Demoniac as Shax was to take it from them.

A nurse walked in, momentarily taking notice of Kim's curious body language, but quickly dismissed it when she began taking Ryan's vitals.

Pulling the stethoscope from her ears, the nurse seemed satisfied. "Doc said you can be discharged, but because it's late, he wants to keep you one more night and let you go first thing in the morning."

Kim lowered her hand, letting it fall to her thigh.

"Agh...." Ryan huffed. His expression screwed into disgust.

Claire rolled her eyes. "One more night is nothing. Quit whining."

One side of Ryan's mouth pulled up. "When I get home, you can come into the apartment, you know. You don't have to sit outside in the Lotus."

"No, thank you. I can't do my job properly and listen to you flap your jaws all night."

"We don't have to talk," Ryan grinned.

Jared stood. "On that note we'll be leaving," he looked to me, "preferably before I vomit cheeseburger in Ryan's lap for insinuating anything remotely intimate about my baby sister."

Claire was speechless, and I frowned. "Ryan. Really?"

Ryan laughed hysterically.

Jared promptly led me to the elevator by the hand. He couldn't get away from Ryan fast enough. Kim followed us into the hallway. Jared pushed the button, and then waited for Kim to speak.

She crossed her arms, already saying what she had come to say. She watched Jared expectantly.

He sighed. "I need more time."

"You promised. What are you waiting for, anyway? Nina is pregnant. The prophecy has begun. It can only go one of two ways now."

"I want to take it back to Woonsocket and spend a couple of days with Father Francis. We could find a weakness. We could find a way to avoid a confrontation all together."

"That's reaching, even for you," Kim said. Her pale cheeks were turning a soft shade of red. Kim being upset was so foreign to me that I almost couldn't process it.

"You and Nina just have a few weeks before summer break. Nina can't miss any more classes, and I can't go without her."

Kim narrowed her eyes. "You think I care about classes? This is serious, Jared. You promised that if I helped you get the book back, you would help me return it to Jerusalem. You promised."

Jared rubbed the back of his neck, clearly frustrated. The elevator door opened, and he pulled both Kim and I inside. An elderly couple walked toward the door. The older gentleman held up his hand, signaling for us to hold the elevator, but Jared quickly pushed the button for the doors to close.

"Jared!" I said, appalled. "Remind me why we can't just let Shax have the damn thing?"

Kim shot a sharp look in my direction. "Because it gives him tremendous power, power that someone from the days of Jesus was so afraid for him to have, they risked taking it from him. Now that your fathers have pissed him off, if we hand over his bible, the first person he'll annihilate with that power is you."

Jared squared his shoulders and lowered his chin. "I understand that you want to return the book and why. Trust me, I do. But when we…once we do this, Kim…it can't be undone. I will never get this chance again."

Kim matched his glare. "Then get it done."

The elevator door slid open, and Kim walked into the main lobby of the hospital. She didn't say another word, and she didn't acknowledge me at all.

Jared and I walked to the Escalade in silence. Both of their arguments made sense. Who could disagree with either side when they both wanted to protect someone they love? My first inclination was to insist Jared hold up his end of their bargain, but protecting me meant protecting our child. Bean was my first priority.

Jared seemed even more conflicted than I. He was a good man, and going against his word clearly bothered him. He was right; we needed to search every clue—every figurative and literal meaning of every paragraph of the prophecy. Forcing Heaven and Hell into a war was a last resort, and we couldn't be sure unless we explored every option.

I slept fitfully that night, dreaming about wars and demons and of Bean. My brain ran incessantly, stuck in a pattern of scaring myself awake, and then falling back asleep, only to imagine a new frightening scenario. In the hospital, in St. Ann's, in the Loft, we fought the demons over and over, but every dream ended the same: Bean would be in my arms one moment, gone the next. Panic would take over my every thought, but we all knew it was too late, and nothing more could be done. Desperation would plague me as I insisted Jared figure out a way to find and save our baby, and then unbearable sorrow when I realized it was over…and then my eyes would open.

"Nina," Jared whispered, following my name with smooth, short phrases in French. For whatever reason, French always seemed to comfort me, and Jared could sense that. His fingers combed through my hair, and his lips grazed the edge of my ear.

The sun cast shadows on every wall of my bedroom. I blinked, trying both to clear my vision and remember what day it was, reminding myself that what seemed like a lifetime of heartbreak was only a dream.

Jared kissed my cheek, and I turned to face him. "That was a rough night," I said. A tear fell from the outside corner of my eye, down my temple.

Jared used his sleeve to wipe the wet line away. "I noticed."

I looked out the window. "You know what will make me feel better?"

"What's that, sweetheart?"

"Training."

Jared nodded. "I thought you might say that. When do you want to start?"

"Tonight, after I put some time in at Titan. Is Bex busy?"

"I don't think so. I'll ask him, but he's always up for some sparring with you."

I forced a sleepy grin. "You should cut in once in a while. I'm sure I bore him to death."

Jared smiled. "We'll see. I'm going to whip up some blueberry pancakes."

"I'm going to whip up a lather in the shower. Do we have salsa?"

Jared's head jerked back a bit. "I think we have some left, yeah. Why?"

"I'm going to dip my pancakes in it."

Jared wrinkled his nose and stuck out his tongue. "So hold the maple syrup, then?"

"No, I want the syrup, too," I said, ambling to the bathroom. I didn't look behind me to see what revolted expression was on Jared's face, but he didn't move from the bed until I turned on the shower.

He was probably beyond disgusted, but it did sound good. What wasn't appetizing about fresh, spicy tomatoes, cilantro, onions, blueberries and pancake batter soaked in maple syrup? My stomach growled. I was suddenly ravenous.

I rushed through my morning routine, and yanked on a Brown University pullover hoody and a pair of jeans. The button was being stubborn, so I sucked in. When I still couldn't get it buttoned, I lay on the bed. Coupled with sucking in, I finally got it fastened. I made my way down the stairs, uncomfortable and stiff.

"We need to do some shopping tonight instead of sparring," Jared said, joining me.

"We can do both," I said. "Just don't take me to a maternity store. I'm not ready for that yet."

Jared shrugged. "Fair enough. I just want to make sure you're both comfortable."

I made a show of looking around the room. "Did you eat my salsa pancakes?"

Jared laughed once. "Absolutely not. Cynthia beat me to the cupboard."

"She's making pancakes?"

"No, and she's not serving salsa, either."

I frowned. "I sort of had my heart set."

Cynthia's high heels clicked against the tile as she brought in a tray and set it on the table. She placed an empty plate in front of me, and then sat a tall glass of an indiscriminate frozen cocktail on the plate. She added a bowl of fresh fruit, a bran muffin, and a slice of tomato.

"What's in the glass?" I asked.

"Fresh fruit, yogurt and peanut butter."

"That sounds awful," I groaned.

"But salsa pancakes are appetizing?" Jared said. I shot him an annoyed glare.

Cynthia nodded to my breakfast. "It's quite good, I assure you. I can't do this every morning. I happened to have a cancellation, but I do expect you to eat well."

All expression left my face. "You know, don't you?"

Cynthia offered a small smile. "I know everything, Nina, dear. Now, feed my grandchild. I'll see you at dinner."

She untied the strings of her apron and hung it over a chair, clicking her heels to the foyer.

I stared at the concoction in the glass. "I officially believe that I will never know what to expect from my mother."

"That makes two of us."

I drank the PB and fruit smoothie—which was actually quite tasty—and gathered my things for class. Jared walked me to the Escalade, but I put my hand on his arm before we left the drive. "I almost forgot. I have to stop by Titan and speak to Sasha."

"Oh, yes. To banish her to the file room."

"Her ridiculous crush is costing me money," I grumbled. "She hired a calligrapher to write names on the new client packets!"

Jared made a strange face, unsure how to react, and then turned the wheel toward Titan. I practiced what I might say to Sasha during the drive. Part of me wanted to smash all of her hopes and dreams like she deserved; the other insisted on breaking it to her gently. By the time Jared pulled up to the curb, I had given up on my dastardly plan of revenge, instead settling on a gentler speech. That decision put me in a less than amiable mood.

"See you soon," Jared said, kissing my cheek.It took some doing to find Sasha, but after looking everywhere else, I headed to the file room in the basement. The room was missing several lights; the only one fully lit was blinking. I stepped in, the concrete echoing under my feet.

"Sasha?"

I slowly walked down the aisle, looking to each side of me.

A small, muffled noise came from a dark corner of the room. The hair on the back of my neck stood up. I was alone, but something was inside that room with me.

I took a breath, and then walked as quietly as I could to the end of the aisle, turning toward the noise. A dark, huddled figure was slumped with its back turned to me. In the failing light I could see it shivering.

"H...hello?"

The figure froze. Adrenaline seared through my veins. Immediately every move, every act of defense I had learned replayed in my mind. My hands balled into fists, and I braced myself for a fight.

"Go away," Sasha hissed. She gasped, and her body shivered again.

Every taut muscle in my body released, and anger served as an outlet for the adrenaline. "What the hell are you doing down here?"

Sasha turned, wiping her eyes. "Peter said Grant was out for the day, and that I needed to straighten up down here until you came in. Does he think I'm stupid?" She stood. "Why would I want to work for someone that doesn't appreciate me, anyway? I wouldn't. I am far too talented to be sentenced to the file room."

"Sasha. You misused company resources."

"It was approved!"

"You're an intern. Interns don't hire calligraphers or order cappuccino machines."

"Grant loves cappuccinos!"

"Then he can buy one for his office."

"He's the CEO!"

"No," I breathed. "He's not. Report to Peter when you're finished with the file room so he can give you a list of new duties. You will work in Peter's department, now, so he is your immediate supervisor, and he will handle your evaluation. If you need anything, Peter will be happy to address your concerns."

"Nina!"

I walked out of the basement and took a deep breath. It was the first time my lungs felt like they were getting air. I noticed another, newer male intern walking down the hall, and called him over.

"Yes, Mrs. Ryel?"

"The lights in the file room need attention. Call maintenance and have the bulbs replaced or repaired immediately, and please help Sasha with whatever she needs. You'll find her at the end of the third aisle. And do not, under any circumstances, leave her alone."

The intern frowned with confusion. "Y-yes, ma'am." He stood there for a moment, every thought scrolling across his face.

"Well? Go."

He nodded, hastily making his way down the hall to the file room, and I paused, disturbed by the distinct Cynthia-like tone in my voice just then.

I rushed up the stairs, squinting from the bright sunlight bursting through the windows of the lobby. When I made it to the Escalade, Jared watched me warily.

"Was there a problem?" he said.

I took his hand. "They were in there."

"Who?"

"They, Jared," I sighed. I put my elbow on the console and covered my eyes with my fingers. "I could feel them." Jared was quiet, so I peeked up at him. He seemed confused. "You couldn't feel them?"

"What makes you think they were there?"

"I was creeped out, for one. I've been around them enough to know what it feels like when they're around. Sasha was down there crying; negative energy in the air; it was cold."

Jared's mouth pulled to one side. "That doesn't necessarily mean that—"

"Just," I sighed, irritated, "this one time, trust me. I'm not a Hybrid, but they were in there. Not many, but I could feel them."

"But…I couldn't feel them. It doesn't make sense that you could and I couldn't."

I shook my head. "I don't understand it." I thought for a moment. "Could you sense me?"

"Yes. You were just fine."

"I was not just fine. I genuinely believed something was about to attack me. You didn't sense that?"

Jared shifted to face me, his face darkened with concern. "You were afraid." His tone was more of a statement than a question.

"My adrenaline was about to shoot through my eyes! I thought your senses were heightened?"

Jared's eyes bounced around the cab of the Escalade as his mind tried to work out the details of this new development. He was clearly not taking it well. He faced forward, and shoved the gear in drive.

"Jared," I said, my voice low and soothing. It didn't work.

He slammed the gear back into park, and his hand flew to his head. He hit the steering wheel. "Just when I think I'm ahead … something else gets thrown at me!"

"Honey, we'll figure it out." I reached to touch his arm.

He gripped the steering wheel. "How can I keep you safe from Hell without being your shadow if I can't trust my senses? If I don't have any to trust?" His eyes were desperate.

"So be my shadow."

Jared laughed once, and then shook his head. "I can't go to class with you. I can't follow you around Titan, Nina."

"You can be within earshot. You said it yourself. You can hear me through the crowd at the Super Bowl."

Jared nodded, putting the gear into drive once more, but he was beyond listening to reason. He negotiated the one-way streets of downtown Providence without effort, and then pulled next to the curb behind Andrews Hall. He opened my door, and gestured for me to cross the street.

"What are we doing?"

"I'm walking you to class. You've only got a few weeks left. I'll wait for you in the hallway."

"Do you really think that's necessary?"

"I'm fast, but so are they. They are capable of a lot of damage in the few seconds it would take me to get to you from here. Without being able to sense when something's wrong, I would feel better being closer than not."

I thought a moment, and then nodded. Anything that was safer for Bean had to be the right answer.

The last few weeks of school came and went without incident. Jared stood in the hallway during my classes, and joined me, Beth and Chad for lunch. Without Ryan around, Josh found another table, and Kim was too angry with Jared to tolerate him.

The crisp air was just a memory by the time my junior year at Brown ended. The Main Green bustled with students who made their way to the Van Winkle Gates to see the graduating class make its last march through.

Before the last stragglers made their way through the gate, Beth, Chad, Jared and I walked to College Hill to beat the rush. Beth prattled on about her family begging her and

Chad to visit over the summer. She barely noticed the congested traffic. She had become a true East Coast woman. Even her accent had diminished. She sounded more like Ryan than her family.

"So what's for lunch?" I asked, tapping Beth's arm.

Jared squeezed my hand. "I thought we would revisit the place of our first date."

Beth slipped me a box, a bit larger than her hand, and without warning, I tossed it to Jared. I loved throwing things at him, because he always caught them. It had become our little inside joke.

"What's this?"

"Your birthday present."

"It's my birthday?"

"It's the ninth, isn't it?" I said with a mischievous grin. "I wanted to surprise you."

"Then I guess it is," he said. He kissed my cheek, and then pulled on the ribbon. "A book?" He thumbed through the pages. "A blank book?"

"A journal. You were down to the last few pages of yours, and I thought it would be a good time to start a new one."

Jared's eyes turned soft, and he took me into his arms. "It is the perfect time."

Chad rolled his eyes, and Beth sighed. "I remember that," she said, her thoughts lost in the sweet, mysterious first days of my relationship with Jared.

"Come on, Ryel. You're making me look bad."

We walked across campus, taking in the atmosphere. Electricity seemed to be in the air, along with the smells of summer. The chatter was louder than was normal; the young faces of students more animated. They would all embark on vacations, travel home, or spend their summer break on the beach or by the pool. I would most likely fill my summer trying to land punches on brother-in-law, or watching Jared read over the Naissance de Demoniac. The beach sounded much better.

Jared stopped in his tracks.

"Oh, no," Beth breathed, looking up at the building that was once Blaze.

I glanced at her, and then followed her gaze. "Shanghai? I thought you said you wanted to go to Blaze?"

Clearly disturbed, Jared let go of my hand. "Did you know about this?" Jared asked Chad.

"No," Chad said, shaking his head. "But I'd never eaten at Blaze, either."

I looked around, and realized we were standing in front of what used to be Blaze. The location of our first date was gone, replaced by sushi takeout. My jaw dropped.

"Seriously?" I said to no one in particular.

Beth's mouth pulled to one side. "I was looking forward to their sweet potato fries."

I felt my eyes bulge. "Jared!"

Chad huffed. "They still have one on the east side. On Hope Street, I think."

"I can't believe this. I just can't believe they…." My voice trailed off, too upset to finish.

Beth rubbed my shoulder. "That has to be upsetting. I'm sorry, honey."

Chad grabbed Beth's hand and stomped up the stairs. "This is not a tragedy. It spoils the sentimentality, yes, but it's still the same building. Make new memories. I'm hungry."

Jared pulled me to his side. "It's bothersome, but Chad's right. We can't do anything about it. If we are in the mood for sweet potato fries, we can go to the east side."

I nodded. "They have them at Cuban Revolution downtown, too." Jared nodded, and then led me up the stairs. I trudged behind him, unwilling to let go of my disappointment.

We stood in line with Beth and Chad. Jared reminded me that because I was pregnant, I should skip the sushi, so I grudgingly looked for something else. Double disappointment for the day. I silently hoped Bex wouldn't be busy later. I had a sudden urge to take a swing at someone.

We went to Shanghai. It still overlooked Thayer Street just as I remembered, and it still had some leftover lighting from Blaze. Beth giggled at Chad's overzealous appetite. Jared smiled at them, and reached under the table to touch my knee. Life seemed so ridiculously laid back that the only issue I had to complain about was the closing of our favorite restaurant. That thought caused the corners of my mouth to turn up, and I continued shoveling my chicken and shrimp Pad Thai. As much as I wanted to hate their food out of spite, it was good. So good, in fact, that my plate was empty before Chad's.

Beth stared at me. "You should have mentioned earlier that you were hungry, Nigh. We wouldn't have waited until you were starving."

"I didn't know I was starving," I said, leaning back in my chair. I looked down, noticing that my stomach had already started to pooch out.

Beth rolled her eyes. "Oh, please. If you even think about saying you're fat...." Her words fell away as she noticed my protruding belly as well. "Food baby?"

I looked to Jared, and nodded. "Real baby."

"What?" Beth wailed.

"That was a productive honeymoon," Chad said.

"When were you going to tell me? I'm your best friend, and I had to find out because you started showing? How long have you known?" Beth was obviously upset, but her high-pitched whines had garnered the attention of everyone in the restaurant.

Jared leaned in and kept his voice low. "Just a few weeks, Beth. You're one of the first to know, I assure you."

Beth frowned. "She's already showing and you've only known for a few weeks? I don't believe it. You're only going to have a real, live baby. Why would I need to know something so trivial? It's not like I need to prepare at work or anything."

I smiled. Beth was grumbling to herself at that point. "I should have told you earlier, Beth. You're right. I'm sorry."

A grin exploded across her face, and she rested her chin on her fist. "You're forgiven. When can we go shopping? Do you know if it's a boy or a girl?" I didn't mirror her fervor, instead sensing the same overwhelming nausea I felt when Lillian bombarded me with wedding magazines two years earlier.

Jared took a breath. "We don't know. It's still new and overwhelming to Nina, so perhaps giving her a break from the reality of it would help the most for now."

"Oh. Right. You're right. We can talk about all that later," she said, waving her hand dismissively.

We finished eating and left. A minute later, we waited at the light—the same light at which Jared had honked at me, nearly scaring me to death, right after we first met. Beth had resorted to not talking at all, instead of risking saying something she wasn't supposed to. Chad tried distracting her with other questions, but she only offered nods or head shakes.

Just as the light turned green, an arm reached across me, grabbing Jared's elbow.

"Long time no see," Kim said.

Beth smiled, but Kim was obviously not in an amiable mood.

"I said I would call you," Jared said.

Kim raised an eyebrow. "I know you did. Three days ago. I'm not waiting any longer, Jared."

If I didn't know of her struggle with exhaustion, I would have thought she'd broken her nose. The purplish skin under her eyes looked like twin bruises. The whites of her eyes were bloodshot, and her shoulders sagged. I knew that look all too well, and I understood her desperation.

"I'm sorry. You're just going to have to."

Kim took a step toward him. "I don't think you heard me. I'm. Not. Waiting. Any longer."

Jared sighed, but he didn't flinch from her glare. "We've discussed this."

"Yes, we have. A lot."

A nervous giggle emanated from Beth's throat, and she shifted uncomfortably. "Waiting for what?"

Jared and Kim looked at Beth, and Kim shot an amused glare back at Jared. "Tell her."

Jared frowned. "You're being unreasonable."

"What are we waiting for? Again?" Beth said, her voice still unsure.

Kim crossed her arms. "My ancestors are Crusade Knights, and I inherited the duty of watching over a book my great-great-times-a-thousand grandfather took from a church in Jerusalem."

"Is it worth a lot of money?" Chad asked.

Beth jabbed her elbow in his ribs.

"Kim," I warned.

"So Jerry over here is half-angel, and he's the only one strong enough to help me get it back without getting myself killed. Only he's being selfish, and even though I helped him save Nina's life, he's not going to help me take it back, now, because he got what he wanted and isn't going to hold up his end of the deal."

"Kim!" I yelled.

Beth began laughing hysterically. "Oh, wow! That's a whopper!" Her Oklahoma accent came back with a vengeance. "Where do you get this stuff, Kim?"

Kim looked to Jared, desperation in her voice and tears in her eyes. "You need me on your side. Don't forget that." She walked away, leaving Beth and the rest of us quiet and unnerved.

Jared watched her trudge back to the Sentra. "We're running out of time."

Chapter Eight
Breakthrough

The oak tree loomed over us, casting a large shadow from the afternoon sun. The sweet summer breeze wafted along the uncut grass, making the delicate petals of the flowering dogwood dance with the violets. Heaven never felt quite as close as when I was on a blanket with Jared by our oak tree, with our names scrawled elegantly in the bark.

Bean had grown for weeks without threat, but Jared and I weren't fooled into thinking we would live the entire summer without event. We enjoyed the peaceful moments while we still had them, and that afternoon was no different.

Jared was studying Shax's book. He hunched over the ugly pages, knees up. One hand held the ancient leather apart while the other rested on my stomach. The book seemed out of place in our quiet, beautiful afternoon.

Jared's phone buzzed. He barely glanced in its direction and continued reading. He did that often when Kim called, resorting to ignoring her instead of repeating his reasons for holding onto the book. I could relate to her misery. Even so, it was easier to look the other way while Jared searched for answers while he could. To admit that to myself made me feel horrible, but it was a necessary evil. The choice to be a better mother than a friend wasn't really a choice at all.

A motor hummed in the distance. "You should probably get your sneakers on," Jared said. "Bex is here."

Bex was bringing firearms today. We would add target practice to our daily sparring session. His motorcycle came to a stop at the edge of my blanket.

I looked up at him. “That blanket is worth more than your bike.”

Bex took off his helmet and snorted. “Negative.”

“Sentimental value,” Jared said, keeping his eyes on the book.

Nearly fourteen, Bex’s body had filled out. He was an inch taller than Jared, and could have been mistaken for a man in his early twenties. Except for the childlike sweetness that remained in his eyes and his occasional displays of inexperience, I would never believe that he was the same person as the eleven-year-old I had met a few years before. It was disturbing.

I must have looked ridiculous in my black leggings and white t-shirt with Bean balled noticeably in front, crouching and ready in front of what looked like a full-grown man. Bex could have wadded me up like a piece of paper on my best day, and I knew if anyone had witnessed a pregnant woman trading punches with someone twice her size, they would have called the police.

“Bex,” Jared warned without looking up.

Bex’s nose wrinkled, irritated at Jared’s instruction. “I know. The subtle distention of her middle section is a constant reminder not overdo it. I won’t hurt your messianic spawn, Nina.”

I shoved the heel of my hand into Bex’s stomach. He barely paused, but it was still thrilling to me that I landed it. “Someone’s been reading the List of Big Words, again.”

Bex glanced to Jared, and then grabbed me. He twisted me around, more forceful than usual, pulling me into his chest. My neck fit snugly in the crook of his arm. “Okay. Now what?”

I stepped on his foot, jabbed my elbow into his ribs, and then threw my head back. Bex dodged, but had he been human I would have cracked his nose.

"Good," he said, nodding.

We went over the same old moves dozens of times, and then Bex showed me a few more. They were more offensive than defensive. Bex seemed to enjoy teaching those more, and I certainly enjoyed learning to attack more than I liked repeatedly attempting to free myself from an assailant.

After an hour, Jared brought the bag of firearms over, and then handed me shooting earmuffs and safety glasses. We walked over to a small hill, where Bex set up several targets. He was as excited as I was, but it didn't occur to me to ask why.

I practiced with a handgun, a rifle, and a shotgun. When Jared and Bex were satisfied with my aim, Bex tied a rope to a branch of the oak tree and hung a large log from it. He unrolled a paper target, and then taped it to the middle of the log. He gave it a shove, and it swayed in a large arc back and forth.

Jared handed me his sidearm. "Less than one percent of your targets will be stationary. You need to learn to hit a moving target.

I lifted the Glock in both of my hand and looked down the sights.

"Anticipation is key," Jared said.

I watched the log for a moment, and then squeezed the trigger. Bex leapt back with a yowl.

I dropped the gun and covered my mouth. "Oh, God! I'm sorry!"

Jared picked up the gun and tried not to smile. Bex, however, was rolling on the ground, laughing hysterically.

I glared at him. "Not funny, you little worm! I could have given birth right here in the grass!"

Bex immediately sobered, looking to his older brother for confirmation.

Jared laughed. "She's exaggerating just a little."

"Again," I said, holding the gun in front of me once more. After six tries, I sighed with irritation and pulled off the earmuffs, letting them fall to the ground.

"You're thinking too much," Bex said. He pulled his gun from the waistline of his jeans and pulled the trigger, never looking away from me. The target had a rip in the center where the bullet made contact.

I blew my bangs from my face. "You can't anticipate something without thinking about it."

Bex lifted his gun and pointed it at me, and I mirrored his action. We were at an immediate standoff.

Bex smiled. "Yes, you can."

Jared palmed my arm and lowered it slowly. "It's called instinct. It's in your blood, Nina. You just need to give in to it."

I looked at the log. "Give in to it," I repeated, raising my weapon.

Bex shoved the log again.

I shut out everything: the breeze, the birds, the strands of hair that kept sticking to my lip gloss. Everything was frozen, even my inner thoughts. My mind focused on the target, and I was in tune with everything. I could feel the movement of the log, the resistance of the rope as it rubbed against the tree branch, and even the wind speed and how it would affect the path of the bullet. I took in a deep breath and pulled the trigger. Bex grabbed the log and it instantly stopped.

"Nice!" Bex said.

The bullet had landed just a couple of inches above Bex's. I smiled, and Jared pulled me to his side, kissing my hair.

After that, Bex took the spare tire from under the rear of the Escalade and fastened a target to the center. He walked to the top of a small hill, and I stood halfway down. He let the tire go, and I took several shots as it rolled down the grass to the bottom, falling on its side.

Bex sprinted to the tire and rolled it over, offering a thumbs-up and a smile.

"You did really well today," Jared said.

I nodded. "I know."

Jared leaned down and touched each side of my stomach with his hands. "Mommy did good today, didn't she, Bean?" He waited a moment, and then stood. "Everything seems to be okay. Your pulse, Bean's pulse, blood pressure and breathing are all normal. I don't think Bean noticed."

"So we can keep going?"

Jared nodded.

I gestured to the book under his arm. "Did you find anything?"

Jared's small smile faded. "Feel like a trip to Woonsocket?"

Bex helped us load the Escalade with our belongings, and then waved goodbye, peeling out on his motorcycle to head home to Lillian.

Jared was quiet during the twenty-minute drive north. His eyes were locked forward, missing the incredible summer foliage on each side of the highway. I allowed it to distract me while Jared silently prepared questions for Father Francis. Poring over the same words over and over, not knowing what to look for, had to be frustrating. I reached my hand across the console, and almost instinctually, Jared covered my hand with his.

Still beautiful, he wore the stress and worry of the years since we'd met only in his eyes. He seemed tired, and desperate, but determined.

He squeezed my hand, brought it to his lips, then reached over to rest his hand on my stomach. He seemed to relax, then.

"Maybe...maybe you're going about this all wrong," I said.

"I'm all ears."

"What if you're reading the wrong book? It's too late to stop the prophecy. What you're looking for is a way to get Heaven on our side, right?"

"That's correct."

"You aren't going to find answers about Heaven in a book about Hell."

Jared's eyes flitted about for a moment, considering my idea. He didn't answer, but he acknowledged my words with a nod. I covered his hand with mine, and let him return to his thoughts.

We passed the rocky wall that welcomed us to Woonsocket, and then made our way to St. Ann's. Yellow tape surrounded the church. The glass from the once exquisitely stained windows had been removed, and the holes that remained were covered with boards and plastic tarp.

Jared parked, and we climbed the steps. He tugged on one set of doors, but they were locked. He tried two others, but they were locked as well. The tarp blew in the summer breeze, flapping against the building. The town seemed otherwise quiet.

Jared turned and noticed a passerby. "Excuse me," he said. "Is the church closed?"

The man shrugged. "Father Francis has kept it locked. He hadn't been actin' right since the explosion." He walked away.

An explosion. Shax and his minions all but tore the church to shreds during our most recent showdown, and it left St. Ann's looking like a war zone. Some construction had taken place, but Woonsocket was no longer the booming industrial hub it used to be. The community that had once pulled together to fund the extravagant adornments of their social center with paintings and stained glass was now preoccupied with a recession and modern priorities.

We walked to a side door, and Jared gave it a light tug. It caught again. "I don't want to leave without speaking to him, and I don't want to break in," he said.

"Call him."

Just as we stepped away, we heard a familiar voice.

"Wait!" Father Francis called, walking briskly from the back of the church. "I'm here, lad!" He slowed to a stop, trying to control his labored breath. "I'm sorry. I was in the back building, praying. It used to be the school, you know." His face dropped. "I'm ashamed to say I feel safer there, now."

Jared cupped the priest's shoulder. "I understand, Father. Some things you can't un-see."

Father Francis nodded, and then gestured for us to follow him inside. We walked behind him, waiting patiently for him to climb the steps into the side door of St. Ann's.

It was cold and drafty. The wooden pews and marble statues were covered with linens. An eerie feeling dwelled within the walls, and I could see why the priest didn't want to be alone there.

The faces of the angels and saints in the paintings looked down on us. I couldn't help but think they seemed sad, waiting for someone to restore their home to its former glory. "Father," I began, pulling my pocketbook from my purse. "I brought this hardship on you. Let me help." I scribbled six figures onto a check.

Father Francis' eyes softened as he took the paper into his hands. "Thank you, my child. We need this more than you know."

"Father," Jared said, pulling Shax's book from under his arm.

The priest's eyes widened and he immediately looked away, shaking his head. "Oh, no! No, no, no. You mustn't bring that here!"

A soft ringing in my ears grew infinitesimally louder, sounding more like panicked whispers. I looked around the room, but we were alone. Just us and the hundreds of people in the paintings on the walls and ceilings.

I looked up. In a scene in which God had cast out the rebellious angels, the artist had drawn them in such a way that the angels seemed to be falling out of the painting—out of the ceiling. I looked at another mural at the back of the church, featuring Navy sailors drifting helplessly in a stormy sea, reaching out to St. Mary. In a moment of what had to be confusion, I could hear their panicked cries. I could hear them all, shrieking and wailing at the sight of the book that brought their home down around them.

I squeezed my eyes tight, and gripped my ears. Their cries became so loud I couldn't hear individual voices, only their frenzied, collective panic.

Jared's fingers touched my arm. "Nina?"

At once, it all stopped. I opened my eyes and looked around. Insanity was the first thing that popped into my mind.

Father Francis nodded in understanding, however. "It gets too loud for me sometimes, too."

I peered around to the different faces in the paintings, unsettled.

The priest looked to the book, and then to Jared. "You can't have that, here."

"I still need your help, Father."

"I've given all I can give."

Jared shook his head. "I can't accept that, I'm sorry."

Father Francis left for the back of the church. Jared pulled me to follow. We kept a quick pace all the way to his quarters, where he immediately made himself a drink. He threw it back, and then made himself another. His hands were shaking, causing the mouth of the decanter to clink against the rim of his glass.

The priest closed his eyes and lifted his chin, taking in another gulp of the amber liquid with one movement. The glass dropped from his hands, crashing onto the floor. Some of the bigger shards made their way to my feet, and I stared at them for a moment.

"Father," I said, looking up at him. "It's almost over. I know you're scared, but we're taking the book back soon."

His eyebrows furrowed. "To the Sepulchre?"

"Yes," I said, reaching out to him. I touched his arm, and he placed a hand on mine.

"You won't make it," he said sadly.

Jared shifted in frustration. "Let's deal with the issue at hand, shall we? I just ask that you sit down with me one last time to try to find another way. Surely our only option isn't to just wait until the baby is born and hope Heaven steps in."

The priest shook his head dismissively. "We've searched every line. There's nothing."

"Just one more time. Please," Jared said. "Before I take my wife and unborn child to Jerusalem, I have to know I had no other choice."

Father Francis glanced at the leather-bound pages and sighed. "Very well." He adjusted his round spectacles, and glanced above him. "Then you must leave, and never bring that thing to the house of the Lord again."

Jared nodded. "You have my word."

The priest brought in an extra chair, and he and Jared opened the book. Immediately the room turned cold, and I wrapped my arms around my middle. The others knew we were here, and that we had the book. The element of surprise long gone, Jared didn't hesitate discussing different passages. When Father Francis would get an idea, the pages would be flipped to one prophecy, prompting Jared to think about something else. The pages would flip the other way. They argued and agreed; each idea led them only to more frustration.

Minutes turned to hours; still they went over each point of the prophecy until it sounded more like chanting than discussion. A strange glow lit up the edges of the windows, and I realized it was the morning sun. We'd spent all night in Woonsocket, and my eyes didn't even feel heavy.

For the first time, Jared looked up from the book to see me fidgeting in my chair. "Hungry?" He said it as if he'd just remembered I was there.

"Getting there," I said, resting my chin on my fist.

He threw the book across the room. It hit the wall with great force and hit the ground with a thud. Despite its age, not a page loosened.

I stood and walked to the small kitchen, found a glass and turned on the tap. My body was just starting to feel the beginnings of fatigue, and the tension in the room made me emotionally tired as well. A copy of the King James Bible sat on the counter. The spine was worn to nearly nothing, and the pages hung at an angle; the book was so spent it could no longer hold itself square. I flipped open the cover, and then pushed several pages with my fingertips.

"We should get you something to eat," Jared said.

I turned to the priest. "What does your Bible say about this?"

Father Francis thought for a moment. "Well, it does have its own version of the end days. It talks about the woman with child."

"I've mentioned to Jared that we're looking in the wrong place. If you can't find the answers in the Bible of Hell, shouldn't you look in Heaven's?"

The priest shrugged. "I suppose so." He walked over to the counter and picked up the book. "It's worth a try. A third of the Bible is prophecy."

I offered Jared my glass, and he took a sip. When he handed it back to me, he kissed my cheek. The two men returned to their chairs, this time opening Heaven's Bible.

Father Francis flipped the pages. "Let's start with anything that discusses women with child in the end days."

Jared nodded, and waited for the priest to find the first passage. They discussed trumpets, and something about seals—I imagined angels opening wax-sealed envelopes the way celebrities do at award shows—and a dragon and a woman with child. I tried to tune that part out, because the sound of it terrified me. But I didn't have the luxury of putting frightening prophecy to the back of my mind. Because of what I had seen the last two years, I knew prophecies were very real possibilities. My only defense against the instinct to run screaming was simply not to hear. The priest discussed literal and symbolic interpretations, among other things that made my head spin. I wasn't sure if it was exhaustion, the fact that I was purposely trying not to pay attention, or that their discussion really was simply over my head. At any rate, I was pregnant, tired, and irritable.

"It would be nice if you two wouldn't talk about me like I'm not here," I grumbled.

Jared's eyes turned soft, and he reached for me. "I'm sorry, sweetheart. We're trying to hurry, but we need to be thorough. This is our last chance."

"Why is that?" I asked.

"Kim needs to return the book to Jerusalem. I've made her wait long enough."

I nodded. Traveling to Jerusalem had crossed my mind many times. Shax and the rest of his minions would not make it easy for us to return his book to the one place he can't go. The Sepulchre was above the tomb of Jesus; the creatures of Hell were forbidden. Even infinite, divine patience refused to tolerate desecration of the Sepulchre. The war could start the moment the plane lands, or they could try to keep us from even getting on the plane. We had no idea what would happen. That was the worst part.

Father Francis looked up from the pages. His eyes were unfocused as he slipped deeper into thought. "There is an ancient Jewish apocryphal text called the Fourth Esdras. The archangel Uriel describes many things about the end of days."

Jared frowned. “I know what you’re about to say, and I know Uriel. Gabriel is the loudest adversary of Hybrids. Uriel is the second.”

“Nevertheless, his prophecy has some merit. He says—”

Jared cut him off. “Father….”

My curiosity and sense of self-preservation outweighed everything else. “Tell me, Father. I want to know.”

Jared sighed, and the priest continued, “He specifically mentions pregnant women in the Fourth Esdras. He says ‘Pregnant women will give birth to monsters.’”

Jared rolled his eyes. “Uriel thinks I’m a monster.”

I hesitated. “What…what kind of monsters?”

The priest glanced at Jared, and then back at me. “He makes many prophecies similar to Revelation. He refers to this as ‘The Beginning of Sorrows’. Jesus also states, ‘Woe to those who are pregnant or nursing babies in those days.’”

“That doesn’t mean anything,” Jared said.

“You need to listen,” I said. “Maybe you’re unable to figure this out because you refuse to hear the truth. Maybe this is out of our hands.”

Jared’s brows pulled in. “Those prophecies state an abundance of Hybrid births. If something like that were happening, we would hear about it. Besides, Bean isn’t a Hybrid.”

Father Francis pushed up his glasses, clearly intrigued. “You know this for a fact?”

“Yes. The only child capable of this kind of reaction from Hell, a child capable of disturbing the Balance, will be more than a Hybrid.”

“Your child isn’t human?”

I wrapped my arms around my stomach, cradling Bean protectively. “You make the baby sound like an abomination.”

"Isn't it?" Father Francis said.

Jared stood. "No. It's a child. Our child." He took my hand and I stood with him.

"Forgive me," Father Francis said. He stood before us. "I didn't mean to offend you. We are in strange times—frightening times. I let panic get in the way of my thoughts. I just don't see how it's possible."

"Nina is a descendant of the Nephilim," Jared said, matter-of-factly.

The priest was confused. "But, this is what you are. Nephilim are children of angels, born of human women."

Jared shook his head. "I am the son of an Arch. The Nephilim bred the likes of Goliath. Giants not meant to blend in. These angels roamed the earth. They had… rebelled."

The priest's eyes grew wide, and I felt mine mirror his. I gripped Jared's shirt. "What are you saying? That I'm a descendant of demons?"

"That's not what I said. We're talking thousands of years ago, Nina. Many things were different back then."

"Rebellious angels were cast out, Jared."

Jared cupped my arms. "My mother is a descendant of Celts. They were savages, Nina. They drank the blood of their dead. I don't personalize it. That's not what I am."

"Then why did you leave that part out?" I covered my face with my hands, ashamed to even look at Jared. He was half angel, and I was carrying around the genes of Hell. No wonder our child was so rare. "Did you know that before?" I asked, my eyes filling with tears.

"No."

My cheeks felt as if they had caught fire. I was hesitant to ask the question that had come to my mind, but I would anyway. I always did, no matter how horrible I thought the answer would be. "Does it change the way you feel about me?"

Jared took my jaws gently into his hands, and he looked straight into my eyes. "Nina, of course not. How could you even think that?"

"Because I don't know how I feel about me, now."

Jared put his lips on mine, and then he pulled me to him. It was my father's last secret, the last thing Jared had tried to keep from hurting me. But, now that it was in the open, everything made perfect sense. I could never quite fit the pieces together until now.

Still, I felt…the only way to describe it was that I felt dirty. After all of that, we were no closer to an answer than when we'd arrived. "Is that what Uriel meant when he said 'monsters'? What will the baby be?"

"Our baby. Bean will be our baby, nothing more. You know what you need?" he said with a small smile.

"What's that?" I said, wiping the delicate skin under my eyes.

"The comfort of experience." Jared tugged on my hand. "Let's invite Lillian to dinner."

Father Francis held out his hand. "We're not finished, are we?"

Jared frowned. "The answers aren't in those books. I don't know what else to do."

"The answer is always in this book," Father Francis said, holding his Bible in his hands. He held it to his chest. "We've just missed something."

"We haven't missed anything. I had hoped He would lead you to the answer, Father, but He hasn't so much as whispered in your ear."

Jared's words sent my mind spinning. Had we missed something? Had the answer been in front of us all along? I clicked through each idea and passage of scripture I'd heard them discuss like channels in my mind. I kept coming back to Shax's book, and returning it to Jerusalem.

"Maybe it's not in my ear he's whispering?" The priest said.

Jared waved him away. "Nina's exhausted and hungry. It's clouding my thoughts. All I can think about is that damn book and returning it so Shax can't get to it and we can concentrate on keeping Nina safe."

"Wait, what?" I said, stunned.

"I have the Jerusalem trip on my mind. I can't focus on anything else. It's maddening."

"He's whispering," I said.

Jared raised an eyebrow. "What?"

Father Francis nodded, and hobbled to where we stood. "She's right."

I gripped Jared's shirt. "The Sepulchre. The only place they aren't allowed to desecrate. The one place the book is safe from Hell's hands."

Jared's eyes lit up like twin fires. "We can keep you safe there."

Chapter Nine
Due

Bex finished the last place setting, and then returned to the kitchen. Lillian sat happily at one end of my mother's long, imported table, Cynthia not so happily at the other. I waited anxiously with them, shifting uncomfortably in my seat. Almost to a beat, Cynthia would shoot me glances of disapproval. She hated it when I fidgeted, but now that I was married, she felt it impolite to mother me. Bex and Jared worked furiously in the kitchen, their laughter and conversation filtering to the formal dining room along with the delicious smells of savory herbs.

Bex appeared again with a basket of hot dinner rolls and a butter dish. His eyes darted to the empty doorway, and then back to the table. "It's about time."

The front door opened, and then I heard Claire grumbling under her breath. She and Ryan made their way to the table like summer and winter—Ryan was all smiles, and Claire sported her usual scowl.

Bex brought in a pot of steamed vegetables in one hand, and a bowl of rice in the other. Ryan pulled out Claire's chair and then clapped his hands, rubbing them together.

"I can help," he said.

Bex nodded once toward the kitchen. "Just pick something and bring it out to the table." He pulled off his apron and took a seat next to his mother.

"I think you should leave it on," Claire said. "Pink pinstripes look good on you."

Bex stuck his tongue out at his sister and then placed his napkin in his lap. Lillian shot a look at Claire and then smiled at Bex. "It looks wonderful, as always, son."

Ryan returned with a casserole dish of scalloped potatoes, and Jared brought in a huge ham. They were laughing about something, and I couldn't help but attempt to sneak a peek at Claire's reaction. She allowed a half smile, but it quickly vanished when Ryan took a seat next to her.

Jared sat next to me, and we began passing around the different dishes, filling our plates. As stressful and dark as the situation seemed, the banter was jovial, and Jared's mood was nearly cheerful. The weight of an answer had finally been lifted, and he felt hopeful again.

Cynthia barely finished her meal when she looked at her watch. "Jared. Bex. Thank you so much for dinner. I do apologize. I have an engagement."

Jared nodded. "Of course, Cynthia. Thank you for joining us."

She paused behind my chair and cupped my shoulders, kissing my cheek. "It was good to see you, Nina dear."

I nodded, and her heels clicked to the front door.

Ryan's brows jumped. "She's not one for family functions, huh?"

"Not really, no," I said.

"Cynthia shows her humanity by way of charities. She's very busy, but she's helped so many people." Lillian said.

"That she has," I said. "Is there pie?"

Jared laughed, and Bex popped up. "No, but there is cake."

"Angel food?" I asked.

"Of course," he said, leaving for the kitchen.

Ryan pulled his fork from his mouth, clearly ready for dessert. "So what's the real occasion?"

Bex returned with the cake, setting it right in front of me. "Trying to keep the pregnant woman fed. It takes a village, ya know."

"Very funny," I said, but I couldn't help from cutting a huge piece. Pregnancy was the perfect excuse for gluttony.

"Ryan has a good point," Lillian smiled. "You're in a very good mood for a change."

Jared smiled. "I took the book to Father Francis."

"Again?" Claire said, surprised.

I swallowed the delicious, spongy bite in my mouth. "We were there all night."

Ryan cut his own piece of cake, but handed it to Claire. "So you found something?"

"Not a damn thing," Jared said, smiling.

Ryan cut another piece for himself, causing a wider smile from Lillian. Claire just rolled her eyes.

"I don't get it," Claire said.

Jared used his fork to attempt to cut a piece of cake from my slice, but I stuck out my elbow to defend my plate. Everyone laughed, including Jared.

Jared finally gave in and cut his own slice. "Nina and I were distracted. All we could think about was getting Shax's book back to Jerusalem for Kim."

Ryan pointed at me with his fork. "She called me today. She's past impatient. She was yelling. I've never heard her yell."

"It's her lucky day, then," I said.

"Oh yeah, why's that?" Ryan said, chewing.

Jared put his elbows on the table and folded his arms. "Because we're leaving for Jerusalem next week."

Claire shrugged. "Well, that's smart. Ryan and I are both starting Brown in the fall, and it's Nina's senior year. It's good to get it out of the way."

Lillian paused. "You're going to Brown?"

Claire shrugged. "Ryan wants to start back…I just thought…."

"No, I'm thrilled!" Lillian said, beaming.

"We're not coming back until Bean is born," Jared said. The entire table was silent. No one moved, and all eyes were on Jared. "The answer has been right in front of us all along. The Sepulchre is the one place I know she'll be safe until she can deliver."

Claire frowned. "You want to live in Jerusalem for nine months?"

"Not an entire nine months," Lillian said. "I'm not exactly sure, but she probably only has a couple of months left."

Jared's face blanched. "What?"

Lillian fiddled with her napkin. "I should have said something, son, I'm so sorry. Nina's situation is obviously different, but a full term Hybrid pregnancy is six to seven months. I assume it's the same, maybe less for Bean."

Bex smiled. "Now you're saying it. That poor kid is never going to get a real name."

I looked down at my stomach. Because of our situation, we had refrained from prenatal care, but I'd just assumed my pregnancy would be a normal gestation. I was measuring a bit larger than normal, but nothing out of the ordinary. Jared assumed it was because of my small frame.

"So…July? August?" I asked.

"Possibly," Lillian answered.

Jared nodded. "Then it's settled. The closer it gets, the more danger she's in. We should leave now."

I shook my head. "I have things at Titan I need to wrap up."

Jared sighed, but agreed. "Okay. We'll all take the week to prepare. We leave on Sunday."

"Sweet!" Bex said.

"Not you," Claire said. "You have to stay with Mom."

"What?" Bex wailed.

Jared glared at him. "We can't leave her alone."

"But I have to go. You know I do!"

Lillian frowned. "Jared, that's ridiculous. You need everyone with you to get her there safe. The second you land, you'll be bombarded. They will do everything they can to keep her from somewhere they can't go."

I swallowed. It was so close. I'd always felt like we had plenty of time before the pandemonium started.

Claire sighed. "We can't leave you unprotected, Mom."

"What about Grant?" Bex said.

"Bex!" Jared yelled. His voice boomed throughout the house. Bex's face turned red, and his eyes immediately fell.

"Grant?" I said, confused. "Grant Bristol?" No one said a word. All eyes were on the table but mine, which danced in every direction. "Titan's Grant? Is a…Hybrid?"

"No," Lillian said, cupping Bex's shoulder. "He's an Arch."

I dropped my fork, and it clanged against my plate. "I don't believe it."

Lillian attempted to soften Jared with one of her sweetest smiles. "It's not a bad idea."

I turned to him, thwarting Lillian's effort. "This isn't something you thought I needed to know? Are you kidding me?" I wailed.

Jared's expression turned desperate. "You can't expect me to tell you about every angel or demon that passes by."

"I work with him, Jared. I…I'm just baffled why you chose to keep it from me! This makes twice today!"

"What else haven't you told her?" Ryan asked, enjoying the show.

Jared shot a death glare in Ryan's direction. "It was his secret to tell, Nina, and it's really not paramount that you know. In the grand scheme of things, it's really minute. You're being unreasonable."

"Minute." I stood up from my seat. "I don't think asking for a little trust, or having the expectation to not be treated like an outsider in my own company or family, is unreasonable. I don't think being upset to be the last to know that I'm pregnant is unreasonable. I am tired of you choosing what is and is not acceptable for me to know, only for me to find out by chance sometime later like a slap in the face!"

Jared's eyes drifted to the floor. I threw my napkin to the table, stomping up the stairs to the bedroom in Oscar-worthy fashion. I sat on the bed, still fuming. A small knock at the door only amplified my anger.

"Go away, Jared."

"It's Claire."

"I don't want to talk to you, either."

Claire, being Claire, walked in anyway. She sat on the bed next to me, crossing her arms. She sat silent for the longest time, and finally took a breath.

"I get it, you know. They don't tell me nonessential information, either. It's crap."

"It's demeaning is what it is." I frowned in her general direction. "I'm his wife. I understand I've been the token human that doesn't understand the rules of the universe, but for the love of all things holy. I know enough by now. He should trust me."

"It's not that he doesn't trust you. He tries to keep your life as normal as possible. He knows how important that is to you."

"It's a moot point these days, wouldn't you agree?"

"I would, but I don't love you like he does."

My mouth pulled to the side. She was fighting dirty. Jared loved me, and at times let that fact cloud his judgment. It was impossible to stay angry at him for it. Jared keeping Grant a secret from me defied logic. It simply didn't make sense.

"He should have a good reason for keeping things from me, and he doesn't have one."

"It's a very human reason, actually."

"Enlighten me."

"Grant's been in love with you for ages. Why do you think Jack was constantly pushing him in your direction?"

"That doesn't make sense, either. Jack didn't want me with Jared because of the prophecy. He definitely wouldn't want me with an Arch."

Claire raised an eyebrow, and the same side of her mouth turned up. "What do teenage girls do when their parents tell them not to do something?" Claire said. "If Jack told you to stay away from Grant, you would have run straight for him."

"Ick," I said. "No one's that stubborn."

"You are."

I sighed. "Why didn't Jack use the same logic with Jared?"

"He didn't have to. He forced Jared to stay out of sight. That solved the problem. Grant didn't take orders from Jack."

"Oh, yes, he did. I saw it on many occasions."

"You saw what they wanted you to see."

"Still doesn't explain why he kept it from me," I huffed.

"Jared might seem divinely perfect, but he's human, too, Nina. He can make decisions based on the fear of losing you to someone else just like any other insecure boyfriend. It hasn't been the first time."

"He's not my boyfriend any more."

"Once he waited to tell you, it was something he'd kept from you. It was already too late, wasn't it?"

"I suppose you're right."

"Of course I am," Claire said, pulling me to my feet. She slapped my backside. "Now go kiss and make up with your husband who is more than likely kicking himself right now."

I walked to the door, hesitated, and then finally pulled it open. Jared stood in the hallway, his hands in his pockets.

I crossed my arms. "You look like you lost your best friend."

"Did I?" he asked, miserable.

My shoulders fell.

"I'm sorry," he said. "I swear that's everything. You know everything else."

"I think I've heard that before," I said, walking to him until I was just inches away.

Jared touched each side of my stomach and looked down, his eyes dark with worry and guilt. I wrapped my arms around his neck and touched my cheek to his. We stood silently for a long while in that embrace. Holding him felt just as good if not better than the first time. The electricity was still there, and I had the same desperate need to be closer to him. He smelled just as amazing, and his skin was still as soft. Too many months had passed since we took a moment to ourselves just to hold each other. I tried to be present in that moment and be aware of everything possible. We would leave in eight days, facing the fight of our lives. I didn't know when this moment would happen again.

His hand slipped to my lower back, and he pulled me closer. I lifted my chin, and his lips touched mine. I dug my fingers into the skin of his arms, and then deeper into the muscle. His tongue slipped into my mouth, but then he pulled away.

"Ahem," Ryan said.

I turned to see the source of the interruption standing next to Claire at the top of the stairs.

"Figures," Jared grumbled.

We returned downstairs together, joining Bex and Lillian in the foyer. I hugged my mother-in-law goodbye, smiling when her enthusiastic hug became a bit too tight.

"I love you," she said, kissing my hair. She looked to Jared. "Be good to each other." Jared nodded, and she waved goodbye.

I walked into the dining room, and Jared, Claire, and Ryan followed.

Ryan and Claire began clearing the table. Ryan smiled and elbowed her. "Your mom loves me."

"She loves everyone," Claire sneered. "You're not special."

"You don't love everyone. I'd say that makes me pretty special…since you do."

Claire glanced at Jared and me, clearly embarrassed. "You wish!"

"Just say it," Ryan said.

"Stop telling me what to do," Claire snapped back.

He crossed his arms. "It's because I'm human, isn't it?"

Claire's eyes narrowed. "Seriously? It is possible that I just don't like you."

"Me?" Ryan said, pointing to his chest. "Nah," he said, dismissing her suggestion. "You're a strong woman. I get it. Not many can handle it that their girl could kick their ass. Even fewer soldiers, and even fewer Special Forces guys. But I get it, and I can keep up with you more than anyone else could. I've had training...and we've pretty much been told by the Creator of the Universe that we have to spend all of our time together. How much proof do you need?"

Claire turned and swiped her leg under Ryan's feet, throwing him to the ground, flat on his back. "First of all, you can't keep up with me. Second of all—"

Ryan kicked forward, and then leapt to his feet. Claire crouched in a defensive position. Ryan smiled at her reaction. "I can keep up with you."

"I doubt that."

"Try me. If I can't, I'll leave you alone."

Claire looked at Ryan from under her brow. Her ice-blue eyes turned murderous, but under them was a mischievous smile.

I frowned. "This is a terrible idea."

"Too late now," Claire said.

She bent her knee and shoved her boot into Ryan's stomach. He flew across the room and flattened against the wall, falling to the ground. He stumbled to his feet and sucked in a few times, the air knocked out of him.

I cringed. "At least she's not wearing stilettos."

Ryan shot an annoyed look my way, and then coughed a few times. He stood on wobbly knees and lifted his hands, palm-out to Claire. "You should know by now that I don't give up."

Claire grinned with devilish intent. "I'm going to enjoy this."

"Not as much as me," Jared said. I glared at him, and he shrugged. "What?"

Claire attacked, and Ryan turned. With a different adversary, he would have turned at the precise time to avoid a landed punch, but Claire was faster than the supernaturally fast—and she preferred kicking.

Claire spun around, her heel making contact with Ryan's backside. He was shoved forward a few steps, and then turned and punched. His hand met the drywall, and it cracked in several pieces around his fist.

"He better know how to fix that," I grumbled.

Claire leaned forward and elbowed the back of his head. Ryan spun around, wrapping his arms around her waist at the same time. He charged forward, and they both crashed into the table.

"C'mon!" I yelled, seeing my mother's imported English dining table in pieces.

Immediately on her feet, Claire grabbed two fistfuls of Ryan's shirt and tossed him into the foyer.

"I love it when you play rough!" Ryan yelled from the other room.

Claire wiped her bloodied lip and licked the crimson liquid from her fingers. "You haven't seen rough yet." She disappeared through the doorway, and I winced when Ryan cried out.

"That's fighting dirty!" he yelled, crying out again.

"We'd better get in there and supervise," Jared said, pulling me into the next room.

Claire held Ryan upside down by his ankle, feigning sympathy as he swiped at her to no avail. He scanned the room and then arched his back, lifting a solid wood statue from the floor, hammering Claire's knee just after getting his hands on it.

She was knocked to the ground, and Ryan fell on his head with a crack. When he stood, a thin line of red streamed from his hairline. "It was worth it," he said, running at Claire.

She flipped backward, and then drew her side arm.

"Not funny," Jared warned.

The gun fired, and Ryan jerked, covering his head with one hand, his crotch with the other. The bullet lodged into the wall—right through the center of Cynthia's prized original Renoir.

"I think…I think I'm going to pass out," I said, feeling woozy. Jared obliged when I hooked my arm around his.

"Should I stop them?" Jared said.

"They won't stop until they're finished being CHILDISH!" I said. "Take it outside!"

Ryan pointed at Claire. "You…you just shot at me!"

Claire rolled her eyes. "You're such a baby. That wasn't even close."

"The bullet blew air by my eyeball!" he said, dramatically pointing to his eye.

"Fine," she said in a huff. "I'll put it away so you don't pee your pants, big Special Forces man."

Ryan relaxed and stood up straight, and then charged her again. Claire rolled her eyes and grabbed him by the throat, stopping him in his tracks. "All you do is run at me. I'm bored."

Ryan took a swipe at her, making strange hacking noises.

I walked over to them, glaring at Ryan, and then at Claire. "He's turning blue."

Claire raised her other fist like she was going to punch him, but then turned it over, casually picking at her nails.

"Claire," Jared growled.

She looked at Ryan and narrowed her eyes. "Tap out."

Ryan struggled to make a noise. "No," he choked. His eyes fluttered as he lost consciousness.

I frowned. "Okay, that's enough. Jared, please make her stop."

Jared took a step, and Claire pointed at him. "Jared Gabriel, don't you dare."

"Claire—" he began, but she held her hand palm-out to her brother.

I glanced at Ryan and then back at her. "It's not funny anymore."

"I don't know," she said. "It's kinda funny."

I grabbed Claire's wrist with one hand and wrapped my arm around Ryan with the other. It was futile, but I hoped Claire would snap out of her rage and realize what she was doing. As if it were nothing, they separated.

"Thank you," I said, helping Ryan to the floor. "Ry," I said, patting his cheek. "Deep breaths." I looked up at Claire to send her a look of disapproval, but her expression took me off guard. "What?"

"I didn't let go," she said, stunned.

Jared's eyes darted between the three of us. "What do you mean, you didn't let go?"

Claire's eyes widened. "She pulled me off him."

"This isn't the time for jokes," I said. "You went too far."

Claire shook her head. "How did you do that?"

She was serious. I had pulled Ryan from her grip without effort. I had barely tensed, thinking Claire had simply decided to let go. "I…I don't…know," I said. I waited for Jared to offer an answer, but he stood speechless.

Ryan stirred. "Did I win?"

Claire frowned. "Of course not, stupid. 'Did I win'," she said, mocking Ryan's deep voice. She rolled her eyes, and then her face brightened. "Stand up, Nina."

"Why?"

"Just do it."

I stood, and Claire took a defensive crouch. In the next moment, Jared was between us. "You have lost your mind!"

"Just one time!" Claire begged. "I bet it won't even hurt her!"

"What are we talking about, here?" I said, my eyes dancing between the two of them.

"I'll do it," Jared said.

"Do what?" I asked. Jared led me to the center of the room, standing directly in front of me.

"What is he doing?" Ryan asked Claire.

"Sssh. Pass out again," she said, impatiently waiting for something to happen.

My eyebrows pulled in. "What do you plan to do?"

Jared steadied himself and squared his shoulders. His eyes darkened, and then he lowered his chin. In the next moment his body relaxed, and he threw his head back. "I can't," he sighed, looking at the ceiling.

"What a wuss!" Claire laughed.

The front door opened, and I closed my eyes, waiting for the painful shrieking of my mother. It never came.

"Uh…what happened here?" Bex said. I opened my eyes, seeing Bex stood frozen in place in the doorway, a half-eaten apple in one hand.

"Nina pulled me off Ryan," Claire said, her voice trembling with excitement.

"Okay. So what are you doing, Jared?" Bex said.

"Nothing," Jared replied, clearly embarrassed.

"He's going to test the theory," Claire said.

Jared shook his head quickly. "No, I'm not."

I crossed my arms. "And how were you going to do that, exactly?"

Jared rubbed the back of his neck. "I was just going to throw it. I wasn't going to…."

"Punch her?" Bex said.

Jared frowned at Bex, and then looked at me apologetically.

"What?" I wailed.

Jared held out his hands. "I wasn't going to land it! Just to see if you would catch it."

Claire puffed, unimpressed. "I was going to punch her," she mumbled.

My mouth fell open.

Bex walked casually across the room, stopping a couple of feet from me. Jared reclaimed my attention when he reached for me again. "Come on, Nina. You don't think I would punch my pregnant wi—"

Before Jared could finish his sentence, Bex's fist hurled toward me with lightning speed. My body reacted, and suddenly his fist was in my hand.

"I'm not holding back," Bex grunted, still pushing his fist toward my face.

Jared's eyes widened. He tried to talk, but the only result was his jaw flapping about.

Bex relaxed and lowered his hand, and then bent down to kiss my forehead. "She's been like that for months. You couldn't tell?" he asked Jared.

"I uh…I could tell something was different. I assumed it was the baby."

"It is the baby," Bex smiled. "Bean is sharing angel juice with Nina. I haven't taken it easy sparring with her for weeks."

"What?" I said.

"What?" Jared repeated.

Bex rolled his eyes. "Remember that time she threw me on my back?"

Jared's eyes dashed to mine. "She really did that?"

Bex frowned. "It hurt, too. I just didn't say anything because I assumed you knew, and this was one of those things you didn't want to talk about."

"He is so like that." Claire said.

Jared was instantly angry. "You were sparring with her on your level? She's pregnant, Bex. Are you insane? What if you hurt the baby?"

I looked down at my protruding belly and gingerly rubbed it with my fingers. "Bean is giving me abilities?"

Bex shrugged. "Bean's full-on angel, Nina. You've got more power than we do, I bet. That's why you could hover during your dreams and climb the walls and stuff. You were pregnant then, weren't you?"

Ryan laughed once. "What? She's Spider-Man, now?"

"That's what I said!" Bex beamed. "Love Spider-Man."

Jared frowned. "You should have said something."

Bex laughed once without humor. "She's your Taleh...not to mention your wife. I thought you knew!"

"You didn't think I'd mention it if I had?"

"No! That doesn't sound like you at all!" Bex snapped.

"He's right," Claire said. "Being forthcoming isn't your strong suit."

Jared turned on his heels, crossing his arms. His biceps bulged over his hands. "I guess you knew, too?"

"Obviously not!" Claire said. "It was my idea to punch her!"

"Well, let's brag about it," I said flatly.

Silence overcame the room while the new knowledge set in. Jared's eyes bounced around different points on the floor while his brain processed a million thoughts a second.

A loud bang sounded from across the room, followed by a vibration in the floor. Claire was lying on her back, looking up at Ryan with a shocked expression.

He smiled. "I told you I wouldn't give up."

Her face flashed red, and I waited for her to send Ryan flying across the room again. But the flush of her cheeks returned to a warm tone, and her eyes softened. A slow, small smile turned up the corners of her mouth. Ryan, without caution, kneeled beside her. His eyes left hers, and then transfixed onto her lips. He leaned in closer. I waited for Claire to grab him by the throat, or kick him in his nether region, but she slowly closed her eyes.

"What in the hell happened in here?" Cynthia shrieked, slamming the door behind her.

My mother's surprise entrance took my attention away for only a moment, and when I looked back, I could see a familiar frustration in Ryan's eyes.

I smiled.

"Someone had better answer me," Cynthia said.

Realization fluttered in Claire's eyes, and she glanced in my direction.

"Karma," I said with a knowing grin. She had made a hobby of interrupting Jared and I when we were falling in love. It was refreshing to see her reaction when the same happened to her.

"Oh, shut up," she said, pushing herself to her feet. She grabbed Ryan's hand and helped him to stand. "I apologize, Mrs. Grey."

"You did this," Cynthia said. Her words were more an accusation than a question. "I expect everything to be in order by tomorrow morning." With that, she left for her bedroom.

Claire surveyed the destruction. "It's going to be a long night."

"I'll help you," Ryan said.

Claire left for the kitchen, and returned holding a large garbage can. She carried it in one hand, picking up the splinters of wood that covered the floor with the other.

"Have fun with that," Jared smiled, taking my hand. "We'll be at the oak tree at first light."

"Oh?" I said with a smile.

Jared glanced at his little brother. "You're coming, too."

"I am?" Bex said.

A wary frown touched Bex's face as his eyes darted between Jared and me. I could tell that he was hesitant to be excited. "Why? Isn't that, like, your breeding ground?"

Jared rolled his eyes. "I want to see what Nina is capable of."

"Sweet!" Bex said, clapping his hands together once. "You ready to spar, Sis?" His hands rubbed together.

A broad smile widened my face. "Oh. It's on."

Chapter Ten
Matches

Jared and I walked upstairs. I went through the motions of my nightly routine in a daze, trying to concede to this new reality. Knowing I had a lot to prove in the morning, it was difficult to sleep. Finally I forced my mind to slow down, and managed to close my eyes for a few hours before the sun breached the horizon.

Once my eyes fluttered, there would be no falling back asleep; no sleeping in. I was wide awake, and my body screamed to get out of bed and get to the oak tree. I didn't bother with a shower, knowing I would be sweaty and covered in dust and dirt within the hour. An oversized T-shirt of Jared's barely stretched over my belly, but it would suffice. I was really showing now, and the thought crossed my mind at how ridiculous I would look, swollen and awkward, while Bex attacked me with gorgeous precision from every angle.

Jared and I met downstairs, where the others were still cleaning. The only person not smiling and joking about the night before was Ryan.

"What?" Jared said, smug. "You don't think Nina can take Bex?"

Ryan pointed at me, but looked at Jared. "She's still pregnant."

Bex laughed once. "Don't worry. Bean's tougher than I am."

Claire thought I should start with Ryan, however. Ryan held out his hands. "What the hell is this? Beat The Shit Out Of Ryan Week?"

"I didn't think you'd mind, since you're always insisting upon getting yourself hospitalized," Claire said.

Ryan's face screwed into disgust. "That was uncalled for."

"The truth hurts, baby."

He smiled. "If you're going to talk to me like that, you can insult me all day long."

Claire pulled her car keys from her pocket, and then pulled on Ryan's hand. "I meant that you're a baby. It wasn't a term of endearment."

"Yeah, right."

Jared squeezed my hand. "The oak tree it is. Are you sure you're okay with this?"

"Does it matter?"

"Yes. I would like to see what you can do, though, don't you?"

I thought for a moment. I had always admired the abilities of the Ryels, but having my own never occurred to me. My damsel in distress days could be over, and I liked that.

"Do I get a shot at you if I beat Claire?"

Jared shrugged. "Sure, but—"

"Then yes."

Jared pretended to be offended. "That wasn't very nice, honey. Not nice at all."

I hooked my arm around his and nuzzled against him as we walked to the Escalade. "A little exploratory domestic violence doesn't mean I love you any less."

The Escalade jostled with the uneven ground of the trail that led to our oak tree. Bex and Claire would be careful not to land a direct hit to my stomach, but my motherly instincts were kicking in, and so were my nerves. I kept telling myself I had already done this: Bex and I had sparred many times, and I got the best of him several times. At the time I thought he was taking it down a thousand notches so that I knew I was improving, but now I knew differently.

Ryan, sporting a standard-issue police T-shirt and a PPD ball cap, took position across from me.

"Until I figure out what I can do," I told him, "try very, very hard not to go anywhere near Bean."

Ryan frowned. "For the record, I feel like I'm having an out-of-body experience, and the rational me is screaming to kidnap you away from this craziness before you get hurt."

"We'll just start slow, and see what happens."

Ryan winced. "I'm about to fight a pregnant woman. This is wrong on so many levels."

"C'mon you weenies!" Claire yelled. "We haven't got all day!"

"I'm not a weenie," Ryan said under his breath.

"You are if you're afraid of a girl!"

Ryan glanced at her with annoyance, and I smiled. "You'll learn whispering doesn't help."

"Okay, let's do this before my girlfriend thinks worse of me."

"Still not your girlfriend!" Claire yelled.

I bit my lip. "Let's try this," I said, shoving Ryan. I used enough strength to push him a few feet away, but instead he flew back, twisted in the air, and then fell, rolling across the ground.

He looked up at me in surprise. "That's cheating!"

"I barely touched you."

"Really?"

"Really."

Ryan pushed himself to his feet, and then jogged back to me, a bit shaken. "I can't let two girls kick my ass in one twelve-hour period."

"Bring it," I said, crouched and ready.

Ryan swung and missed a dozen times before I tried punching him. My fist caught him in the gut, and he landed nearly in the same place as before. He stood up, but then doubled over, trying to catch his breath. He took a step, and then bent down again, holding up one finger.

"Sorry!" I called.

"My turn!" Bex said. He wasted no time, and I could see in his eyes that playtime was over.

He lunged, and I moved. Blocking each of his punches, I used Claire's leg sweep, knocking him to his feet. He jumped up, missing the first punch, and then landing the next. It stung, but it felt like I had accidentally walked into a door instead of the full power of a Hybrid pounding into my jaw.

"Oh!" Jared yelled. His hands were on his head, his fingers intertwined. He hated this. He had spent his life protecting me, and now that we were married and I was pregnant with his child, he was allowing me to be a guinea-pig-slash-punching-bag.

"You okay?" Bex said, breathing hard.

I frowned.

"Oh, God, I'm sorry, did I hurt you?" Bex said, lifting my chin to see the damage.

"Again," I said, squatting defensively.

"No!" Jared yelled. "No, we've seen what she's capable of. That's enough."

I shook my head. "I'm fighting a thirteen-year-old, Jared," I said quietly. "I wasn't trying that hard."

Bex crouched. "That's insulting."

He lunged again, and although our movements would have blurred to the human eye, I had no trouble keeping up. Each move Bex attempted seemed nearly in slow motion. Within seconds, Bex was in the air, and then flat on his back.

"My turn!" Claire said, pulling on fingerless leather gloves.

I steadied myself. Claire had always frightened me. Bex, I had sparred with before; I was familiar with his moves. But it had been months since Claire and I had practiced together, and I was unfamiliar with her strategy. Still, I didn't want to make Jared worry, so I planned to step up my game a notch. I couldn't let Claire punch me. Jared would feel guilty enough. Not to mention that even though she loved me now, Claire had been waiting for this moment a long time.

She glared at me from under her brow as she always did to intimidate an enemy. That part I was familiar with. She would not hold back, and she wasn't afraid to hurt me.

This was going to suck.

Bex helped Ryan to Jared's side, and Ryan fell onto his knees, sore and demoralized.

"Get her, Nigh!" Ryan yelled.

"Hey! Whose side are you on?" Claire said.

I focused. Claire Ryel was the best of the best. Demons feared her. She was Earth's deadliest weapon, undefeated by anyone she'd ever come up against, and I was about to deck her. Once Claire returned her attention to me, I swung. Claire took the punch, and it almost knocked her off her feet. She looked at Jared, rubbed her cheek, and smiled with bloody teeth. "She hurt me!"

I didn't let my guard drop for a second, knowing Claire was too competitive to quit. Her ice-blue eyes sharpened and her vicious glare targeted me. "I love you, and I'm sorry for the ass-kicking that's about to commence."

"No, you're not."

"You're right. I was just being polite."

Knowing that she had watched me wait to be attacked with my last two opponents, I took the first shot. She dodged, but in the next moment, my foot connected with her chest, and I sent her flying forty feet into the one muddy section of the entire field. She emerged, wet, dirty and pissed off. She flung her hands outward, letting the excess mud spatter to the ground. "You really went there, didn't you?"

I smiled. "I did."

She sprinted toward me and grabbed my shirt. I was soon in the air, but landed on my feet—just short of the mud.

"Nice try," I smiled.

Claire was unhappy. She tried repeatedly to push, shove, throw, and punch me into the mud, but I either blocked her or put her there instead. After half an hour, her platinum hair was tangled and brown, and we were both filthy and panting. She was filthier than I, but coming into contact with someone covered in muck made it impossible to emerge unsoiled, and Claire was definitely a full-contact adversary.

"Enough," Jared said, walking out to meet us. He wiped a chunk of mud from Claire's face. "You've made your point."

"I'm…not…finished with…her yet," Claire breathed.

Bex had been laughing uncontrollably since the first time Claire found herself in the mud, but with one glare from his sister, the laughter silenced.

"Okay," I said, breathing hard. "Now you?"

"No."

"No?" I said.

"Chicken!" Ryan said.

Jared frowned. "We've seen what we need to see, and I don't want you to get overly tired. You may have angel blood running through your veins, but you're still human. Until we know for sure how your body will handle the stress, I don't want to push it too far."

I nodded. "You're right. I can throw punches at you anytime."

Jared laughed, and then put his arm around me as we walked to the Escalade. He was thoroughly enjoying my new Yes, Dear attitude. The truth was I couldn't live with myself if something happened to our baby.

Ryan took off his coat and draped it around Claire's shoulders, and then used his hand to scrape the rest of the mud from her face. She was never happy to lose a fight, but the excitement we all felt for this new development was evident in her eyes. "I want a rematch after Bean is born!" she yelled.

"No way!" I called back. I looked to Jared. "She's not serious?"

Jared tried to subdue a smile. "Of course not." His attention was diverted from the path to the road. Kim's Sentra barreled toward us.

The Sentra stopped abruptly, and Kim emerged, slamming the door behind her.

Jared raised his hands. "I know you're impatient, Kim. We're leaving next week, okay?"

When she was close enough, I gasped. Her clothes were covered in blood. "Well, that's just great, Jared. Unfortunately for my uncle, it's too little, too late."

"What happened?" Jared said, equally alarmed. Bex, Claire and Ryan gathered around.

Ryan grabbed Kim's arm, but she pulled away. "Oh my God, Kim. Are you okay?" he said.

Kim didn't look away from Jared. Her eyes glossed over. "I told you. I told you we needed to get it back."

"I'm so sorry, Kim," Jared said.

"Sorry won't bring him back. I helped you, and when it was my turn, you dragged your feet until someone I loved was killed." She turned and walked toward her car.

"Sunday, Kim," Jared said, calling after her. "We leave Sunday."

Kim's arm shot into the air and her middle finger pointed toward the heavens. A moment later, she was gone.

"Poor Kim," Ryan said. "What do you think happened?"

Claire crossed her arms, watching the Sentra disappear into the distance. "They're sending a message. If it were demons in true form they wouldn't have been able to get to him. They must be shelling."

"Shelling?" I asked.

"They're taking human form," Jared said.

Ryan nodded. "Like possession."

Claire frowned. "No, like shelling. They take over the body for a short amount of time to achieve a purpose. It doesn't leave the body weakened, and the human has no recollection or aftershock."

Jared rubbed the back of his neck. "It's starting."

"It sure as hell is," Claire said, heading quickly toward her Lotus.

"It's a good thing I was quitting to go back to school, anyway," Ryan said, following Claire. "If I would have asked for more time off to go to Jerusalem, they would have fired me."

Claire put a hand on Ryan's shoulder. "They were going to fire you, anyway."

Ryan's head jerked in her direction. "Huh?"

"Because you suck."

Ryan shrugged off her hand, and then used all of his might to shove her. She didn't budge, only turning long enough to offer a small, amused smile.

"I don't suck. You suck," Ryan grumbled, climbing into her car.

Chapter Eleven
Last Minute Forgiveness

So much to do. So much, so much. Repetitive grumbling hissed from my lips as I rushed around the house. A week wasn't long enough to get my life in order. I scrambled around the house, up and down the stairs, trying to maneuver around my growing stomach. It became rounder and fuller every day. As I packed, Agatha worked overtime trying to finish the laundry, and Jared was constantly up and down the stairs, fetching clothes and medical supplies. It wasn't until he phoned in a favor to a friend for bags of saline, IV tubing and needles, and anticoagulant that I realized I wouldn't have my baby in a hospital—not even at home. Bean would be born in a dark, timeworn cavern under the city of Jerusalem, away from modern medicine, but just beyond the reach of Hell.

Seven days didn't seem like enough time, but knowing that demons were shelling, it was also too long. Anyone we happened upon could try to kill us. Any human was a threat. Beth, Chad, even Ryan or my mother. The thought of my mother as a demon made my blood run cold. She was already frightening enough as a human.

Grant needed to be informed of my upcoming absence, but something kept me from dialing the numbers. Knowing he was an Arch—a fallen one, at that—made me feel uneasy. I had been rude to him, even insulted him at times. Being kept in the dark seemed to be the theme of my life, and yet this time it felt like a violation of my trust by everyone. Not to mention the unspoken competition I felt between us was forever ended. He had won. Every jab at my expense, every flirtation was only him goading me, and

I played into his hand every time. Knowing that made future conversations with him difficult. The urge to admit defeat might come, and that would be the ultimate humiliation. Nope. Absolutely not. Wasn't going to do it. Jared was his celestial BFF. He could talk to Grant.

"Sweetheart?" Jared called from the hall.

I shoved more clothes into my suitcase and then zipped the lid shut. "In here."

He chuckled. "I know. Bex called. Grant will keep an eye on Mom. He said he needs to speak with you."

"You talk to him. You know the details of the trip."

"I don't know the details of Titan. He wants you to go in tonight. I'm going to let Bex follow you in while I run to a friend's clinic to get the rest of the supplies, and then I'll be by."

"Jared—"

He pulled me to his side, his arms surrounding me. It just occurred to me why the temperature of his skin didn't feel as warm as usual. I was running the hybrid fever as well. That was one thing I would be glad to have back once Bean was born: Jared's warmth had always been so comforting. Now that it was gone, I mourned its loss a bit.

Bex burst through the front door and sprinted up the stairs, stopping just short of us.

Jared tensed. "What? Is it Mom?"

"No. Why?"

"Why else would you barge in and run full speed up the stairs like that?"

Bex shrugged. "I don't know. I just felt like running. What's the big deal?"

"The big deal is that at any moment someone we care about could die. Don't do that to me."

"Okay," Bex said, taken aback. "I'm sorry."

Jared stomped down the stairs and slammed the door behind him. Bex looked at me. "I didn't mean to."

I put my hand on his shoulder and squeezed. "It's okay, Bex. He forgets you're just a kid, I think. You're doing great."

Bex's half-wounded, half-appreciative smile offered little persuasion that my pep talk did him any good. He waited for me to dress for the office, and then I allowed him to drive the Beemer to Kennedy Plaza.

"You are so much like your brother," I told him as he opened my car door.

"I wish he'd see that."

"He does."

"I'll walk you to the door. With them shelling, we can't be too careful."

I nodded. Although I felt bad that Bex had to babysit me once again, I was glad he was so close. The sidewalk was an obstacle course, and as usual I didn't choose the correct shoes. My high heels landed unbalanced on broken cement more than once, and my pregnant body wasn't in its most graceful state—angel-blood-amped or not. If Bex's newly thick and bulging arms hadn't been there to grab me, I would have rolled both of my ankles at the very least.

"Okay. You made it. I'll wait in your car for Jared."

I nodded. "Sounds like a plan, kiddo."

"Nina?"

"Yep?"

"Think you could stop calling me that? I'll be fourteen in a few weeks, and it's awkward when people hear you. I look older than you."

"Do not."

"Do so."

"Fine," I grumbled. "My apologies, Mr. Ryel."

"Bex will do."

I pushed through the glass door, frowning. I wasn't sure when Bex had grown up, but it was unsettling. My boot heels clicked across the tile floor, muffling when I reached the elevator. The building was quiet, making me even more nervous to meet with Grant.

The elevator opened, and I stepped into a dark hallway. "Grant?" I called. Everything was quiet. The sounds of the copy machine, the phones, the clicking of keyboards, and conversation were notably absent. The nervousness I'd felt about speaking with Grant was overshadowed by something else. My body was on alert. Something was off.

A faint glint of blue light trickled from under my office door. I blew out the breath I'd been holding. Get a grip, Nina. You bested Claire today. Whatever is behind that door, you can handle.

I gripped the knob and turned, trying to keep the fear at a manageable level. When I realized who was at my desk, I was instantly angry.

Sasha, leaned back in my chair with her ankles crossed and on top of my desk, held the phone to her ear with one hand, and curled a strand of her ginger hair around a finger of the other. "Oh stop," she laughed, slightly swaying back in forth in my custom-made Aero chair.

I swung the door open, hoping to surprise Sasha so much that she fell onto the floor. Instead, she glanced at me and then continued talking without pause. "Ugh, and did you see the shoes she wore? I thought about giving her a mercy-nudge into that mud puddle just to cover them up!"

"Sasha," I said, trying to keep my voice calm. "Hang up the phone, please. We need to talk."

Sasha rolled her eyes. "I need to go, Mom. Someone needs her office for the first time this week—coincidentally when I'm on the phone. Okay. Bye," she said, returning the phone to its cradle. "You have the last cord phone in this entire building."

"It was my father's."

"So?"

My first reaction was to run at her full speed and tackle her bony ass to the floor. Then she wouldn't be in my chair complaining that it wasn't fit to her standards.

I closed my eyes, took a deep breath, and began again. "I'm not changing anything in this office. I like it the way it is…because it is, in fact, my office. Which begs the question: What are you doing here at ten o'clock at night?"

"What are you doing here?"

"Answer the question, Sasha," I replied, exasperated.

"I was working," she snapped. She pulled a file off the desk and held it against her chest as she approached me. "Trust me, your office was happy for the change."

I started to cross my arms, but forced them to stay at my sides. "What exactly do you hope to accomplish here by insulting the CEO of the company? How far do you expect to get here, Sasha?" I hated how arrogant that sounded, but I was genuinely curious.

"Grant is the CEO as far as we are all concerned."

"What you should be concerned about is the company you'll be applying to after you graduate. Who do you think will sign your recommendation letter? Who do you think will have the final say on your reference report?"

"You wouldn't."

My eyebrows popped up. "You've made an enemy of me from day one. You can't expect me to feel sorry for—"

"Grant has plenty of positive things to say about my time here."

"Grant likes your short skirts and that you have coffee waiting for him every morning. Even if he did somehow notice the insignificant tasks you do complete, he would also see how many mistakes you make. You are not the asset to this company you believe you are, and you're a bi—" I stopped, catching myself.

"I'm a what?" she goaded.

"A bit rough around the edges."

She narrowed her eyes. "I know you're the princess of Titan. That doesn't mean you get everything."

"What on earth are you talking about?" I said, wrinkling my nose.

Sasha stuck her hands on her hips. "Oh, enough already with the oblivious routine. You may have some people fooled, but I'm not one of them," she said, poking her chest with the last few words.

Frustrated, I closed my eyes, shook my head and sighed. "If you don't wish to resolve this, fine. But stay out of my office unless you have my verbal permission." I opened the door, gesturing for her to leave.

Sasha's arms crossed tighter, and she lifted her chin in defiance. "Truth hurts?"

"I honestly don't have time for this."

"You just threatened my career. Make time," she said, pushing the door shut.

"What career?"

"Better than a fake one."

"Are you serious? You're bitter because I'm taking my father's place in the company? As if you wouldn't, had you the opportunity! What father doesn't want their child to take over the family business?"

"You're never even here!"

"What is it that you want, Sasha? My job?"

"No! It's absolutely ridiculous that you have this huge office right beside Grant that you're never in! What a waste of company resources! Grant keeps this company running while you're off doing God knows what with your husband-slash-stalker…it's disgusting," she said, her face screwing so tight, the skin around the creases in her face turned white.

"Disgusting?"

"Yes! When you do decide to show up, you're so busy flirting with Grant that you still don't get anything done. What will happen to this company if Grant decides to leave? It's doomed!"

Sasha's words turned a light on inside my head, and I stood there in shock. "You're in love with him," I whispered.

"Oh, please," Sasha said. "You must be losing sleep again."

"You're in love with Grant."

Sasha's mouth fell open. "Am not!"

I pointed at her. "You're in love with him, and you've been pissed at me this entire time because he flirts with me!"

"You think I'm jealous of you? That's just the most ridiculous…," she trailed off, laughing to herself. Her face turned red, and the she took a step forward. "I don't see what anyone sees in you. You're not talented…at anything…you're not that smart, definitely not that attractive, you have no fashion sense, and you have the personality of a rock."

"Tell me how you really feel," I said, incensed. "I don't care what Grant sees. I'm married to the most perfect, amazing, handsome man in the universe." Although it was the truth, I inwardly cringed at how sophomoric it sounded.

"You don't care? Then why did you stick me in the bowels of the file room? I know you wanted me out of the way!"

I wanted to tell her that Grant was the one that cast her away, but that was more cruel than I was capable. "You can have Grant. I never wanted him," I said. Even the thought of Grant, of me and Grant…ew.

"He's not yours to give away!" Sasha howled. "You want to know what I can't stand about you? That! That right there! That snooty, presumptuous, overconfident tone you have when you have zero redeeming qualities! Your father thought you hung the moon, Grant thinks you can do no wrong, your best-friend-slash-assistant treats you like a queen, and your husband should have never given you the time of day. Now, you're pregnant and gloriously happy. I'm not jealous, Nina, I'm revolted! You don't deserve anything you have!"

"Maybe you're right."

"What?" Sasha said softly, clearly caught off guard.

"I don't have any redeeming qualities to speak of. I don't know why Grant has that ridiculous crush on me—if that's even what it is—and I am the first person to admit that I don't deserve Jared. He probably just fell in love with me because it's his job to be around me twenty-four-seven, and he didn't have time to date. He disagrees, but I've always thought…."

"Well," she cleared her throat, "you're not…you're not that bad. I mean, you're not funny at all but sometimes you make Grant laugh. And I've seen you be sort-of kind to Beth. Once. No, you don't have any redeeming qualities, but since when does anyone need to be extraordinary to be loved? Most people are average. Not me, of course, but it's perfectly fine that you are."

I took a deep breath. "I can see why you're upset with me. I haven't handled our situation in the best way. I should have talked to you. I didn't realize…I mean, looking back, I knew about Grant. But I thought it was the position you wanted, not necessarily him. Now that I know, I get it. I don't think he's all that attractive, but I see why others do."

"He's very cute," Sasha sulked. "He really does care about this company and the employees, and he's so smart—and sweet. When he's not trying to figure out how to keep Titan on top, he's talking about you. It's infuriating. You are never kind to him."

I frowned. "I'm not. I will try to work on that."

"No! Don't do that!" she said, shaking her head. "I just meant that...don't go out of your way on my account."

"I'm sorry. I would like us to get along better," I said. Now that I knew the source of her disdain, it was easier to understand the motives behind her hateful remarks. "You still can't put your feet on my desk."

"You're right. Totally out of line. I apologize."

I wasn't sure what to say next. We had never been civil to each other, and now that we had come to an understanding, all that was left was an awkward silence.

"I was, er…I was just about to get some coffee. I'm going to be here all night reorganizing the file room. It's atrocious. So…do you want some?"

"Coffee?"

"Yes," Sasha said, trying a smile.

"Here," I said, pulling a twenty dollar bill from my pocket. "I can't drink coffee, especially not the sludge in the break room. I'll grab me an apple cider and you a coffee at that place on Spruce. It's my favorite."

Sasha snatched the bill from my fingers. "I'll get it. I need a break, anyway. I just need a flashlight."

"Why?"

"I had to park four blocks down in that parking garage because of the construction, and the lighting is nonexistent."

"Why don't you take my…." I had to stop myself and think. Jared was surely back by now, but he couldn't take her in the Escalade, for many reasons. My car was parked at the curb just outside. The only people I had allowed to drive it were Jared and Bex, and that was only because they had supernatural powers of precision and lightning reflexes. It was too late, now. I'd opened my mouth, and a retraction would shake our already fragile cease-fire. I would have to let Sasha drive the car my father had given me.

"Why don't you take the Beemer?" I said, nearly choking on my words.

"Are you sure?"

"Yes," I said, holding out the keys. "Just be careful, please."

Sasha smiled. "What do you want?"

"I'll have a large hot apple cider with caramel. Oh, and a slice of their Lemon Velvet cake."

"I know it's summer, but I can get you an iced coffee if you'd prefer." I shook my head, and Sasha's expression changed quickly from confusion to understanding. "Oh, right. The baby. Okay, I'll be back in twenty."

I smiled. "I'll be here."

My keys jingled in Sasha's hand as she disappeared behind the elevator. I leaned against the wall, wondering if I had just made the biggest mistake of my life. How could I trust Sasha with my most precious possession? She hated me.

I bit on my thumbnail, and paced back and forth a few times. I thought about the different items in my car. Would she go through it? Was anything incriminating inside that might hint at the truth about Jared? My cell phone rang in my pocket. I quickly fished it out.

"I'm fine," I said.

"Then why is your blood pressure going through the roof?" Jared said. His voice alone slowed my heart rate. "I can stop her if you don't want her to take your car."

I walked through my office to the large window, looking down to the street below. "Yes, because that won't look suspicious at all." The lights of Fleet Rink were bright enough to illuminate the entire block, and I watched as Sasha followed the sidewalk, her red hair bouncing against her silk olive blouse. The headlamps of the Beemer blinked, and a short blip sounded when the alarm was deactivated.

"Her car seems in good shape," Jared said, trying to comfort me. He was in the Escalade across the street, pressing the cell phone against his ear as he smiled up at me.

I took a deep breath. "I don't know why I'm worried. It's only a mile awa—" I began, but the words were cut off by a loud boom. In the same moment, the space where my car once sat turned into a billowing fireball. The glass vibrated, but it didn't break. The windows of the Escalade didn't fare so well. I could see Jared's shocked expression as he sat in the driver's seat. Flaming debris shot into the sky and fell into the street.

"Oh my God! Help her, Jared! Help her!" I screamed.

"Stay inside!" Jared yelled over the noise. He jumped from the Escalade and ran to the roaring flames. He covered his face with his arm, testing different sides of the car. I could see from three stories up that he couldn't breach the flames. Even if he had, Sasha was gone.

Jared watched the fire in horror, grabbing each side of his blond hair with his fists. He shook his head, and then grabbed his knees, leaning over. After a few moments, he ran back to his Escalade and took off at full speed. The wheels squealed against the pavement.

I ran to my desk and grabbed at the phone with trembling hands. I tried to dial 911, but my fingers shook so much that I kept hitting the wrong keys. After the third try, Jared was beside me.

I collapsed into him, tears finally welling up in my eyes. "What happened?" I cried. "Where did you go?"

"I wanted them to think I panicked and drove off. It was a bomb, Nina. They wired your car with a bomb."

I paused, my eyes widening. "I killed her. I gave her the keys to my car and sent her to her death! Oh my God, Jared, she's dead! She's only twenty-two years old! She just got off the phone with her mother not half an hour ago!"

Jared hugged me to him, unable to find words of comfort. "I should have sensed it. I should have smelled it—something."

"Nothing?" I said, looking up at him with wet eyes.

He shook his head. "Not a damn thing. The baby and how it affects your body saturates my senses. They must have wired it after you arrived at work. I don't understand. I wasn't half a block away. I should have seen it."

"We have to call the police," I whimpered.

"Let someone else do it. If whoever placed the bomb somehow mistook her for you, it may buy us some time. That's why I made such a show in the street. They're probably watching."

"Who?"

"I don't know. Must have been a shell. There's no way to tell how many are around."

I nodded, and Jared pulled my hand, leading me to the stairwell. He held his finger to his mouth, and then opened the door. We descended four flights of stairs into the basement level, and then sneaked out an access door to the alley.

My shoes tapped against the wet pavement and sloshed through puddles. The moonlight glistened on the wet pavement we walked upon. Jared led us through labyrinthine alleyways cluttered with green trash bins and litter until we finally reached the Escalade.

"This wasn't your fault," he whispered.

"Then whose fault is it?" I sobbed, hitting the door with my fist. "I want to know! I want them to be held accountable for taking an innocent person's life! She was mean and spiteful, but she had her whole life ahead of her! It's not fair!"

"No, it's not. It's sloppy. They've never made a mistake like this."

"You think it was a mistake?" I sniffed.

"One way or another."

My face fell again. "She was in love. With Grant, and she never told him."

Jared frowned. "I'm sorry for Sasha. I'm sorry for her family when they learn of her death, but we have a bigger problem here. We're leaving in one week, and you won't be allowed to leave the country if you're involved in an investigation. We have to explain why she was in your car, and why your car was there and you weren't. That's after they declare it wasn't you in the car. That could be a while."

"Stop."

He thought for a moment. "We'll have to go away. Write a note to Beth explaining that we went on a short getaway and that you left your car keys on the desk in case she needs it, and I'll have Bex put it on the floor under your desk in your office so that it looks like it fell."

"Stop, Jared."

"We'll go away for a few days. Figure out our next move."

I squeezed my eyes tight. "Just stop it!"

"What?"

"It won't matter."

Jared grabbed each side of my face and looked into my eyes. "Don't do that. You're not going to give up." One hand left my cheek and touched my stomach. "We have a reason to fight more now than ever."

His cell phone buzzed in his jacket pocket. "Ryel. She's fine, but it was her car. No, her car exploded. They wired explosives to it. I'm not sure, yet. She let Sasha take it for coffee. No," Jared said, his voice low. "We're going to leave town for a few days; buy us some time. Send Bex. I need him to run a note to Nina's office. Bye."

Sirens sounded in the distance. Jared put his phone away and cupped his hands over my shoulders. "You with me?"

I nodded. "I need paper and a pen."

Jared patted his jacket and pulled out a pen, and then he blurred out of sight. A few moments later he returned with a pink memo pad. I scribbled a few lines to Beth explaining my impromptu vacation and the location of my keys in case she needed to move my car, and then signed it. Five minutes later, a motorcycle pulled into the alley.

Bex planted his feet on the ground and pushed the visor of his helmet up. "Whatcha got?"

"Put this in Nina's office, under her desk as if it fell. We need to explain this away."

Bex pulled off his helmet and grabbed the paper. "You guys staying here or…?"

"No. We're leaving town for a few days. I'll call you when we get there."

"Where?"

"I don't know, yet," Jared said. "Stay out of sight, and go straight home to Mom."

Bex nodded once, and then sprinted down the alley toward Titan. The sirens grew closer. Jared squeezed my hand and kissed my cheek. He opened the passenger door, and brushed the broken glass from the seat, and then repeated the process on his side. We drove south, stopping just outside of town. Claire and Ryan were waiting in Ryan's Tundra truck.

"I figured you would need a vehicle with windows for your road trip," Ryan smiled, tossing Jared the keys.

"Thanks," Jared said.

Claire pointed to the bed of the truck. "We brought your luggage. Good thing you were going on a trip, anyway." I nodded, feeling a little lost. Claire offered a sympathetic expression and a hug. "Sorry about Sasha. You'll be soaking up the sun on vacation, and I'll be here finding out who tried to kill you. Whether they're human or not, they won't bother you again."

I frowned, and then tears pushed over my eyes and fell down my cheeks. I squeezed her tight.

"Don't worry," she said, making a point to look into my eyes. "This will all be over soon."

Chapter Twelve
Road Trip

South on Interstate 95. With my head rested against the passenger side window, I kept the beat in my head with the white lines as they zoomed past and out of sight. My body felt empty and numb; I didn't know if I was awake or asleep. Traumatic events should have been second nature to me. Maybe that was why I wasn't a crying, shaking mess. I wasn't coping—or maybe I was. Maybe I was simply feeling acceptance, but it was hard to know without feeling anything.

Jared moved a piece of hair from my face. "Why don't you try to sleep?"

"I don't know if I can."

"Try," Jared said, rubbing my arm. It was just a comforting gesture; we both knew I wasn't cold. Bean coming sooner rather than later suddenly seemed a relief. Summer was unbearable for any pregnant woman, but considering my heightened temperature, it could mean trouble. Jared's hand left my arm and rested on my stomach.

My eyes finally shut sometime soon after entering the Bronx, and didn't open again until we were just south of Philadelphia's city limits. It was still dark when I awoke, my hair plastered against my cheek, warm and moist between my face and the console. Jared had made the distance in half the time it should have taken.

It wasn't long before I processed where we were and why, and then the tears came. "Oh," I said, wiping my cheek. Being unsettled and upset was a strange relief. I was normal, after all.

“It’s going to be okay, sweetheart,” Jared said, leaning over to kiss my hair.

“Have you heard from anyone?”

He nodded. “Claire shot me a text. They put out the fire and found the body. They think it’s you. Everyone will probably find out in the morning.”

“My mother….”

“Claire already informed her. She will play dumb and devastated to the police. She knows the routine.”

I let a puff of air escape my lips. “At least she won’t think I’m dead.”

“It could be Monday morning before anyone notices Sasha is missing.”

“I don’t know,” I said, picking at my fingernails. “She was on the phone in my office talking to her mother. They seemed close. Her family could file a missing persons report today or tomorrow.”

Jared nodded, deep in thought.

It didn’t feel right letting Sasha’s death go unannounced. If she typically spoke with her mother daily, she could be waiting for her call, her worry turning into panic. My hand drifted to my midsection, resting over the bump that protected our child. Sasha was someone’s daughter. Her mother had brought her home from the hospital, taught her to crawl, walk, and raised her to the young woman she is. Was. That woman, who loved Sasha more than anything else in the world, was sleeping peacefully for the last time. The moment Sasha crossed her mind—the moment it occurred to this woman to call her daughter—would be the first moment of thousands that she would feel a horrible sick feeling in the pit of her stomach. More guilt washed over me.

“Stop, Nina. It’s not your fault,” Jared said.

"I don't suppose we can tell Beth?" I asked, already knowing the answer.

Jared only offered an apologetic expression.

We pulled into a gas station for the second time. Anyone else would have thought twice about stopping at such a nefarious-looking place in the wee hours of the morning. Bars guarded the windows, and several unscrupulous characters loitered next to the front door. Jared, however, stepped out and walked past them as if he were at the mall.

I waited in the truck hoping none of the people staring back at me would become curious enough to wander over. Jared was only inside for a moment, and then he emerged, holding a bottle of water and something deep-fried and stuffed with cheese and chicken.

He frowned as he handed them over. "It's not the healthiest thing, but I thought it would tide you over until we could find a decent restaurant."

I took a bite. It was disgustingly wonderful.

Just as Jared pulled back onto the highway, my cell phone buzzed. The display lit up, and I instantly tensed. "It's Beth," I said.

Jared sighed. "You have to let it ring."

"She is probably sick with worry. I can't just let her think I'm dead."

Jared took the phone from my hand. "I sympathize, I really do. Beth doesn't deserve that, but we don't have a choice."

I shook my head and looked out the window. Jared was right: Beth didn't deserve a friend like me. She had only been patient, honest, kind, loyal, and protective. I couldn't imagine the despair I would feel if I answered a call that Beth's car had exploded with a charred body inside. My heart ached for her, and if I wasn't riddled with guilt before, now I was so ashamed I could barely stand to be in my skin. Tears welled up in my eyes and fell down my cheeks. If Beth ever found out that I knowingly allowed her to suffer over my death, she would never forgive me—and I would never expect it from her.

The phone stopped ringing, and the voicemail chimed, letting me know she'd left a message. I held out my hand to Jared, but he shook his head.

"Do you really want to hear the worry in her voice? You feel bad enough."

I covered my face with my hand and shook my head. "This is awful, Jared. This is so wrong."

Jared leaned over and kissed my temple. "I'm so sorry, Nina. I'm so, so sorry."

I looked over at him and could see he was just as upset as I. If he could find another way he would, but once someone knew about our life there was no going back. I didn't want that for Beth, either.

We continued south, and by daybreak reached Maryland. The morning sun glistened on a sign that read Eden Pop. 793. Trees lined the median on one side of the road; railroad tracks on the other. Other than a few billboards and a patch of land used for tractor sales, I couldn't see much of Eden.

"That's an interesting name," I said.

"It fits, too," Jared said, straight-faced. "The town is just as hard to find as the garden."

"Ha, ha," I teased, unimpressed with his joke. "So do we have an actual destination?"

Jared smiled. "We do, now. When I saw we were on Ocean Highway, I thought of the perfect place."

"Which is....?" I trailed off.

"Virginia Beach."

I smiled. "I've never been there."

He met my eyes, matching my expression. "I thought it would be a relaxing place for you to wait while the investigators figure out what happened, and then when they contact us—and they will—we will return in a few days, upset and flustered."

I frowned. Jared's plan wouldn't work. If anything, once the Providence PD followed the breadcrumbs we left for them, we would look more suspicious. Jared's loft had already been declared an act of arson, and they had assumed it was him. Unable to prove anything, no charges were filed. But now that my car had also been targeted, he would be under investigation again. If they found out we were there at the time of the explosion, they could charge and hold us for a number of things. With every thought, my concerns compounded.

"It's not the first time I've had to explain myself to the police. I promise there is no need to worry. We'll explain our version and leave for Jerusalem as planned. If I can kill a dozen or so dirty cops in one night and keep our names out of it...."

"But her family. Don't you think the police stopped looking back then because they dug deep enough to see what was going on? Sasha's family will want answers."

"Ryan and Claire will take care of it. The family will have answers. They'll just have ones that don't imply either of us. You have a bodyguard that everyone knows about, Nina. Now everyone will know why. You're a target, and Sasha was collateral damage. It's not far from the truth, actually. The only difference is that we won't have to explain why we fled the scene."

Jared took my hand and kissed my fingers, and then pressed my knuckles into his chest. "I'm sorry about Sasha.

She didn't deserve to die, but you can't blame yourself for her death. If it's anyone's fault, it's mine."

I stiffened. "How can you say that? You couldn't have known—"

"I should have known. That very easily could have been you." He frowned at the thought. "I'm glad it was her and not you. I know you're wallowing in guilt about what her family will feel when they get the call, but I want you to think about the moment that car exploded. If it wasn't her? Honey, I would have watched my wife and child's death in the same moment. You can't wish that for me." He released my hand and wiped his eyes with his thumb and index finger, and then sighed. "I'm just glad it wasn't you."

I wanted to tell him that it shouldn't have happened at all, but I was afraid it would only make him feel worse. "First the loft, now the car," I sighed. "We won't have anything before long."

"We need to take out whoever the hell knows anything about explosives, that's for sure." He laughed once, sounding exhausted. "This being so in tune with you and Bean that I'm missing important things like a bomb on your car is also a negative." He shook his head. "It was ignition-based, so it couldn't have been there before you left for Titan. It had to been set up between the time you got there and when it blew. Bex would have sensed it. The only time they would have had a window is after I arrived."

"How is that possible? You were in the Escalade a few feet away."

"Exactly," he said, his expression unsettled. "It was difficult to focus before…."

"Before what?" I asked, knowing better. Jared had become skilled at leaving me out of the loop. It wasn't like him to slip.

He replied with only a sigh, but he was visibly upset. It was then that I made a decision. I no longer wanted to be in the dark. I was a mother now. With so many important things at stake, it was time I took an active role in the effort to save our lives.

"Tell me," I said.

"After we…I've been more in-tuned to you for a while. I had just become used to wading through the mess to get to the basics of what I used to feel when you…when we…."

"This would be a good time to forget your usual hour-long explanation and just get down to the naked truth."

"The baby. I sense it, too. It's amazing, but it's also distracting. Very distracting."

"You sense the baby?" I smiled. "So is Bean your Taleh, too?"

Jared frowned. "This whole situation is unprecedented. That would mean the baby is human, and that's obviously not the case. Maybe it's because the baby is a part of you. I just don't know."

From that point on, Jared remained silent except for the few times we made pit stops. As the sun began to set, we had just breached the outskirts of Myrtle Beach. I couldn't help but think about the fact that Sasha's mother hadn't heard from her for a full day, and at any minute they would go to her home, and the panic would begin. Sasha would be reported missing any moment. The guilt began to close down around me once again, so much so that it was hard to take in the beauty ahead.

While we were eating a late lunch, Jared had called ahead and reserved a condo at Myrtle Beach's northernmost point, the Grande Dunes Oceanfront. As we pulled up to the resort, I gasped at its extravagance. It worsened my sense of guilt.

"What is it?" Jared said. I could see the hope in his eyes. He wanted this to be an escape, but I couldn't stomach maternity massages and facials knowing my friends and Sasha's family were going through hell.

"I appreciate what you're trying to do. I really do. But this is not a real vacation. We're hiding out while most of the people I know think I'm dead, and Sasha's family frantically search for her."

Jared nodded and squeezed my hand. "That's the idea, but I'm not pitching a tent on the beach for my pregnant wife. You deserve a little comfort while you're busy stressing out for everyone."

"'A little comfort' would be the Super 8 down the road, Jared. This is a resort."

"It's beachfront, and the ocean will clear your head. C'mon."

Jared checked in while I tried to seem completely normal about the fact that we brought two large full suitcases for a quick getaway. The staff was too pleasant, almost eager that we had arrived. I thought that strange for two reasons: One, Jared called for reservations just a few hours before; and two, we weren't celebrities. Their behavior quickly had me convinced that they were shells, and they would attack us at any moment.

"Sweetheart?" Jared called over his shoulder.

I glared at the girl behind the desk. Her blonde spiral curls bounced against her full, pink cheeks. Her warm brown eyes were glazed over with the absolute captivation she felt standing before Jared. I remembered that feeling. Jared was ridiculously beautiful, and his looks and confidence alone must have made them think he was famous in some way. Okay, maybe they weren't demons with skin, but that girl was still looking at my husband as if she wanted to eat him.

"Just fine," I said with my best fake smile. Other than watching a colleague I'd known for three years turn into toast before my eyes, I wasn't sure why I was in such a foul mood. Girls like that behaving in a completely understandable way hadn't affected me in years. I couldn't remember the last time I'd rolled my eyes at waitresses or coeds nearly slobbering over Jared. It could be several things, but I was sure my rounding form was the culprit.

Jared returned to the luggage, and to me. Inside the room, Jared placed our luggage on the mattress, and looked around. The room was spacious and light, not unlike any other hotel room I'd spent time in.

"This is nice," Jared said.

"Have I ever told you that you suck at small talk?" I smiled. I walked the few steps to reach him, and then pressed my forehead against his chest.

Jared laughed and kissed my cheek. "Yes."

I went to the bathroom and splashed water on my face. The puffy towels smelled sterile and flowery, a quick giveaway that we weren't at home. I groaned and stretched. A belly nearly in full bloom and a long road trip didn't mesh well together. I felt stiff and groggy.

"Nap or beach?" Jared said. He pulled off his boots and slipped his bare feet into a pair of leather sandals.

"Both sound equally appealing, but a walk on the beach after being stuck in the car is the better option."

"Agreed," he said, holding his hand out to me.

We lazily walked to the near-private beach of the Grande Dunes, letting the new summer wind whip around us. The scene looked like a postcard; everything I imagine the perfect beach to be. Jared picked a spot and unfolded a blanket. He sat with his elbows resting on his knees as he looked out toward the ocean.

"It's almost like being back in Little Corn."

"Almost."

Jared peered up at me. "Sit with me."

I fidgeted, knowing I was about to play into my childish insecurities. "They were attractive."

"Who?"

"The girls behind the desk."

Jared laughed once, and then crawled onto his knees. He leaned toward me and placed his hands on each side of my belly. "Nina, there has always been something about you that I couldn't shake. Even when I didn't want to love you, I was drawn to you. I couldn't think of anything else. Now you're my wife, and you are carrying our child. There is nothing more beautiful than that. When you're sweaty and exhausted holding Bean, then that will be the most beautiful thing I've ever seen. When I see tears fall from your eyes when we send Bean off to the first day of kindergarten…that will the most be the most beautiful thing I've ever seen. When you comfort me each time we send our kids to training; on every one of our anniversaries; and when your hair turns gray. Every one of those moments will be the most beautiful thing I've ever seen."

He nuzzled his nose into my belly, and then wrapped his arms around my middle. "You always say the right thing," I whispered, touching his ears.

He looked up at me. "If the impossible happened, and something more beautiful existed, I wouldn't notice. You have my constant, undivided attention. You always have."

I smiled. "Only because I pay you."

Jared's white, wide grin was a contrast against the tan tone of his face. "Not any more. When you marry your boss, you can pay yourself."

I playfully nudged him in the ribs; he hugged me to him. Resting on the blanket, we watched the sun slowly melt into oranges and purples until it sizzled against the ocean. I wondered if the sky looked the same on the other side of the world. If once we arrived in Jerusalem, if we would see the sun again until the baby was born.

I relaxed back against the blanket, looking up at the sky. The stars were visible on the eastern half of the sky, but they were still burned out by the sun in the West. Jared grabbed my arm, and I froze.

"What is it?"

Jared smiled and pulled out his Glock. "You almost laid on my sidearm."

"You brought your gun? Worried the grains of sand would shell?" I smiled.

"When the others start shelling, it's impossible to know who's a threat and who's not. That's why we can't get to the Sepulchre fast enough as far as I'm concerned. I almost wonder if they didn't blow the Beemer on purpose. If they knew our plan—and I'm sure they did—if they didn't kill you in the process, they thought it would keep us from leaving. Bex has a harder time sensing them, so I know with my…distraction, it could be dangerous."

I nodded. "It's not fair that with everything else we're dealing with, your senses are overwhelmed, too." I frowned. "Now that I think about it, none of this is very fair."

"Considering the circumstances, I think it's clear we have some fans up there. We have Eli and Samuel vying for us. That's a huge advantage in and of itself."

"It doesn't feel like it," I grumbled.

My cell phone rang. It was Beth again. I closed my eyes tight while Jared took the phone and pushed the silence button. He buried it into the tote I had carried with me to the beach and then pulled me against his chest.

"You can tell her goodbye before we leave. She'll only feel this way for a few days and then you can comfort her. She'll probably tackle you and forget all about it."

"No, she won't."

Jared took in a deep breath and wrapped his arms tighter around me. "I'm just trying to help."

"I know. I know you are. It's just that I feel I'm hurting her intentionally. It's not fair that she is the only close friend that isn't in the loop."

"Do you really want to expose her to all of this? More importantly, do you think she can handle it?"

I shook my head. "No. I know you're right. I don't want to tell her, I just feel like a jerk. 'Jerk' doesn't even cover it. I'm a bad friend—a bad person."

"She'll be able to close her eyes every night not wondering what's with her in the dark, Nina. I'd say you're being kind."

"Maybe. Can you imagine her reaction when she finds out we're leaving for Israel in a few days? She's going to freak out. I don't even know how to explain it to her."

"Then don't. It's not a necessity to tell her we're going to Jerusalem. Just say the West Coast or something."

I pressed my lips together in a hard line. "I'm tired of lying to her, Jared."

"I know."

The stars had crowded out the last colors left behind by the setting sun, and the ocean was as black as the sky above. I might have been chilly at night by the water a few months before, but with the warmth of Jared's arms coupled with my own elevated temperature, the sun might as well have been bearing down on my skin.

The wind rolling off the water blew my hair into Jared's face, and he turned his head, blowing the strands from his mouth.

I smiled, but my amusement quickly faded. "Speaking of Jerusalem…."

"Yes?"

"If they know we're going, won't they try to stop us? If it gets worse than a car bomb we're going to be busy. What if they wire the plane?" I laughed once without humor. "What if they shoot us down?"

"That is a possibility. But we're prepared."

Dread settled over me. We were vulnerable on the plane, and it was a ten-hour flight.

"We'll land, get you and the book to the Sepulchre, and wait it out underground until you deliver."

"You make it sound simple, but you forget demons will do everything they can to stop us."

"We just have to get you there. It's smooth sailing after that."

"You hope."

The skin around Jared's eyes tightened. "I'm going to stop by the warehouse before we leave. Talk to Eli."

"I thought he said to come to him when we only had one question to ask?"

Jared kept his eyes on the ocean. "I don't think the question is ours to ask."

Chapter Thirteen
The Road Home

We revisited that spot on the beach many times over the next two days. Jared sat with me and watched the waves roll onto the sand, and the water carry distant ships slowly across the horizon. We discussed our upcoming trip to Jerusalem, but Jared kept most of the details to himself. He didn't want to worry me with the truth of what he saw coming. Although I was much stronger than I used to be, that didn't change the fact that I was carrying our child.

The only sound was the wind and the intermittent waves sizzling against the sand, but my mind was crowded and loud. Sometimes I would close my eyes tight and try to push out the hundreds of frightening thoughts in my head, but then I would see Sasha. No matter how tight Jared wrapped his arms around me, or how hard I tried to pretend we were in Little Corn, thoughts of demons, and Sasha, and bombs plagued me.

My cell phone rang several times. Beth's phone number dominated the call log, and my voicemail, with her frantic pleas. Sasha hadn't come to work, and it was clear she was also missing. Before long, other people began to call. Even Cynthia, although I assumed it was just to keep up pretenses for the police. As far as they knew, she was afraid I was dead or missing.

By the evening of the second day, Jared's phone buzzed. "Ryel." Jared listened for a moment, gave a quick affirmation, and then hung up. "The investigators expect the results of the dental records any minute. It won't be long."

"Well, that's good news, I guess."

Sasha's family learning that it was her remains the police had found inside of my vehicle wasn't a good thing, but it was a means to an end. It all was. The true good news was that I could finally call Beth.

Claire was right, within the hour, she texted a confirmation. When Jared gave me the go-ahead, I dialed Beth's number.

"Where in the hell have you been?" she wailed. "I thought you were dead!" Her breathing quickened until sobs developed in her throat, followed by a pause in the form of muffled noises before Chad came on the line.

"Uh...hello?"

"I'm so sorry," I said. "I left a note. I thought everyone knew I was gone. Jared and I needed some time away, so I turned off my phone. I feel awful."

The last bit was true. I could hear Beth sobbing in the background; hearing Chad try to comfort her only made me feel worse. Between consoling her, he tried to fill me in on what had happened. He described the scene at Titan, the police tape, the lines of employees waiting to be questioned, and the blackened asphalt where my BMW burned into the night.

Before long Beth took the phone back and put it to her ear. "My life has been miserable. Everyone at Titan either spread rumors, or spontaneously burst into tears, or alternated between irritated and hateful. Did you know Sasha is missing, too? It's insane!"

"Missing?" I said, trying to keep my voice steady. The guilt weighed on me with every lie I told.

"Oh my...oh my God, Nina. The last person to speak to Sasha was her mother. She said Sasha was working late at Titan the night she went missing. Do you think it was her in your car? I mean...if it wasn't you, then who?"

"I...I don't know. Maybe you should say something to the investigators."

Beth began to cry again. "That poor girl. You should call your mother, and then call Providence PD and tell them you're okay. You'll probably have to come back right away." She sniffed again. "I'm sorry in advance if I smack you upside your head for scaring the beejeezus outta me."

I laughed once. "You're forgiven."

"I'm just glad you're okay. As much as I loathed that woman, I hope it wasn't Sasha, either. That's an awful way to die...Nina?"

"Yes?"

"Someone put a bomb on your car."

"It certainly appears that way."

"But...doesn't that...doesn't that bother you?"

I sighed, resolved to tell her at least some of the truth. "I'm used to it, Beth. Why do you think my father hired Jared?"

Beth didn't speak for a long while, and then finally managed a whisper. "I guess I didn't think about it. I'm sorry. I remember Mr. Dawson, but I...I didn't know things were so frightening for you."

"I'm at the beach, Beth, and I'm married to my bodyguard. Don't worry for me, okay? We'll talk when I get back."

Beth blew a deep breath of relief into the phone. "Please hurry. I need to see you."

"Jared is already packing."

I sat in the truck, dreading the long car ride home while Jared checked out at the front desk. He jogged to the Tundra, and slid into the driver's seat, leaning in to kiss me. "I know it was stressful, but I cherished these last three days with you. When we go away, it's easy to forget about the rest of the world."

I grabbed his hand, holding it tight. He knew as well as I did that our return would stir a hornet's nest. We had just enjoyed our last few days of peace, and now we would be fighting for our lives. I touched my stomach, and Jared reached over to touch the same spot with his free hand.

His blue-gray eyes darkened, and his brows pulled in. I nodded, knowing exactly what was on his mind. He leaned in for a kiss, soft and slow. His lips pulled at mine the way they did when we first met, as if it could be the last time. He pulled away, and then pressed his forehead against mine. We sat there in silence, in our emotional embrace. Neither one had the courage to cry or speak, just in case it became overwhelming.

Jared put one hand back and wheel and shoved the gear in drive. "Okay," he sighed. "Back to Providence."

The drive home seemed to take less time. Jared made me repeat the story we would tell the police over and over. I had recited the words dozens of times when the twinge hit.

Jared immediately looked down to my stomach, and then his eyes met mine. "Are you okay?"

I grimaced. "Maybe we could pull over for a moment. I should walk, I think."

The Tundra made a gentle turn to the left, pulling into the gas station we had stopped at on the way to Virginia Beach. A familiar group of transients idled in the parking lot. Jared opened my door, and kept close as we made our way into the store. To escape the eyes of the quiet group as we walked past, I kept my eyes on the asphalt, noting the grease spots and wads of old gum. I wasn't sure if it was their presence, but something seemed off, and I could tell that Jared felt it, too.

Jared held the door open for me, and even though I let out the breath I'd been holding, the heavy feeling only became worse.

Meandering in the aisles with no real goal, I stretched my back and neck, picking up a package of something and then setting it back onto the shelf. A roach crawled from behind bags of crackers and then disappeared. I lurched back my hand, and glanced around. I didn't recall the store being quite so filthy the last time we were in, but my memory consisted of a quick trip to the bathroom.

One of the fluorescent lights blinked and buzzed overhead. From my peripheral vision, I could see that the man behind the counter was staring at me. He was of small build, and dark-complexioned. His lack of expression made me instantly nervous. I'd seen that look before.

I heard the cooler doors shut, and then Jared rounded the corner with two large bottles of water and a forced smile. He held out his hand, pulling in his fingers twice to signal me to come to him. The air around us felt stale, and my heart began to thump loudly against my chest.

"You don't have long," the man behind the counter said, glancing to my protruding belly.

I instinctively touched my stomach with my free hand.

Jared cautiously approached the cash register, keeping me a safe distance behind him. He took another step and paused. "Are you okay?"

The man was panting, his body swaying in a rhythmic movement. Sweat glistened across his face and neck, and dampened his white polo shirt. The darkened circles under his eyes made his sunken eyes seem even more alarming.

When offered no response, Jared took a step back and threw a ten-dollar bill onto the counter. "That should cover it."

The man looked down at the folded bill before him, and then closed his eyes. He pressed his fingertips onto the counter, and then his body vibrated for a few moments before he snapped straight. He peered up at Jared. His eyes had changed; now obsidian orbs bulging from their sockets.

Jared put his hand on my chest and nudged me toward the door. "It's time to go."

I stumbled back, reaching blindly for the glass door behind me. The small man jumped into the air and landed in a crouch on the counter. "I'm going to gut her like a fish." The sound of his voice was terrifying; a combination of a small child and the hiss of a snake.

I pushed open the door and ran head first into one of the large men that belonged to the group of bikers in the parking lot. He had a long, gray beard, and wore riding leathers. Forgetting my new strength, I plowed over him, knocking him to the ground. The man looked up at me with shock and confusion. Within seconds, all expression left his face, and the blackness of his pupils spilled into his irises, and then to the whites of his eyes.

I scrambled away from him, and then Jared grabbed my arm, pulling me to the Tundra at full speed. The passenger door slammed in my face, and then Jared was next to me.

"Seatbelt!" he commanded.

I grabbed for the clasp, trying in vain to remain calm. The small, dark man galloped toward us on all fours. Jared stomped on the gas pedal. The nozzle was still tucked in the Tundra's gas tank, and after a quick yank, the line came free of the pump, dragging behind us as Jared fishtailed onto the highway.

I rolled down the window.

"What are you doing?" Jared yelled.

"Your gun!" I said, my heart pounding against my rib cage.

"Here!"

He pulled his Glock out from behind him, and placed it on the seat between us. I grabbed it, and then leaned out the window. Jared grabbed a fistful of my dress to keep me from tumbling to the road below. The small man stood in the parking lot, chin down, watching us flee with his unnatural black eyes. I stretched out my arms in front of me, and pointed the gun at him, aiming at his forehead.

"What are you doing?" Jared yanked on my skirt, pulling me into the cab of the truck. "You can't kill him!"

"Why in the hell not? He was going to kill us!"

"Once the demon leaves, the Shell is human again. He's an innocent, Nina." Jared pressed a button on his door, and my window rolled up, cutting off the wind that had blown my blonde hair into a wild mess.

I turned to keep an eye on the Shells. There was no telling how many had turned. The fuel line swaying against the asphalt distracted my attention. The nozzle finally broke free of the Tundra, and rolled into the ditch. A loud boom vibrated the truck, and a ball of smoke and fire rolled into the sky. The small man still stood in the street, glaring at us, just in front of the roaring flames.

"Jared!" I cried.

"So much for that," Jared said, frowning. He peered into the rearview mirror to assess the damage. A column of fire shot up from fuel pumps. It would be a miracle if any of the people we'd left behind survived.

"Those people," I moaned, touching the palm of my hand to my forehead. My eyes filled with tears, and I turned to face the front.

A few miles later, two large fire trucks, a pumper truck, and an ambulance raced toward us. All four vehicles ran hot, full lights and sirens screaming, fading away as they passed. The ambulance trailed behind, but the second its back bumper was in line with ours, it flipped around.

"Jared?"

"I see it," Jared said, grabbing his side arm from the seat. He reached over, pulling my seat belt tight, and then without slowing down, jerked the Tundra to the right, turning one hundred and eighty degrees until we were face to face with the black-eyed ambulance drivers. Jared held his Glock outside of the window and aimed, shooting at their tires. The ambulance fishtailed, and then Jared jerked the truck again until we were once again facing north, with the ambulance behind us.

The ambulance skidded, and then tumbled forward, finally cartwheeling across the road and into the field on the opposite side.

As I watched it seemed to happen in slow motion, but within seconds of seeing the emergency vehicles, Jared had taken out the ambulance's front tires and righted the truck so we could go about our journey. My mind hadn't quite caught up with the events, but my heart was ripping through my chest.

"I thought you said not to kill them!"

Jared put the gun back in the seat and peered into the rearview mirror. "I hope they're not dead."

He picked up his phone and held it to his ear. "Claire. They're shelling. I need backup." He snapped the phone shut, and then pushed the phone under his thigh.

"Is she coming?"

He nodded once. "They all are. We just have to get to them." The Tundra surged forward when Jared stomped on the gas. The speedometer climbed from seventy-five, to eighty-five, then ninety-five. The engine screamed a deafening soprano as Jared desperately tried to get us closer to his sister.

"Maybe we lost them," I said, more to comfort myself than to convince my husband.

Jared reached his hand across the console and gripped it around mine. We were vulnerable, and he knew it. Any human we came across was a threat. Jared's hand squeezed tighter, and all color left his face.

"I can't decide if I should turn off the highway to a road that's less traveled, or stay and cut down on time."

"This particular stretch didn't seem busy when we came through. Maybe we'll get lucky. It's the cities I'm worried about."

We passed only a car or two over the next ten minutes. Every time I saw something in the distance, I tensed and waited. Each time the car would pass without so much as a wave, and the adrenaline would absorb back into my system. I was beginning to feel sick and dizzy after an hour, but I knew we couldn't stop.

"They're up to something," Jared said. He was squinting, trying to focus as far out as he could to see any impending danger.

"How long before we meet Claire?"

"I don't know when they left. I'm assuming right away. Considering the time of the call and how fast Claire drives, I would say less than an hour. Maybe half that."

I nodded quickly, trying to make myself feel better. "Thirty minutes. We can hold on for thirty minutes. What could they possible throw at us that we couldn't handle for that long?"

Jared didn't speak for a solid minute while he studied the road ahead. When he finally focused on a tiny dot in the distance, his face fell, and his breath caught. "Oh, my God."

I knew my human eyes wouldn't have been able to make out the dark blur several miles ahead, but Bean gave me focus I might not otherwise have had. The long, dark blots on the road, dancing against the heat off the asphalt, barreled toward us.

It wasn't until I tried to form a sentence that I realized my mouth was gaping open. "What do we do?"

Jared released my hand and reached under the seat. He offered me an extra handgun, and then put both hands on the wheel.

A caravan of Army vehicles, a Humvee, three Jeeps, and a large supply truck moved toward us at full speed. The back of the truck reminded me of a covered wagon, only one covered with camouflaged tarp.

"You've got to be kidding," I said, breathless.

"They're probably on their way to Fort Story," Jared said.

"I don't care where they're going. This is why things have been so quiet, Jared. Hell knew about that caravan and planned to shell them the second they crossed our path. You have to leave the road."

"They'll just follow."

I sighed in frustration, and then looked down at my watch. "Maybe they aren't armed."

"That FMTV transport has an armored cab. It could obliterate the Tundra if I let it get close enough."

I turned to him and tried a nervous smile. "Please don't."

Jared returned my smile, and then nodded, gripping the wheel. He pressed on the gas. I wasn't sure what he had decided, but he had a plan. It was possible that the drivers of those trucks wouldn't shell at all. We could pass them without a problem like we had the previous ten or so vehicles. That, of course, was just empty hope. I could feel a strange burning deep inside my bones. Every one of those soldiers had already turned.

Chapter Fourteen
The Most Important Thing

The Jeep passed first, and then the Humvees. I was just about to allow myself hope when the transport truck jerked into our lane. Jared didn't twitch; he just drove faster. The needle on the speedometer vibrated at one hundred miles per hour. I gripped the door handle so tight that my knuckles turned white under the pressure. I trusted that Jared had a plan, but at the same time, soaring down the road to meet an armored truck in a head on collision didn't sound like a good idea to me.

"Hang on, sweetheart," Jared said, his voice low. "When I get out, take the wheel."

"When you get out?" I said, instantly panicked.

In a move that was so smooth it seemed choreographed, Jared swerved to the right and jerked the wheel again in a nearly perfect half-circle around the Army truck. As the Tundra spun off the road, Jared opened the door and stepped out, shooting directly at the Army truck's tires. I heard several popping noises, but I was focused on grabbing the wheel and getting my foot on the break. Although I was terrified, the move was effortless, and before I had time to be afraid, the Tundra had come to a stop on the shoulder.

I peeked over the steering wheel to see the truck skidded to a stop, all of its tires blown. Jared held one of the soldiers in the crook of his arm. The soldier went limp, and Jared lowered him gently to the ground. I counted eleven men on the ground, all of them unconscious.

Jared's eyes met mine, and then he looked behind him, noticing the other vehicles circling around. He took off in a sprint, pointing behind me. I turned to see two shiny dots in the distance. I squinted, focusing in on the objects, and made out a motorcycle and a black sports car. It was Claire's Exige, traveling at a speed manageable only to Earth's most badass Hybrid.

I turned the wheel and stomped on the gas, picking Jared up along the way. My foot was flush against the floorboard as we raced toward our family.

Jared had barely broken a sweat.

"Are you okay?" I asked.

"Yes. The shells don't have the strength of demons because they don't have the same hold on them that they do when they take the time to possess. I didn't want to kill them, so I incapacitated them."

"Will they come after us after they wake up?"

"It's possible," Jared said, turning around. "Faster, honey."

The jeeps and Humvees were gaining ground, and with a quick calculation, I figured if we were lucky we would reach Claire when the Army vehicles caught up to us.

Jared leaned out the window and aimed at the tires of the first Jeep. His gun clicked, and he popped out the clip. He leaned into the back seat and pulled out a bag, dropping it to the passenger floorboard. It was full of ammo and handguns.

"Where the hell did that come from?"

"Claire helped me pack." He shoved another clip into his gun and flung his top half out the window.

He got off only a few more shots before ducking back inside. The Exige swerved to one side of the road, and Bex's motorcycle went to the other, creating a clear path for us. I looked to my right, and everything went from hypersonic, to a snail's pace. Claire came into view, and half of her mouth was pulled up into a smile. She winked. Ryan was in the passenger seat, showing me his fist. His index finger and pinky was up, and his mouth was open, his tongue hanging out.

When they passed, I pulled off to the side of the road and made a wide turn. One of the soldiers manned the turret of one of the jeeps, aiming in Bex's direction.

"What should I do?"

Jared reached over and turned off the ignition. "We wait."

Claire drove until she was behind the caravan, and then flipped around, pulling alongside one of the Jeeps. Her tiny arm appeared outside her window, gun in hand. She pulled the trigger once, shooting out the front tire. The Jeep swerved out of control, and then cartwheeled toward the Tundra.

"Jared?"

My husband held my hand. "It's fine."

The Jeep continued to roll at us, end over end.

"Jared!"

I pulled the keys from his hand and shoved the keys in the ignition, and then paused as I watched the Jeep skid on its side and come to a halt inches away from our bumper. My heart started beating again and a puff of air escaped my lungs.

Gunfire drew my attention down the road. The Exige fell behind what was left of the caravan, driving strangely straight and at a decent speed for a moment before Claire popped out of the passenger side, In the next moment, Bex was next to her on his Ducati. As if they'd practiced the move a million times, Claire jumped onto the back of Bex's bike—backward—with two guns.

Bex pumped his wrist, and the motorcycle took off like a rocket. Claire's platinum hair whipped into her face while she took out another Jeep's tires, but the soldier on the next Jeep began firing on them.

Bex maneuvered close to the Jeep and then he jumped off his bike high in the air, flipped, and landed sure-footed behind the soldier. After a short scuffle, the soldier flew off the Jeep and rolled onto the shoulder. Claire flipped around and drove the bike next to a Humvee, punching through the class and pulling the driver from his seat and into the road. The Humvee fishtailed and then rolled six times, finally slamming into a tree.

Claire skidded the bike to a stop, and then hopped off of it, pulling the remaining soldiers out of the Humvee. She checked each for a pulse, then picked the Ducati off the ground and pushed it to the Tundra. Ryan slowed the Exige to a stop just a few feet away, and then got out.

"Glad this is fun for you," I said.

Ryan's eyes immediately fell to my stomach. "Whoa, Nigh, how long were you gone? You look ready to pop."

I rolled my eyes, and then my eyes drifted behind Ryan, to the Jeep approaching slowly. The Jeep parked, and then Bex stepped out, frowning at Claire. "Did you scratch it?"

Claire shrugged. "It'll buff out."

The scene behind them looked like the aftermath of war.

"Should we call an ambulance?" I asked.

"I already did," Ryan said, crossing his arms across his chest.

Claire fiddled with her hair, knotting it into a bun. "They won't remember anything, so we should move out before any of them come to." She handed Jared a set of keys. "The Escalade is good to go. You can pick it up at Mom's."

Jared wrapped his arm around Claire's head, trapping her in the crook of his arm, and then gave her a quick kiss on the head. "Thanks, kid."

Claire pulled away with a smile, waving him away dismissively. "We were bored, anyway."

Jared punched Bex in the arm. "Nice moves, little brother."

Bex lifted his chin and smiled. "I'm a beast. Wait 'til we get to Jerusalem."

Jared and I returned to the Tundra, with him back in the driver's seat. In a caravan of our own, we returned to Providence. The Exige behind us, the Ducati in front, we raced home. Sandwiched between my brother and sister, I felt at ease, completely different from an hour before. I leaned back and took a deep, relaxing breath. Jared smiled and reached his hand across the console. We intertwined our fingers, and I watched the different terrain pass by my window, unfazed by what might be ahead. I knew I was safe, and in that moment, that meant everything.

Just after sunset, we pulled into Lillian's drive. Bex pulled into the yard, and held the door open for me. Claire was next, and she and Ryan walked together up the sidewalk. They were elbowing each other and smiling, still happy and excited. Ryan didn't seem affected in the least, and it was at that moment that I knew they were truly meant for each other.

Jared patted Bex on the shoulder as he walked by, and then took my hand, guiding me into the dining room. Lillian was expecting us, and the table was already set. She brought out a large plate of brisket, and placed it in the middle of the table. Claire disappeared into the kitchen, and Bex followed.

Lillian pulled the oven mitts from her hands, and then wrapped her arms around my neck. "Look at you! Darling, you look wonderful! How do you feel?"

"Big," I said, only half-kidding.

"It doesn't take long," she said. Her smile was as warm and bright as the sun.

Lillian had always made me feel so loved and welcome. I was sad that she wouldn't be there for Bean's birth.

"Oh," she said, touching my cheek. "What is it?"

"We're leaving soon."

She offered a comforting smile. "I know. But the next time I see you, you won't just be my favorite daughter-in-law, anymore. You'll be the mother of my grandbaby."

I leaned into the crook of her shoulder, and she hugged me tighter. "You probably haven't had a home-cooked meal in a few days. Let's eat."

At the table, Claire and Bex were chattering excitedly about the encounter with the Army trucks, and Ryan was busy stuffing food in his mouth. Lillian cut her food into small, bite-size pieces, smiling as she listened to her children talk about their day.

Jared smiled, amused at how Claire and Bex took turns with each sentence of the story. He held a fork in one hand, and touched my knee with the other. I noticed the end of the table had an extra, empty place setting.

I leaned into Jared's ear. "Is Lillian expecting someone else?"

Jared looked down to the plate, and then shrugged. "Er...Mom? Is someone else coming to dinner?"

Lillian's eyes brightened. "Yes. I didn't have much notice, so I extended the invitation a bit late."

The doorbell rang, and everyone at the table traded glances. Lillian patted her mouth quickly with the napkin and then pushed her chair away from the table.

The familiar sound of clicking heels echoed through the entry, down the hall, and into the dining room.

"Oh, Nina, dear!" Cynthia said, her arms outstretched.

I stood, a bit startled when she took me into her arms. "Hello, Mother."

Cynthia relaxed her grip and held me at arm's length. "I heard what happened. I trust you're all right?" I nodded and she continued, "And the baby?" I nodded again, and she pulled me against her once more. "That's very good news. Good news, indeed."

It felt a bit strange to have her at our dinner table, listening to the chaos and wreckage Claire and Bex described. She didn't seem affected, however.

After Bex served dessert, I realized it would be our last time for several months to see Lillian, and Cynthia, and that we were all trying very hard to pretend it wasn't. The Ryels were a practiced family at this sort of thing, but I struggled to keep the sadness away. I caught Cynthia more than once glancing in my direction. I wasn't sure if it was my belly that held her curiosity or the fact that she wanted to memorize my face in case we never saw each other again.

After a proper amount of post-dinner socializing, Cynthia excused herself, citing a previous engagement. I walked her outside, and watched with a smile as Robert got out of the car and opened the back door for Cynthia.

Cynthia looked down at her expensive shoes, and then laughed once. "I could've been a better mother, Nina, dear."

Her words caught me off guard. I wasn't sure how to reply, but even if I had been, she didn't give me the chance.

"It's always been hard for me. I was never what one might call a natural-born mother. These instincts that people talk about...well, I never had them. Your father was always so good at hugs and kisses. I suppose I envied him for that." She dabbed her nose with a tissue, and then looked up at me. “I do love you. If you’ve ever questioned that, please accept my sincerest apology.”

I grabbed her hand and offered a smile. I could feel my eyes threatening to tear. “I love you, too. I’ll see you soon.”

Cynthia took me in her arms, and beyond her thin shoulder and the porch light, I saw Robert’s shocked expression. She let me go, and without looking back, she left, her heels clicking against the pavement until she disappeared into the car.

I wasn’t ready to meet the curious stares of the others. I walked around to the back of the house, and leaned against a beam of the back porch. Murmuring caught my attention, and I saw Ryan and Claire sitting on the porch swing, looking up at the sky.

She was giggling, and he nonchalantly rested his arm on the back of the swing behind her. She didn’t lean away, and I smiled at the scene.

“I had fun today,” Ryan said, watching for Claire’s reaction.

“I couldn’t tell.” She rolled her eyes, but couldn’t hide her smile.

“My favorite part was when we traded places in the car.”

“I bet it was.”

They exchanged stories about the battle with the shells, and laughed as they teased each other. Every time Claire was in Ryan’s line of sight, his eyes lit up, and his grin was so innocent and animated, it was infectious.

Ryan pushed back against the swing, and again they sat quietly, with just a few residual giggles interrupting the still night. Claire held her feet out in front, her tan legs a perfect accessory to her cutoff jean shorts and casual pink tank top. The black combat boots just made her outfit more ‘Claire’.

Ryan rubbed the back of his head, trying to seem casual. "I gotta tell ya. I'm a little nervous about the trip."

Claire turned to him, squaring her shoulders. "Are you scared, little girl?"

Ryan huffed, playing off her taunt. "Scared. Psh. I can handle it. I'm nervous about how it's going to turn out. What if something bad happens?"

Claire's playful smile melted, and she faced forward. "It won't."

"But, what if it does?"

"Then I'll fix it. I always do."

"What if something happens and you can't fix it?"

"I don't know," she said. "That's only happened once."

Ryan squared his shoulders, facing her completely. "You mean your dad?"

She only nodded.

"Have you ever been up against something like this?"

Claire paused for a long time. I wished that I could see her expression. I wasn't sure if she was annoyed at his line of questioning, or she was afraid of the answer.

"Hey," Ryan said. When Claire ignored him, he tapped her shoulder. "Hey." She looked at him, then. "I'll be right behind you. And I don't mean that you can't take care of yourself, because we all know you can. I just mean if something happens, I'm not going anywhere. Whatever you need."

Claire took a breath. "I just assumed you already knew, but now I realize you don't. Jared is the last line of defense, so if we lose them, we won't know it. Do you understand?"

After a pause, Ryan nodded.

Claire continued, "The baby she is carrying is the most important thing. We have to protect it until we can't."

"The baby is important," Ryan agreed. "But you are the most important thing to me."

Claire watched him, and then her eyes fell to his lips. Ryan's eyes turned soft, and then he leaned in.

Watching them suddenly felt wrong. I turned, trying to find the best way to escape. The way I came seemed to be the best exit, and I took a step back.

Claire smiled. "You've watched this long, you might as well stay and watch it play out."

"I'm...I'm sorry," I said. My face instantly flushed.

Jared appeared at the back door, holding it wide open. "Everything okay?"

Ryan laughed and shook his head. "It was."

"Oh," Jared said with an awkward look. He and I traded glances, and then he retreated into the house.

Claire giggled, and then punched Ryan in the thigh.

"Ow!"

"Wait up!" she said, following me to the front yard. She was at my side in less than a second, and hooked her elbow around mine. "I meant what I said you know."

"Which part?"

Claire stopped, her face fell, and she lowered her chin so I could see directly into her eyes. "I don't know how all this will play out. Knowing Jared, he has a plan B, C, and D, but if something goes wrong, we'll just figure something else out. The only other option isn't an option." I shook my head, and Claire pulled me into her chest with a tight squeeze. "Piece of cake."

Jared stood at the Escalade with keys in hand. "We should get going. We still have to stop by the warehouse."

I nodded, and then waved to Claire. Ryan walked up behind her, putting his hands on her shoulders. It was so natural to see them standing next to each other, I couldn't remember what it was like when Ryan didn't know the Ryel secret, and he and Claire didn't spend every waking moment together.

"See you on the plane," Ryan said with a contrived smile.

I paused. "I'd understand if you didn't want to go."

Ryan shook his head. "I'm a marine, Nigh. I live for this shit."

Jared tugged on my hand. When we reached the Escalade, he sighed.

"You're worried for them."

"No," he said, starting the engine. "I'm worried for us, and what we'll have to put up with when they don't have an impending war to keep them entertained."

Chapter Fifteen
Questioned

Jared drove across town, and then took the highway that would lead us to the warehouse. Once we exited the highway and hit a dirt road, I knew we were close. The night sky was clear, and every star in the universe seemed to be present to watch over us. No wind, not even the sound of crickets or cicadas played for us as we parked and walked down the gravel drive. Jared unlocked the large, rusted lock of the gate, and then I followed him to the side door. Jared pushed the button, and then waited.

Accustomed to waiting ten or twenty minutes, I settled in, but the door immediately clicked, and Jared pulled me inside.

"Now, that's service," I said, smiling.

Jared smiled back. "He's expecting us."

"Isn't he always?"

The full moon let in the only light, casting large shadows across the vast cement floor. My sandals scraped against the dirt, and echoed throughout the building. Jared walked across the room, stopping in the middle.

This time was different from the visits we'd made before. This time, I could feel Eli. I could almost smell him. It seemed like he was closing in; that he was in the next room and making sounds to signal he was heading our way, but there was no sound. I could only feel it.

His energy grew stronger, and then he was standing in front of us. The same ensemble as usual, I smiled at his casual sandals. I withstood the urge to hug him. He had saved our hides the last time I'd seen him, but I didn't know where we stood now.

Eli's smile was immediate and sincere. "Hello, Nina. You look positively radiant! Doesn't she look radiant, Jared?"

"She does," Jared said.

"Time is so inconsistent between planes. It seems like I've been waiting ages for you two. I trust the family is doing well?"

"So far," I said.

Eli held one arm across his middle, and touched the other hand to his mouth as he feigned being lost in thought. "Hmmm...you're going on a trip, soon? Leaving this weekend?"

Jared nodded.

Eli's eyes widened. "I heard. You really aren't going to make this easy for the dark side, are you?"

Jared took a breath. "You don't seem concerned."

Eli laughed once. "It's hard to be concerned when nothing is a surprise. Just once I'd like to say, 'Ohemgee!' you know?"

I laughed, and Eli nodded, glad for my reaction.

Jared released my hand, and then rubbed the back of his neck. "This is no road trip. We need protection in the air."

Eli pulled his mouth to the side. "He'll remain neutral."

Jared frowned. "How can I protect her if the plane goes down? This opens us up to any amount of obstacles. Power failure, engine failure...if we end up in the water, we could wind up in a storm with fifty-foot waves. That's not balanced."

Eli nodded. "True. I'll put Samuel on it. Make sure things stay fair. Deal?"

"Good enough," Jared nodded. "One more thing...."

"Oh, you're ready, are you?" Eli said, his eyebrows shooting up.

I couldn't help but smile. "That looks awfully close to surprise to me."

Eli grinned from one ear to the other. "It feels like it, too. I should probably say, 'Ohemgee' to make it official, right? Ohemgee! You're ready?"

Jared smiled and then looked down, nodding. "We're ready."

"For what?" I asked.

Eli's expression softened. "The last question. The child is special, Jared. The first angel born to earth. As you already know, this child is capable of much, and has powers beyond your comprehension, but your wife is your only responsibility."

Jared frowned, trying to understand what Eli was trying to tell him.

I gripped Jared's arm. "But I thought once the baby is born, it's protected. Isn't that true?"

"Yes," Eli said. "But Jared is not its protector. He is yours."

Jared put his hand on mine. "Ask your question, Eli. Ask the only question left."

"Can you trust her?" he said.

"Nina?" Jared said. He looked at me, confused.

I could see Eli staring at us. His words were soft and slow. "A mother's love is everything, Jared. It is what brings a child into this world. It is what molds their entire being. When a mother sees her child in danger, she is literally capable of anything. Mothers have lifted cars off of their children, and destroyed entire dynasties. A mother's love is the strongest energy known to man. You must trust that love, and its power. Can you do that?"

Jared never took his eyes from mine. "Yes."

Eli nodded. "Then have confidence to carry out your plans."

I looked to Eli to tell him goodbye, but he had vanished. I took a deep breath, and threw my arms around my husband. "Do you feel better?"

"Not that I think you incapable, but I'm not practiced in the art of spectating."

"He just told us we could go to Jerusalem and be safe! He just said everything will be all right! Didn't you hear him?"

Jared frowned. "I heard him tell me to hand you total control."

I smiled. "And I heard you say you would."

Jared nodded, clearly frustrated. "I know. I will." He took my hand and led me to the Escalade. I shot him a warning glare, and he winced. "I swear."

"I don't think he means that I should lead the operation. My love for our child will keep it safe. I take that as a good thing, and it sounds very simple."

"Too simple. I don't want you thinking we're going to land and take a taxi to the Sepulchre and everything work out as planned. It's going to get messy, very fast."

I squeezed his hand. "We can do it. We have to."

Jared took my face in his hands and pressed his lips against mine. I grabbed his blue T-shirt in each of my fists and pulled him closer. My stomach kept us farther apart than usual, but I was as close as I could get for the moment.

"Whoa!" Jared said, backing away.

I grabbed my stomach and laughed. "You felt that?"

"Of course I did. Think Bean's trying to tell us something?"

"That we're grossing him out?"

Jared opened my door and helped me in. "Oh, now it's him?"

“I don’t know,” I said. “I’m playing around with both.”

Jared shut the door and in the next moment, slid into his seat. He shoved the shift into gear and then pulled away, a residual smile on his face.

I leaned over and hugged his arm, leaning my head on his shoulder. For the first time in a long time, tomorrow didn’t seem so ominous. Eli gave us all a bit of hope.

My cell phone rang, and I fished it from my purse, reading the display. “Hi, Beth,” I said.

“How long have you been in town?”

“A few hours. I know I said I would come over. We had to see Lillian and Cynthia, first.”

“Okay, I get that, but you could have at least called!”

I frowned. I was failing right and left at friendship. “Okay. Let me make it up to you. I’ll meet you at the pub in twenty minutes.”

“The pub? Really?”

“Yes. I’m sure you need a drink. I’ll call Ryan and Claire. They can meet us there.”

“Just like old times!” Beth squealed. “I’ll tell Chad!”

I dropped the phone into my purse and smiled. “She hung up on me.”

Jared frowned. “Do you think it’s wise to meet in a public place after the day we just had?”

I looked out the window. “This is my town. I dare them.”

Jared chuckled, and then took my hand, kissing my fingers. “You’re very attractive when you’re feisty.”

I grinned over his compliment, and watched Providence pass by as we made our way to the pub. Once in a while I would sneak glances at him. Jared hadn’t changed much since we met. He was still the tall, blond, movie-star-handsome man that sat next to me on the bench almost three years before. His chest and arm muscles still caught my eye when they moved and flexed under his shirt; his blue-gray eyes still made me pause. Life couldn't have spiraled out of control anymore than it had, but I wouldn't trade it. A different life didn't even appeal to me at that point. Despite that we were about to run for our lives, I had everything I'd ever wanted, with a man I loved desperately. Was the danger, stress, and fear worth it? Damn right it was.

The neighborhood around the pub had deteriorated since my freshman year. The streets seemed darker, and instead of college students congregating outside the front door, those loitering were much older, wearing sad stories on their faces. Jared pulled into the parking lot across the street. Nearly hopscotching my way around the puddles in the road, I ignored the stares of those standing outside, and led Jared into the pub. Tozzi was no longer behind the bar. In his place was a large woman with long, yellow hair. She didn't greet us when we came in.

"New management, I'm guessing," Jared said as we found a table. "I guess Beth hasn't been here lately, either, or she would have said something."

"It's a shame. Some of my favorite Brown memories are of this place."

Jared put his elbows on the table and settled in, smiling. "You mean the first night we danced?"

I rested my cheek on the palm of my hand, shooting a flirtatious smile across the table. "That's exactly what I was referring to, yes."

The music was loud, so I resorted to texting Beth to see if she wanted to meet elsewhere. I felt safe anywhere if I was with Jared. Although Chad was no pipsqueak, I couldn't imagine she would be comfortable here.

Seconds after I sent the text, Beth and Chad pushed through the door. Beth's eyes were wide as she looked around, and only slightly relieved when she recognized Jared and me. She waved at us, and then pulled Chad hastily across the room to our little corner.

"What in the hell happened to this place?" she said.

I leaned into the table. "Do you want to leave?"

"Why?" Chad said, puffing up his chest. "I'm ready for a beer."

We ordered, then Claire appeared, with Ryan right behind her.

One of the men whistled, and then slapped Claire's backside. She jerked to a stop, and with her stiletto boots, kicked the leg of the chair the man was in. It splintered, sending him tumbling to the ground. Neither Claire nor Ryan glanced behind them. They simply continued to our table as if nothing had happened.

One of the misfits at the man's table stood, and then Jared pushed himself away from the table, rising until his six feet, two inches towered over his challenger. Even from across the room he was intimidating. When the friend promptly took his seat, Jared did the same.

"You always have to make an entrance," Jared grumbled to his sister.

"I'll never get his greasy fingerprints out of this fabric."

"That's what you get for wearing pleather," Ryan joked.

"This is not pleather," Claire seethed. She jerked her head, shaking her bangs from her eyes. Her ice blue irises glowed against her nearly white hair, and I silently hoped that Bean looked just like her. A little nicer, of course, but physically, Claire was the perfect female specimen.

Beth filled us in on the magnitude of emotions at Titan, the rumors, and how well Grant was handling it all. The longer Beth talked, the hotter the pub became, as more grungy bikers and seedy individuals flowed through the door. Hearing Beth over the noise became more difficult for Chad, but Jared and I only pretended to struggle. To me, Beth sounded like she was talking directly into my ear.

A fight broke out, and Jared stood. He was on high alert, waiting for the crowd around us to shell. I watched the scuffle until they were thrown outside, and then I breathed. Jared was right. I was too confident. Even with the added security of Claire and Ryan, Chad and Beth could easily be hurt if the rowdy crowd inside shelled and we had to fight our way out.

"Maybe we should find somewhere else," I said.

"I agree," Beth jumped in.

"I'll get the tab," Jared said.

Claire rolled her eyes. "You guys are babies."

Beth and I left Claire and Ryan sitting at the table, walking together toward the door. Just a few feet away, we waited for Chad and Jared to pay the bill. Chad was laughing at something Jared had said. I smiled. There was something so satisfying about Jared socializing with someone other than our inner circle. It made him more...human.

Spending time with people who didn't know our secrets was relaxing for me, and it seemed to be that way for Jared, too. In that moment, I accepted my choice to keep the truth from Beth. Not only was it for her own safety, but I could rationalize that it was for my own sanity as well.

"You've really popped!" Beth said, gesturing to my stomach.

Instinctively I put my hand on my rounded belly. "Crazy, isn't it? It seems like it happened overnight."

Just then another fight broke out. People were punching and shoving, their bodies bouncing against each other like pinballs. I desperately tried to find Jared in the chaos, but when a line of sight finally opened up, he was no longer beside the bar.

Knowing the safest place for us was outside, I hurriedly opened the door and pushed Beth into the night air. The fighting spilled out onto the sidewalk, forcing Beth and me farther away. I tried to keep her out of harm's way, tugging on her until we found ourselves in the alley.

"Oddly enough, I feel safer in the dark," Beth whispered.

Yelling and breaking glass sounded just around the corner, and I decided to stay put. We waited for Jared and Chad, but the minutes passed, and I fought away feelings of panic. I imagined they were fighting their way out of the pub in that moment, and at any second they would come around the corner.

The small space between the two buildings didn't allow for much light. I felt a chill down my spine, and the hairs on the back of my neck stood on end. From each end of the alleyway, whispers floated from the shadows.

I squeezed Beth's hand. "We should see what's taking so long."

Beth nodded. We took a step, and then froze. A large man that I recognized from the pub stood in the way, his eyes bulging black spheres. His mouth moved, but he spoke in a different language. Something I'd never heard before.

Beth let out a small gasp, and she took a step back, pulling me with her. A dark metal side door opened, and the bartender stepped out. Her expressionless face and dark eyes signaled that she had shelled as well.

"Ooooooh sh—" Beth began, but I pushed her against the brick wall, right beside a dumpster.

"It's okay. Jared and Chad will be here any minute," I said. I turned, holding up my hands in a defensive pose.

The two shells approached me, the woman with a frightening smile and a knife in her hands.

"Chad!" Beth yelled. "We're in the alley!"

"Help!" I called. I could still hear yelling from the sidewalk fight. It would be difficult for anyone to hear; not that any of them would come to our aid. I deduced that Jared was dealing with shells of his own, or he would already have reached us. The shells came closer, and I braced myself.

"Crap," I said.

The woman lunged at me, and I dodged. I kicked, buckling her knee. Her head hit the brick cement wall just a few feet from Beth's feet. Beth covered her mouth and let out a yelp. The bartender regained her footing, blood dripping from her hairline, and took a step toward Beth. I picked up a branch beside the dumpster and swung with both hands. The woman fell to the ground. The knife clanged against the asphalt.

Beth leaned over, picked up the knife, and held it in front of her, shaking. "Don't go near her!" she said. "She's pregnant!"

The man smiled, and spoke something inaudible once again. He ran at me, and I jumped over him, letting him careen at full speed into the brick wall. He stumbled back, and I attacked. My hands balled into fists, and I punched his face over and over, and then grabbed his leather jacket with both hands and threw him to the ground. He grabbed my ankle and yanked, knocking me off my feet, but within seconds, I was standing, my hands out and ready.

My senses were heightened again, signaling that additional danger was coming, but it was too late. Someone burst out of the shadows and hooked an arm around my neck.

"Leave her alone!" Beth said, running at us with the knife.

I held out my hand, palm out. "Stay against the wall, Beth!"

She stopped mid-step, confused, and then I jerked my head back, hitting my assailant in the nose with my skull. I turned to see another man, this one skinnier and lanky, on the ground. Blood was spattered on his cheeks and forehead.

The larger man came at me with the branch. I used my forearm to hit it out of his hand, and then shoved the heel of my hand into his throat. In Claire-like fashion, I spun around, kicking him in the head. He fell to his knees. I reared back my hand and punched him with my fist in the jaw, knocking him out cold.

The skinny man kicked my back, and I fell to the ground, but caught myself before I fell flat.

"No! Nina!" Beth screamed.

I turned around, and threw every one of my limbs at him, kicking and punching. We were half way down the alley before he finally swung and punched me in the face. Half-surprised that he had landed a punch, half-amazed that it didn't hurt, I paused. Taking advantage, the skinny man lunged at my middle. My motherly instincts kicked in, and rage welled up inside of me. I moved to the side, and his fist landed against the brick.

Seeing that he'd left his side open to attack, I reacted, shoving my elbow into his throat, and then with one hand, I picked him up, and with all of my strength, I cried out, simultaneously throwing him against the opposite wall.

He rolled to the ground, and didn't get up again.

Beth ran to my side and threw her arms around me. I could hear her heart thumping against her chest, and she could barely catch her breath.

Jared and Chad rounded the corner, both disheveled. Jared's terrified expression melted into relief, and his shoulders fell.

Chad's eyes were wide, his breath labored. "Beth!" he cried, jumping over the bodies in his way.

Beth released me and ran into Chad's arms, immediately breaking into loud sobs. It was then that Chad noticed the limp bodies on the ground, and his eyes met mine. "What the hell happened?"

Beth held up her hand, palm out. "Don't say it," she said, sniffing. She wiped her nose and took a step toward me. "I love you, but please don't tell me how you did all of that. I honestly don't want to know."

"Well, I do," Chad said.

"It's better that you don't," Jared said, shouldering past Chad. He reached for me, and I fell into him. "Every last one of them shelled. It took forever to get out the door."

"It's a shame, but we're not going to that pub again," Chad said, shaking his head. "It's been taken over by misfits and criminals."

"Where's Claire and Ryan?" I asked.

Chad rolled his eyes. "Cleaning up. I think they're enjoying themselves."

We walked around the corner to find Claire standing alone, her arms crossed. Ryan grabbed a man twice his size and head-butted him.

"The PD will be here any minute," Jared said.

"I know," Claire said. "But I find him strangely attractive right now."

Jared rolled his eyes and led me to the street, and Beth and Chad followed. When we reached the parking lot, Chad took a deep breath. His hands were trembling, as were Beth's. I felt so sorry for them. They didn't deserve to be dragged into our mess.

"Beth," I said. I licked the blood from my bottom lip. "We're going away."

Her eyes shot up. "Again? But, you just got back."

"I need you to cover for me at Titan. Work under Grant. We'll be gone for the summer."

Beth left Chad and wrapped her arms around my neck, squeezing me tight. "I just need to know one thing: Are you going to be okay?"

I smiled. "Yes."

She nodded, taking a deep, cleansing breath, and straightened her shoulders. "I'll take care of it."

"I know you will."

Chapter Sixteen
Direct Flight to Hell

My hands shook. The seat belt clanged as I tried to buckle it for the fourth time. Claire was two feet away, stuffing her carry on in the overhead bin. Jared was outside, directing baggage and making doubly sure the preflight check had been carried out at least three times. Bex's deep voice hummed from the back as he joked with Ryan. His nervous energy was evident in his tone, and even though he was trying to play it off, it was there.

The sun had set, and because of an earlier light summer rain, the tarmac glistened. Jared was pointing in every direction, answering questions, his expression severe. I was glad that he was able to burn off some of his anxiety by choreographing our departure.

"Oh, for Pete's sake, Nina. Here," Claire said, snapping my seat belt closed.

I sighed, and nodded in thanks, and she left me for Bex and Ryan. I rested my head against the seat and took a deep breath. My nerves seemed to take a back seat when I watched Jared work outside, so I tried to keep my concentration on the window.

A dark figure approached Jared. Kim. She was unhappy, and when I realized she would ride with us for the duration of the trip to Jerusalem, my anxiety level doubled. We had all abandoned her. She was left to fight alone, even after she was promised for some relief. She had helped us, and we turned a blind eye while she lost sleep and her uncle. I was afraid of what she would have to say to me. And she had plenty of time to either let me squirm, or call me out.

She held out her hand. With the abilities Bean had given me, I could hear her dry voice.

"The book."

Jared put the Naissance de Demoniac in her grasp. "I know you don't believe me, but I am sorry."

"I believe you." Her voice was tired. Any sign of the Kim we once knew was as nonexistent as our former life. She took the book and held it to her chest, and then pulled a cell phone from her pocket. As she walked to the steps of the plane, I heard her sigh.

"Dad. I have it. We depart in ten minutes." She clicked the phone shut.

I wiped my moist brow.

"What's your deal?" Bex said, tapping my shoulder. "You sick? You look sick."

"I don't feel well."

His eyebrows turned in, deepening the same line that gave away Jared. Bex sat in Jared's seat, and patted my hand. "You have Kim, the human demon repellant, three hybrids, and a cop/ex-special forces guy on this plane. Not to mention you're kind of a badass yourself these days."

"Bex," I warned.

"Sorry. Don't tell Mom."

Kim boarded the plane. Her clothes were stained and wrinkled, hanging from her gaunt body. The dark circles under her once-soft brown eyes appeared like purple bruises on her ashen skin. She only carried the book in her hand, and the phone in her pocket. No luggage, no carry-on. She had one mission, and one mission only. Nothing else mattered.

Her eyes met mine, and she froze. Ryan passed my seat, and approached her. They traded glances, but no words were spoken. Ryan kissed her bony cheek, and she let her body weight lean against him. He supported her weight for a moment, and then squeezed her tight before letting go. She used the seats to support her weight as she approached me.

"Hi," she rasped.

My eyes filled with tears. Nothing I would say would be adequate. I didn't deserve to talk to her.

Bex stood, and then helped Kim into the seat he occupied. She turned to face me, and her chin lowered. "I don't blame you."

I pressed my lips together in a hard line. An apology seemed insulting; I could barely look her in the eye.

"I don't. I just wanted you to know that, you know...in case we crash and burn in a few minutes."

I stared at her in disbelief, and then the corners of her mouth turned up, and she winked and left.

Settling back into my seat, I took a deep, not-so-relaxing breath. The small crowd loading the plane had dissipated, and Jared made one last sweep of the plane before boarding.

"This is it," Jared said to us all. "From the moment we depart until we land, it's out of our hands."

I reached out to him, and he grabbed my hand, sitting in the seat beside me. He kissed my fingers, and closed his eyes. I waited for several moments, but he stayed still and silent. I turned to see Bex and Claire, eyes closed. Bex's lips moved in prayer.

Guilt washed over me. They didn't need to be on the plane. Bex didn't, either. If Hell pulled a fast one and the plane went down, we were helpless to stop it. I knew they didn't question their presence, though, but that only made me feel worse. It was all of us, or none of us, and the display of the lengths our mismatched family would go to for each other brought tears to my eyes.

Jared wiped the tear that raced down my cheek. “Ready?”

I nodded, forcing a smile. “I was born for this, right?”

“We all were.”

The engines whined, and the plane wheels began to roll. The wing lights blinked against the fuselage, casting a red glare at half the time of my heartbeat.

“Try to relax,” Jared whispered. His voice held no conviction. He knew they were just words.

We all waited for our impending death, knowing our chances plummeted the second the plane was in the air. The flight to Jerusalem was long—too long to cope with constant fear that every jostle or noise would signal our fall from the sky.

I turned to look at my family. Claire and Ryan were in deep, quiet conversation. Bex sat next to Kim, chewing his pinky nail, and Kim stared blankly ahead. The engines whined as the wheels rolled forward. The pilot taxied on the runway, and after a short pause, the plane surged forward. The sudden acceleration of the aircraft pressed my back into the seat. I closed my eyes, trying not to feel every flaw in the runway, or the wind resistance against the wings. My new abilities were exciting, and at times had saved my life, but for the first time, I wished for the aptitude to turn them off.

As we raced faster and farther down the runway, I imagine the tiny wheels, and how on earth at that speed the plane didn’t veer off into the grass, or a building. At that point, everything that could possibly go wrong before we even got off the ground flashed through my mind, and my heart pounded so hard against my chest wall that I thought I would die of a heart attack before we left Providence.

"Nina," Jared said in a smooth tone. He leaned into my ear, and his lips brushed against my skin. He pulled my arm across him, and kissed my neck. I gripped his shirt, my knuckles white. I was relieved to be in the arms of my husband, but for all the wrong reasons.

"I'm afraid," I said, stuttering.

"I know." He gently held my jaw with both of his hands, and lowered his chin. His dark blue eyes met mine. "We're going to make it. I won't let anything happen to you."

"Don't start making promises you can't keep, now."

He kissed me, hard and purposeful. Once, I could have become lost in a kiss like that, but the wheels were leaving the ground, and we were now a large and easy target.

"Nina, you have to have faith."

My eyebrows pulled together. "Someone is going to have to give me a reason. I'm all out of faith." The plane dipped a bit before making a sharp turn.

"Look at how far we've come," he said, smiling. He meant to be comforting, but I could see the fear behind his eyes.

I buried my face in the crook of his neck, and squeezed him to me. My eyes shut tight, trying to push away the overwhelming feeling that we had been deceived, corralled into this deathtrap —the one place Jared couldn't control.

The plane righted itself, and then climbed effortlessly into the night sky. The lights below appeared to shrink, until they seemed like glowing clusters of fireflies. Everything else on the ground was black and ominous.

Jared was unfolding a map of the old city, sprawling it across his lap. He used his finger to trace different routes to the Sepulchre, then sighed. "I wish we'd had enough time to send someone ahead. To shape the battle space."

I touched his free hand. "I don't know what that means, but we'll figure it out."

He paused. "I apologize for the military jargon. I'm just in that mode at the moment."

"I understand," I said. The stress he suffered was nearly visible. The pressure was crushing him.

His eyes slowly fell on where my fingers touched his skin, and then closed. He took a deep, faltering breath, and exhaled. "I am terrified of losing you. The routes, the possibility of last minute change of plan, everything that could possibly go wrong has ran through my mind so many times, I doubt I'll ever forget. I love you so much, Nina. I love our child. The fear of failing you weighs so heavy on my mind, I feel like I'm going crazy."

I turned in my seat to face him. My eyes bore into his, filling with tears fueled by every emotion. "If I've ever believed in you, Jared, it's now. Whatever happens, whatever crosses our path, I know you'll make the right choice." I pulled his hand to my round belly. "We both believe in you."

"Claire has spent quite a bit of time there." He turned and gestured at her to join them.

"We're setting down in Ben-Gurion airport," he said, pointing to the map.

Claire nodded. "It's about forty-one kilometers from the center of Jerusalem. We head west here, toward Nesher, and then take this right, here, to Route Forty-five-oh-three."

With his finger, Jared followed the road, and shook his head. "But this is a main road. Shouldn't we try some back roads?"

Claire shrugged. "I say get there, Jared. We're going to get the shit kicked out of us on any road we take."

I frowned. "That doesn't make me feel better."

Claire raised her brows. "Nina, you should prepare yourself. Think of every war movie you've ever seen on TV. Loud noises, yelling, guns, and things blowing up around us. We're going to be shot at, chased, and running for our lives the second we touch the tarmac. You're going to have to listen, stay focused, and follow orders, or we're not going to make it. Get it?"

My head bobbled, trying to process the war zone she described.

Her eyes left mine to return to the map. "That tunnel could be a problem. We could detour here," she pointed, "and skip across to rejoin the main road here, skipping the toll."

"If we can just get into the Old City, we'll be home free. The Sepulchre is just there," Jared said. He pushed his lips back and forth with his fingers, a million decisions flipping through his mind.

They pored over the map, discussing different roads, buildings, and blind spots. Even though they were kind enough to speak in English this time, as much as half of their discussion was lost on me with phrases like Black Swan, Belay, and Schwerpunkt.

Claire shook her head. "I brought the new rifle. Ryan and I could stay behind. I could cover you."

Jared thought for a moment, but shook his head. "Too risky. What if you get trapped?"

Claire frowned. "That's insulting."

"It's not just you, Claire. You have two of you to watch out for."

"I know that, but he—"

"Claire?"

Claire's shoulders dropped in resignation.

"We're not leaving anyone behind. We stay together."

"Copy that."

They spent another hour coming up with Plan Bs, and Cs, and Zs. If something went wrong at this corner, we would take that alley; duck into that building; cut across that roof. Areas of concentrated population were to be avoided at all costs, but the Sepulchre was in the center of the Old City, and a popular pilgrimage. Our fight wouldn't end until we were safe inside the tomb.

I shivered. How anyone could feel safe in a tomb was beyond me, but it was the one place Hell wouldn't go. The book was proof. I turned to see Kim staring at the book in her hands.

She sensed me looking at her, and her eyes jumped up. I was immediately embarrassed, but she showed a glimpse of my friend, letting the corners of her mouth turn up. The action seemed unnatural for her, and it only lasted a moment before she was blank-faced and once again staring at the book.

Claire stood and crossed her arms. "Six hours 'til arrival. I'm going to ready the weapons."

She didn't get halfway down the aisle before the plane trembled, and then shook. Jared looked at me, and then behind him. Claire held onto the tops of two seats on each side of her.

"Probably just some choppy air," Ryan said.

In that moment the plane bounced violently, sending objects from the overhead bins to the floor. The lights flickered, and I held my belly with one hand, and gripped Jared's arm with the other. Claire's outline flashed by as she made her way to the cockpit.

"Is it turbulence?" I shouted. The engines whined in a way I'd never hear before, and I could feel the plane descending rapidly. The plane took another dive, and then leveled out slightly. "Jared?" I cried.

"Claire will handle it," he said, covering my hand with his.

The cabin went dark, and red emergency lights cast frightening shadows. After another dip, the emergency oxygen masks fell from above.

"Doesn't that mean we've lost pressure?" I said in a panic.

Jared leaned over to look out the window, and I did the same. Blackness covered the ground below. No glowing fireflies, no tiny lines of traffic. We were over ocean, with no hope of making an emergency landing.

The plane leaned to the left, pushing me against the window. It was then that I saw it: Moonlight flickering against the waves below. We were just a few thousand feet from crashing into the water.

"Nina!" Jared said, unbuckling my seat belt. "Come with me. I'm going to open the emergency exit door, and when I tell you, we're going to jump."

"What?" I said. "Jump from the plane? Are you crazy?" I could see real fear in his eyes, and for the first time, I knew Jared had made a decision out of desperation.

Claire burst out of the cockpit and looked Jared, shaking her head.

Jared gripped my hand and pulled me to my feet. Before I could speak, we were at the emergency exit. Jared grabbed the lever with both hands, but I stopped him.

"We need to do this now!" he yelled.

I shook my head. "I can't."

"You can!"

I looked around me to the frightened faces of Bex, Kim, and Ryan, and then Claire.

“Why are you just sitting there?” she cried, “Help us, dammit!”

Jared’s arms tensed against my strength, but I refused to let him pull the handle.

I closed my eyes, trying to block out the noise. “Help us,” I whispered. “We need your help.”

Chapter Seventeen
Departure

The plane trembled like an earthquake. The engines whined, and the emergency oxygen masks leaned forward as the plane plummeted toward black water.

Claire shrieked. I was afraid to open my eyes, hesitant to see what unimaginable horror had caused her to scream. I popped one eye open, and then the other. Even in the dim red light, I could easily make out Claire's tiny arms wrapped around a large, dark figure. The lights returned to normal, and the shaking immediately stopped. The plane leveled out as the high-pitched cry of the engines quieted to a smooth, low hum.

Jared stopped trying to open the door, and he stood, moving slightly when every muscle in his body relaxed at once.

Bex hopped to his feet. "It's about freakin' time!" he said, slapping the top of the seat in front of him. After collecting himself, he turned to Kim.

"You okay?"

Kim's expression remained blank. "Why?"

She winked at me, and an uncontrollable grin stretched across my face. I was beginning to see traces of my friend again.

Samuel stood at the front of the aisle, a large, white smile a contrast against his black face. "I apologize. The best way to describe it is that I had to wade through some red tape."

Claire released Samuel and playfully punched his arm.

Jared raced up the aisle and then paused. Samuel opened his arms wide, and Jared fell into his chest, hugging him as well. Samuel laughed, his voice bellowing, filling every space in the cabin. I didn't realize that I was still tense until Ryan spoke into my ear, causing me to jump.

"He wasn't on the plane before, was he?"

I shook my head, smiling. "Nope."

A loud popping noise echoed when Samuel patted Jared on his back. "I can only go as far as the outskirts of Jerusalem, but I'm going to join you, if you don't mind."

Jared laughed once. "Not at all." I joined him at the front of the aisle, wrapping my arms tightly around him. I sighed. "I admit it. I was scared to death."

Jared shook his head. "I was ready to jump from a crashing airplane with my pregnant wife. I think I win this one."

I agreed without pause. "Touché."

Samuel walked back and forth along the aisle for a while. We all watched him quietly, but the fear and apprehension was gone. When Samuel would pass our seats, Jared would squeeze my hand. I kept trying to use my new and crude sensitivities to recognize a dark presence, but I either wasn't doing it right, or Samuel had given them a severe enough warning.

Before long, Jared's breathing evened out, and then his fingers relaxed around mine.

I fell asleep soon after. A tiny baby boy in my arms, swaddled in the softest blue cotton, smiling and content in the shade under our oak tree, saturated my dreams. He smiled, his bright blue-gray eyes glimmering in the summer sun. His pinky finger was no longer than my pinky nail, and I kept kissing his hands over and over, unable to feel his skin against my lips enough times.

Time passed quickly there. Before the end of the day, he was a toddler, and then grade-school age. He didn't appear older than he was, like Bex always had. He was perfectly human, and yet flawlessly beautiful like his father. By the time the shadow under the oak had faded, my son was a man, as tall and distinguished as Jared. I watched all of this in awe, but a little sad at the same time. It had gone by too fast. I wanted more time with him. I wanted to start over. A strange mixture of pride and sadness surged through me, and I remembered how just a few hours ago I was pregnant with him.

The shade now a shadow, my son walked over to me and held out his hand. He looked so much like his father. "It's time," he said with a small smile. My smile.

"Time for what?"

"The end."

My eyes popped open. Jared had left his seat, and I could hear him conversing with Bex and Kim somewhere in the back of the plane. I rubbed my eyes, and turned to my right. Samuel sat across from me, his massive frame nearly too large for the seat.

"Did you sleep well?" he asked.

"I did, actually."

He smiled. "I know. I was just being polite."

"Oh. Right." I maneuvered my body out of my seat, stretching.

Jared's eyes met mine, and he stood, moving to the side.

"Again?" Bex teased.

"Yes, Bex. I'm pregnant. When you have a full-grown infant doing a handstand on your bladder, I'll keep track of how many bathroom breaks you take, mmk?" I waddled down the aisle, passing Ryan and Claire, who didn't seem to notice my presence. I noticed that Ryan's pinky was overlapping Claire's however, and she wasn't beating him to a bloody pulp for it. I smiled, and made my way to the lavatory.

I opened the door and frowned. I felt like Winnie the Pooh trying to squeeze into the honey tree. I looked down the aisle, meeting the inquisitive eyes of my husband. "I always feel I'm going to get stuck in there."

Jared laughed. "If you do, I'll get you out."

Bex held up a white bottle. "I have lotion. That should help."

I rolled my eyes and made my first attempt to navigate the small space.

Without event—or lotion—I returned to my seat, but not without the irritating snickering of Kim and Bex.

"Shut it," I grumbled, glaringly aware that my penguin walk only made their laughter more boisterous.

I turned my attention back to Jared. "I don't suppose you've thought about the little things."

"Such as?"

"Bathrooms? Sleeping arrangements? Privacy?"

"All luxuries that won't be readily accessible."

"Pardon?" I said, my eyebrows shooting up two inches. "I'm heavily pregnant, and there's no bathroom?"

Jared shifted nervously. "Yes."

I sighed with relief, and looked to the ceiling. "Oh, thank God."

"But...not like the facilities you're used to."

I peered over at him.

He shifted again. "It's more like a...a...hole. In the ground. But there is running water below so it's not as bad as it sounds."

My face screwed into disgust. "You expect me to balance this," I said, pointing to my belly, "over a hole?"

"You have Claire and Kim to help."

I crossed my arms and faced the wall. "Not funny."

"It can't be helped."

I relaxed, and covered my face. "I'm so sorry. I sound like a brat. It's just…" Tears burned my eyes. "It's not the way you imagine your pregnancy, you know. Not that I ever really imagined it, but living the last few weeks of my pregnancy in a moist, dark hole, with medieval accommodations and the birth," I said with a faltering breath. "I'm scared to death. It's going to be painful, and I trust you, but...not being in a hospital, or even have a midwife there. I'm afraid I won't be able to do it."

Jared wrapped his arms around me tight. "It is. But, Claire and I have researched it to death, talked to every medical professional we know, and brought every supply we'll need."

"I'm still scared," I said. A tear fell down my cheek.

Jared rested his cheek on my hair, and his fingers pressed into my skin. "I'm going to love you through it."

I nodded, and pressed my face into his chest.

Claire tapped Jared on the shoulder. "We need to ready the weapons and check the supplies."

Jared nodded and released me. Everyone looked to him, and he gestured to everyone. "We have a lot of gear to hike through the city. The most important packages are weapons, med supplies, and rations. These will be carried by myself, Claire and Bex. Ryan, you'll be extra eyes on the book, but stay close to Claire."

Ryan nodded.

Jared continued, "Kim, stay close to Bex. If any one gets separated, hold your position and we'll double back. Under no circumstances is anyone to go off alone. I don't care if you're in a panic, or you see a better way to go. Fracturing the group puts us all at risk, so we stay together. Got it?"

Everyone agreed.

The pilot announced the beginning of our descent. Claire and Bex had already brought the supplies and weapons packs to the front, and we were prepared to scramble to the waiting vehicle.

Jared was clearly anxious, but Samuel didn't seem fazed.

I nudged my husband. "Samuel said he would ride with us to the old city. Does that mean things will be calm until then?"

"I don't know. We should be prepared for anything."

I nodded, and wiped my sweaty hands on my pants.

Claire and Ryan both had AK-47s slung around their shoulders, pistols in the pockets of their cargo pants, and communication devices in their ears. Claire passed two more to Bex and Jared, and they spoke quietly to each other, testing the clarity and to see if they worked correctly.

The more they rushed around to prepare to land, the more nervous I became.

Claire handed me a vest, and Jared encouraged me to put it on. I watched Claire hand the same vest to Kim, Bex, and Ryan, and I realized they were bulletproof. Mine was surprisingly light.

Jared bent down to ensure my laces were tied and secure.

"Really?" I said. "I'm not a toddler."

"I'm just covering all the bases, sweetheart."

Kim and Samuel sat back, barely noticing the activity around them.

"Ryan," Claire barked. "Hand me the fifty-cal. The launcher is in pack two."

Ryan nodded, and rifled through one of the larger duffels. He handed her what looked like a heavy backpack.

As the wheels touched the runway, Claire and Ryan put on their own dark sunglasses and stood by the door, assault rifles in hand. I unfastened my seat belt, and Jared took my hand. “Kim and Nina in the middle, Bex bring up the rear. Claire and Ryan on point.”

At the door, Samuel closed his eyes and whispered something both beautiful and menacing, and then opened the door. He walked out, and stood, his arms crossed, on one side of the stairs.

“It’s quite safe, I assure you,” he said, his deep voice echoing. The tarmac was empty except for our waiting Humvee. It was borrowed, light tan, and gauging by the bullet holes, had already seen action in its lifetime.

Claire took off her sunglasses and looked up at Samuel in awe. “It’s going to be like this until we get to the old city?”

“If not, I’ll take care of it, but it would be a waste for them to attack any earlier.”

Claire elbowed him in the stomach, but he didn’t flinch. “You let me get all dressed up for nothing.”

Samuel smiled. “I thought you’d be happy. The Humvee matches your clothes.”

Claire looked down at her olive green tank top and light tan cargo pants, and then feigned irritation. “Not good enough.”

Samuel’s hand swallowed Claire’s small shoulder. “Once you reach Jerusalem, I promise you’ll use your fancy vest more than you’d like.”

Claire and Jared traded glances.

“Sounds like a party,” Ryan said with a grin.

Chapter Eighteen
Sepulchre

Loading the Humvee only took a few minutes, and then we were barreling down the highway, weaving in and out of traffic. Bex drove, Claire sat in the passenger seat, and the rest of us piled in the back. Jared barked directions at Bex, securing packs and loading weapons at the same time. Knowing he was in protector mode until we were all safely tucked under the Sepulchre made me miss him, but I had to let him focus. The more miles Bex put behind us, the more my fear threatened to take over.

Kim scooted closer to me and grabbed my hand.

I looked over at her sheepishly. "Are you scared?"

"I'm about to piss my pants."

I nodded quickly, glad that I wasn't the only one not looking forward to a battle.

Ryan was humming along to a song inside his head, tapping his fingers to the beat against his assault rifle.

"You weren't kidding," I said.

He looked up. "What?"

"About the party."

He smiled. "What can I say? I miss it."

Kim laughed once, incredulous. I couldn't even manage a reaction.

"Oh c'mon," he said. He gestured to us, "You two get to see me in action for the first time. Who can say their friend has gone off to war and then they get to watch them work? No civilians, I guarantee it."

"It's going to get bad," I said.

He shook his head and smiled. "I'm counting on it."

As usual, Ryan's casual demeanor made my anger boil just below the surface. "What if something happens to you? Do you know what that means for Claire?"

"This isn't my first rodeo, kiddo."

Kim leaned forward. "It's not your moment to impress her, either. This is serious. Quit screwing around and focus before you get us all killed."

While Ryan and Kim bickered, I leaned up to look out the window. The scenery didn't look so different. Retail stores, traffic, and pedestrians. The only things that seemed foreign were the sun and palm trees. We could have been in California. I settled back against my seat. For reasons I couldn't explain, the familiar surroundings made me feel better.

The Humvee took a sharp turn, shoving me against Kim.

"Bex?" Jared called.

"They're shelling, but they're keeping their distance. I'm just trying not to get boxed in."

"Patience," Samuel said.

Jared nodded, and then fastened an extra ammo belt around him. I crawled to the closest mirror, and watch as civilian cars and pickup trucks crowded the sides and behind our Humvee.

Bex swerved to the right, nudging one of the cars off the road. Claire readied her weapon.

"Just wait," Samuel said. His voice was even, creating a strange calming effect.

I watched him for a moment. "Why can't you stay with us until the Sepulchre?"

"So that you may rise above your struggle," he said. "And because that was the agreement. I will keep you safe throughout the flight and trip to Jerusalem. Then you must rise above your struggle. Only then will you appreciate your plight." He shrugged. "It is the way of the humans. It has always been the way."

I wasn't exactly sure where he was getting at, but I didn't want to question him more. He wasn't as practiced as Eli at human relations, and I had a feeling that no matter how in depth he explained it, I would only be more confused.

Kim leaned into my ear. "He means he can't just give us a Get Out Of Jail Free card, because it behooves our character to struggle before success. God is all about being fair and not interfering."

"And Hell is the opposite," I groused.

Another swerve threw me into Kim. "I'm glad you're here." I said, righting myself.

One side of her mouth turned up. "I'm not."

"Plan B," Bex said. "I'm taking the next exit!"

Samuel held up his hand. "Stay the course. Think of them as an escort."

"Not the good kind."

As we approached the city, the cars and trucks around us became more uniform, and it was evident that everyone around us had shelled. I peeked out of the window to see the sedan running alongside us. It contained a woman in her mid- to late twenties. An empty car seat was in the back.

I closed my eyes. When Samuel left us, they would attack, and we would have to kill them.

"Jared?"

"Yes?" he said, albeit distracted.

"That woman over there," I said, nodding in her direction. "She has a baby."

Jared barely glanced at her. "Yeah?"

"We can't kill her."

The woman looked at me, her eyes bulging and black.

Jared drew my attention away from her, gently turning my jaw to face him. "She can't kill you, either. We're going to make plenty of tough decisions between now and then. Let's not dwell on the shells. We can't."

I nodded, but Ryan glanced at the woman in the car, and was visibly unsettled.

Jared grabbed the barrel of Ryan's weapon and jerked it. "Everyone can shell. Everyone is a threat. The demons are counting on you to see the human and hesitate. Hesitation will get you killed. Got it?"

"Got it."

"Five minutes!" Claire called.

Everyone tensed. Bex flew through traffic, trying to leave the shells building up around us behind, but every time he gained ground, the drivers of the cars ahead shelled. The stores and houses seemed to be almost on top of each other, covering the gentle hills. Many of the buildings—especially the older ones—were made of rectangular rocks and castle-like in shape. Trees peppered the landscape, unlike the vast desert I had expected.

The sun was blindingly bright, glaring off the road and buildings. Kim squeezed my hand when we passed two statues of knights on horses, flying flags and proclaiming victory over the land. It was dizzying to think of how many empires had tried to own this land, and how much blood had been shed for a claim to it. We were going to be the numberless battle in that holy city. Not to own it, but survive it.

Jared looked at me. "Stay close. Never leave my side, for any reason. Keep your eyes and ears open."

I nodded. "I love you."

He managed a small smile and shook his head. "I love you," he said, pulling me to him. He planted a quick kiss on my lips, and then the Humvee stopped.

"Damascus Gate less than one klick!" Claire yelled.

Jared looked to Samuel for explanation, but he was gone.

Bex turned, his face intense. "Shells coming over the hill!"

"That's it! We're on our own!" Jared yelled. He took the safety off his pistol, and grabbed a fistful of my vest.

Claire and Ryan left the Humvee first, and Jared and I followed. The bullets were already flying, landing in the sand at my feet. We hunkered down in a small alley just inside a stone corridor until Kim and Bex joined us, and then Jared silently ordered us to move.

Claire pointed further inside the corridor. "Damascus Gate. Markets and pedestrians. No good."

Jared nodded once, and then we moved out. Claire took to the street with cover fire, running at full speed to the next alley. People walking in the street would run, and then suddenly stop to follow. Jared pulled me across the street, and a large man with military fatigues ran at us. Claire put a bullet in his head in less than a second. Jared didn't bother to slow down. We jumped over the corpse and caught up.

Duck and cover seemed to be the plan of action for the next two streets. The Old City was a series of narrow rock roads and corridors lined with trinkets and rugs for sale. We reached the end of one road to find ourselves at the beginning of a marketplace. Claire froze, and we stopped abruptly behind her. A hundred or so people stopped, slowly turning around. They eyes of men, women, and children were black as night and bulging from their sockets.

"Move," Claire said, waving us back.

Jared turned on his heels, leading us to the next building and up a set of stairs. We climbed to the roof, with the mob just behind Bex and Kim. Jared took a few wide strides and then we leapt from that roof to the next. He wanted to continue, but I refused, waiting for Kim. Once they breached the top of the stairs, I saw hands clamoring over bodies, the shells trampling each other to get at us. Bex was focused, but Kim's eyes bulged.

"Just hang on to him!" Claire called.

Bex, still running, hugged Kim to him, and when his feet left the roof, he cradled her to his side like a football. His landing was smooth, but Kim had to take a moment we didn't have to get her bearings. The mob still came at us, most of them falling to the alley below when they tried to make the jump.

My hands flew to my mouth. Children were among those falling to their deaths.

We made the jump four times, and then descended a set of stairs that lead us to another series of corridors.

Jared hunkered down, letting Kim catch her breath. "We're in the Christian Quarter. The Sepulchre is two klicks away. We're going to take the west bypass. It's a high traffic area for tourists with high rock walls on each side, so we're going to have to mow a path."

"Copy that," Ryan said, cocking his rifle.

Jared began to speak again, but a small group of young men shot at us from above. We ran again, dodging shells and bullets. Bex followed up the rear, turning and shooting as he ran. Ryan and Claire were at the front, their rifles against their faces, pointing the barrels in every direction they looked. As many times as I had tried to imagine it, we really were in the middle of a war. The sounds of the

AK-47s trading shots and the bullets ricocheting off the walls and roads just made me run faster.

Already exhausted, Kim had trouble keeping up, and Bex kept encouraging her to keep moving. We took cover behind dumpsters and parked cars every few seconds, and the noises around us paused ever so often when we hunkered down, and began sounding like a familiar beat.

Claire and Ryan would reload at nearly the same time, and then we'd start again. Jared would drop a clip and reload as we ran, and Bex did the same. At one point, he pulled a second pistol, turning to lay down more cover fire until Jared yelled for him to keep up. He was next to Kim in less than a second.

Shells that were unarmed simply tried to grab us, but the demons were still human on the outside, and Ryan quickly learned how to incapacitate them. He would use his elbow or the butt of his gun, and shoot the ones he didn't have time for. I noticed most of his bullets landing in their kneecaps or shoulders, hoping to give them a chance once the demons let them go.

In the court of the Church of the Holy Sepulchre, a large crowd obstructed the two giant wooden doors that led inside. They stood like statues, their arms calmly at their sides, their black eyes and ashen skin confirming control by the demonic. Some of them were civilian, but most were in fatigues, holding AK-47s. The building itself was massive, much larger than I had imagined, made of stone. I suddenly felt much better about being holed up in there for the next sixty days or so, but the high rock walls made it impossible to do anything but initiate a head-on invasion.

"Should we wait until dark?" Bex asked.

I grabbed his bloodied shoulder, pressing my palm against it. "You're hit."

He winked. "It's not bad. So...should we wait?"

Jared shook his head. "We just need to get in there."

Kim sighed. "But how? There are hundreds of people out there."

Claire pulled a pin from a grenade. "Like this." She rolled it into the crowd, and in seconds a large explosion blew people and body parts in different directions. A huge brown cloud of smoke filled the area and Claire and Ryan ran full speed into it.

Jared grabbed my sleeve and we followed. We didn't get five steps before a hail of bullets rained down on us. Jared was hit several times and faltered. A bullet ripped through my arm. At first it didn't hurt, but the closer we got to the Sepulchre, the more the burning surged through my veins. The memory of the pain in my leg at the Japanese restaurant in Providence immediately came to the forefront of my mind. Jared flipped around, and emptied his pistol into the dissipating cloud. He pushed me forward, and Claire and Ryan took me into the church.

"She's hit!" Ryan said.

They had already cleared the main room. Ryan tied a piece of cloth around my arm while Claire took out the shells in the rest of the church and secured the entrances. Jared, Bex, and Kim came into the doors as one unit, with Kim sliding in on her knees. Bex slammed the door closed behind them, and immediately covered the window.

After a few minutes and sporadic gunfire, Claire returned. "We only have a few minutes before they reorganize. The barricades won't hold for long. We need to get underground."

I winced as Jared tightened Ryan's tourniquet. "I thought they couldn't come in here."

Jared frowned at the dark red saturating the cloth on my arm. "It's the tomb they can't violate. The church and basilisk itself are fair game."

Bex glanced back from the window. "Whatever we're doing, let's do it fast."

The cloud from the grenade had cleared, revealing dozens of mutilated corpses on the ground. More shells were crowding the Sepulchre, and were now climbing its walls and beating on the doors.

Jared lifted Kim off the floor. "You have the book?"

She nodded, breathing hard.

"You ready to do what you came here to do?"

"Yes, and it's about damn time, Ryel," she said, tightening her grip on the pack.

We retreated into the church, passing extravagant garnishing of gold, marble and artwork. Candles lined altars, and pictures of the crucifixion of Christ. We passed a set of stairs that made Claire pause before advancing into the Sepulchre of Jesus.

"Where do they lead?" I asked.

Jared glanced at the stairs only briefly. "That would be the stairway to Calvary. Christ climbed those steps on his way to be crucified."

We continued through a large clearance to another room that held a smaller space within. You could walk around the center room to the next section of the Sepulchre, but Claire advanced inside.

"Is this it?" I asked.

Jared squeezed my hand. "The Holy Sepulchre."

We filed in, and everyone dropped their packs. I was confused. The adornments around the room signaled a holy place, but all this time, my mind pictured an underground cavern.

"This can't be it. How can we protect ourselves in here?"

Claire sighed. "Not in here." She pushed the altar to the side, revealing an ancient steep staircase. "The true tomb is hidden below. It's hidden from the public."

"I'm having my baby in a hole," I said, more of a statement than a question.

Bex laughed once. "Uh...is there room in the inn?"

My stomach lurched, and I grabbed Jared's arm.

"Nina?" he said, immediately worried.

I grabbed my belly with both hands and groaned. "Give me a minute," I said, panting.

Claire took a few steps down. "We don't have a minute."

"Let's get her downstairs," Bex said, checking outside the room. "They're coming."

Claire clicked a flashlight onto her rifle and ducked down the staircase. Ryan followed, and then Jared, Kim and I went down next, with Bex closing the opening behind us. The stairway opened up into a stone hallway that led to a massive cavern. Damp, dark, and drippy. Just as I had imagined.

"Feeling better?" Jared asked, touching my protruding stomach.

I nodded, still looking around the room. The flashlights illuminated giant stone arches lining the vast space, accessing lateral halls.

"Where do they lead?" I asked.

"Tunnels. Two hundred yards either way isn't protected. They won't come down here, but don't wander."

"I won't."

Kim pulled the Naissance de Demoniac from her satchel, and pointed her flashlight around the room, settling on what looked like a formerly adorned altar. She walked over to it slowly. Even in the dim light, I could see her body shaking uncontrollably. Ryan and I walked behind, watching her hold the book in front of her.

"I did it," she said, staring at the book in awe. "We're free."

Ryan put his hand on Kim's shoulder as she placed the book on the altar. She fell to her knees, and we fell with her. In the next moment, the ground began to shake, and small bits of rock fell to the floor. A piercing roar echoed through the tomb, causing us all to cover our ears. It was one voice, but also many, wailing, yelling, cursing utter foulness...and then it was over. Silence.

Kim looked back at Jared, and he offered a knowing smile. She had completed her mission, and freed her family of the duty of protecting the Naissance de Demoniac from a constant, powerful enemy.

"I guess I can go home now?" she said.

"You can," Bex said. "But you're on your own, and this place is crawling with shells."

"We could use you here," Jared said, "to help with the birth."

Kim smiled at him. It was a relief to finally see the two come to terms. The air was immediately lighter between them.

"I wonder if you still have your superpower?" Ryan said.

Kim punched him in the gut, and he doubled over. "It would appear so."

"That wasn't what I meant," he coughed.

Chapter Nineteen
Trapped

It's hard to keep one's days and nights straight when underground. If it weren't for the family full of Hybrids, I would have been alone while keeping my strange hours. Whether it was the baby, or the less-than-comfortable blow-up mattress we slept on, or the constant dripping in the background, it was impossible to sleep. Regardless, I took naps at one to three hours at a time, around the clock.

Ryan and Kim didn't seem to have the same problem. Even though his mattress was noticeably close to Claire's, she made a point of keeping her distance now that we were all safe. As the days wore on, Ryan grew less happy about her cold demeanor, and the grumbling turned into full-blown arguments.

It was difficult—after we'd spent so much time dodging and preparing—to sit and wait. As much time that went into planning our escape into this tomb, no one, it seemed, had planned for the suffocating time spent underground.

Jared and I tried to make the best of it: talking to my belly, spending quality time together, discussing the birth. I wasn't sure how I felt about Jared delivering our baby, but of all the people trapped in the tomb with us, Jared was my top pick.

After thirty days of darkness, tasteless rations, and the same close company, life in the tomb began to wear on all of us. Even Bex's bright and cheery demeanor began to show signs of waning. Poker and gin rummy only entertained for so long, and radio reception was hopeless in the deep of Israeli rock. Stories in the evenings were something I looked forward to, and it gave me a chance to get to know everyone better.

"So, that was the first time I bested Dad, although I'm pretty sure he let me win," Bex said with a broad smile.

"I remember that," Claire said. "He didn't let you win. He wouldn't stop talking about it after you went to bed."

"Really?" Bex said, his eyes bright.

"Really."

Bex's smile faded. "He died four days after that."

Everyone lowered their chins, unsure how to advance the conversation.

Jared finally spoke. "That must've been hard on you, Bex. I don't think I ever asked you if you were okay."

Bex shrugged. "I was, I guess. What else could I be?"

"In pain," Claire said. "We were all so wrapped up in our own, we didn't even try to help you through it."

"I missed him. And then...I missed you guys. I was glad when Jared brought Nina around. The family kind of came back together, then. Now we have Ryan."

"We don't have Ryan," Claire said.

Ryan shot her a dirty look, and then softened his features for Bex. "Yes you do, man. I'm here if you need me."

Claire rolled her eyes. "What would he need you for? To help with a school bully?"

"To talk to," Ryan said. "You know, what we used to do before you became so hateful and mean."

Claire crossed her arms over her knees. "You don't give me a choice," she mumbled.

"What?"

Ryan's acerbic tone lit Claire's eyes. "You don't give me a choice!"

"C'mon, guys," I said. It was far too claustrophobic, even in the large cavern, for anyone to fight.

Ryan stood. "What kinda choice would you like? The one that includes you stalking me all day without us talking? Or the one where we get along?"

"We can get along without you trying to land the unattainable blonde!"

Ryan's mouth fell open. "Is that what you think I'm trying to do?"

Claire stood, meeting his glare. "Just...back off."

Ryan took a step forward. "I love you. I love you, and you act like I'm some random frat boy trying to get lucky."

Jared sighed. "I should have packed ear plugs. I have nowhere to go."

"You just…." Claire trailed off.

I knew she must care about him. She had bit her tongue to keep from hurting his feelings, which Claire never did.

Ryan took another step. He was only a few inches from her face. "Say it."

"I've told you. A million times! It's not going to happen."

He shook his head. "No, say you don't love me. Say you don't see me in that way and I'm just a helpless human to you. Say you hate me! Say something! I'm tired of your vague excuses!"

"I don't need excuses!" she yelled. "I don't want that!" She pointed to us. "I don't want a family like I had or they have! You want children! You want a normal life, Ryan. I'm not it!"

"I just want you! Whatever that is, I want it!"

Claire frowned. Her body shook with anger. She grabbed his collar with both fists. Ryan leaned away slightly and winced, waiting for her to land a punch on his face. Claire's lips pursed together, and then she pulled him to her, pressing her lips against his, hard.

"Agh," Jared said, turning.

Ryan paused in shock, and then his body melted against hers. He wrapped his arms around her, pulling her closer, and she wrapped her fingers around the back of his neck. The kiss was so intense that it looked nearly painful.

Bex giggled, but they didn't hear him. After a minute or two, it was uncomfortable to watch, so we all meandered to the other side of the cavern. Jared seemed to be in a foul mood, which bothered me. Why he was so against Claire and Ryan was a mystery to me. They were perfect for each other, and clearly loved each other.

"I wonder if that will happen for me," Bex said, glancing back.

"Don't look. No telling what's going on back there," Jared said, picking up a rock and throwing it.

"It might," I said, smiling. "Don't listen to Jared. He knows I'm the best thing that ever happened to him."

Jared grabbed my hand and squeezed. "Of course you are. Why would you believe I've thought otherwise?"

I shrugged. "You're so against them." I gestured behind us. "Like my mother was so against us. Because it makes things hard."

Jared pulled me closer and wrapped his arms around my knees. "I just don't like Ryan. It has nothing to do with you, or us."

I raised an eyebrow. "Why don't you like him?"

Jared shifted nervously. "Ryan is the closest I've come to losing the love of my life. That's not something you get over."

I touched his face. "I love you. Ryan loves Claire. Get over it."

Jared laughed once, and looked to Bex. "I hope it happens for you. I really do."

Bex rolled his eyes and stood, walking to the back of the tomb where the altar held the book. Kim spent a lot of time in that area, even slept there. Bex sat next to her, and their voices became a stream of quiet conversation.

I balanced on all fours trying to navigate my large body to a standing position. Just as I pushed myself from the rock floor, my stomach clenched, and I stumbled. Jared caught me, but I couldn't stand straight up.

"Contraction?" he said, frowning.

"I don't...I don't know," I said, breathing through the pain.

Bex and Claire were immediately at our side, with Kim and Ryan trailing behind.

"The baby?" Bex said. "Should I set up?"

"No," Jared said. Let's let her rest. See if it eases up."

Claire nodded, and assisted Jared in helping me to our makeshift bed. My feet up and relaxed, I tried to think about something else other than whether the pain would return. Labor was going to be a nightmare if I had to look forward to hours of that. I had hoped that my new abilities would anesthetize the pain a bit, but if the previous encounter with contractions had been any indication, I was screwed.

The pain crept up again, like a wave swallowing me whole.

"Breathe, sweetheart."

I sucked in through my nose and blew out from my mouth, but it didn't help the pain. A large fist had gripped my uterus and was digging in its fingers while I suffered the worst case of food poisoning ever recorded—that was what I felt.

"Should we set up?" Bex said again.

"No," Jared said firmly. "We're just timing them now."

We waited several minutes, and then I felt another contraction, but it wasn't nearly as painful. They became less frequent and painful before stopping all together. Everyone in the room breathed a collective sigh of relief when Jared deemed the event a false alarm. He wouldn't allow me to sit up, though, or even leave the bed after that. He or Claire would walk me to the hole in the floor if I needed to relieve myself. It was half-humiliating, half-frightening. My body hadn't felt like my own for quite a while, but now there was no control over the situation.

We had no idea what went on in the world aboveground. I wondered what Beth and Chad were doing, if they worried about us, and about Cynthia and Lillian. If they leaned on each other for support, waiting to hear their grandchild had been born and that all of their children were alive. Even though I knew I needed to stay positive in those last difficult days, lying in bed with nothing to do but read the same magazines or think, my mind effortlessly traveled to less trivial things.

Checkers and chess were no longer entertaining. Even watching the others play cards irritated me. We were nearing the end of July, and I was so large I could barely maneuver. I had to let my mind wander to get away from the darkness of the tomb, from the fact that we were living in a tomb at all, and the dripping. For the love of all things holy, the dripping. That sound alone nearly pushed me out of my mind.

I would close my eyes, and pretend I was at Brown on the Main Green, lying with Jared while the summer air weaved through the trees. I blocked out the echoing and murmuring inside the tomb, and replaced it with laughing and jovial sounds of flag football on warm days, and the wonderful smells wafting from the Gate. Even my dorm room at

Andrews was an escape. Mostly, I concentrated on our oak tree, and the loft. I still mourned our first home, but in my mind, it was untouched. Recalling every memory of every place I'd spent with Jared was the only thing that kept me sane at that point. That, and watching Claire and Ryan fall in love. Their sweet conversations, and the way they reveled every moment with each other, kept me away from the darkness.

As the first of August came and went, my memories became harder to enjoy. They just mocked me. Us. Our faces had all grew pale, begging to see the sun again. Not even the promise of safety was worth this. Quiet times with Jared were something I had always wanted, but not in this prison. Not in this tomb, where I already felt dead.

A small twinge in my stomach made me hold my breath. It went away, but soon another came, and then another. They were stronger, and the more I hoped they would go away, the quicker and more intense they came.

I tried to breathe, but the air was so stale. When I tried to concentrate on breathing through the pain, all I could hear was the water dripping. Always dripping. It was maddening. I was in labor, and going to give birth inside a drippy, cold hole in the ground.

"No," I whispered.

Jared read a book a few feet from the mattress, noticeably waiting for me to tell him I was uncomfortable. I didn't want to say it. Speaking the words made it real. There would be movement towards the supplies, and the unpacking of all the medical paraphernalia I didn't want to see.

Before another contraction came, I pushed myself out of bed. "I have to get out of here."

Jared put down his worn copy of The Catcher in the Rye, and turned to face me. When he saw I was standing, he stood, too. "Nina, you have to lay down."

"I can't," I shook my head. "It's enough, Jared. I can't stay here, anymore. We need to find somewhere else."

"There is nowhere else."

I bent my knees and awkwardly bent over to pick up a few of my things lying around the bed. "Well, we can't stay here. I can't...I won't have my baby here."

Jared sighed. "Nina, stop. You're being irrational."

"Okay, so I'm irrational. But, I'm going to be irrational outside, where I can breathe."

Jared tried to touch my hand, but I pulled away. "You know you can't," he said.

"I can, and I'm going."

Ryan crossed his arms. "Then go."

"What?" Jared seethed.

"She's stronger than all of us. If she doesn't want to stay, we can't make her."

"See?" I said to Jared, pointing to Ryan. "He listens to me. You're not listening!"

"Sweetheart," Jared said, holding his hands in front of him. "You know what's waiting up there for us. We'll be attacked the second we breach the stairs."

"Just for a minute," I said, trying to nonchalantly slide by him. I grabbed my stomach and hunched over a bit, trying to casually weather another contraction.

Ryan touched Jared's arm. "Jared, we got through an entire city of shells. If she wants to breathe some fresh air after nearly sixty days in a cave, I say let her."

"You don't have a say, so shut up," Jared said through his teeth.

"I don't either?" I said. I hobbled toward the entrance slowly, but Jared matched every step.

"Of course you do," he said. "Just...just let me think for a minute."

I closed my eyes tight. They twitched every time the drops of water slid from the rock wall to the ground. "That's the problem. I can't think in here. I can't breathe. I can't sleep. I feel like I'm dying!"

"Jared," Ryan began.

"Shut the hell up!"

"Maybe we all need some fresh air," Bex said.

With wide eyes, Jared and Claire craned their necks at their little brother.

Jared's jaws worked under his skin, and he struggled to relax enough to speak to me in a calm voice. "Nina, for all we know the devil is up there. They will stop at nothing now."

Ryan shrugged. "Sometimes you gotta dance with the devil to get out of Hell."

The further we got to the entrance, the darker it became. Bex had set up twin-head industrial light stands around the perimeter, so bright that at first that when they were all lit, it felt like day. Now the shadows they cast were just another reminder of our prison.

I moved quickly to the doorway, and Claire grabbed my wrist. "Maybe we should sedate her?"

I yanked my arm back, easily shouldering past her. "You're not keeping me here against my will! I know I sound crazy! I feel crazy! This place is making me crazy! I don't want to leave forever. I just...I just want a couple of minutes of sunshine. Just a moment to feel alive again."

Ryan appeared in front of me, holding up his hands. "Whoa, buddy. You're getting yourself all worked up," he said. He spoke through nervous laughter, trying to lighten the mood. "You need to take a minute to think about this. No one is making you stay, but maybe if you think about this a little more, you'll reconsider."

Jared looked to me with hope in his eyes.

"I thought you were on my side," I said.

"I am, Nigh. I've always been on your side."

"No one's on my side. No one hears me."

Ryan relaxed a bit. "Just try to clear your head and think about it. You're not a prisoner here. You're here to keep the baby safe until it's born."

I nodded. "Okay, I've thought about it. I can't stand it anymore. Who wants to have their baby in a tomb? Not me. This was a bad idea. I just need to go. I have to go."

I made my way to the entrance that led to the stairs, but Jared stood in my way, his fingers digging into my shoulders. "I can't let you go, sweetheart. If you go upstairs, they'll kill you."

"But, we...you...you need to get me out of here, okay? I don't want to be here any more."

Jared nodded, his voice low and calm. "I understand. As soon as the baby comes, we'll leave. I promise."

I shook my head, the tears cascading down my cheeks. I took a step back. "No. No, I don't want to have the baby here. I can't stay here another night. Not another second."

"That's a prize-winning freakout, right there," Kim said without emotion.

Jared grimaced. "You're not helping, Kim. Listen," he said, returning his attention to me.

My body shook. I was in control of nothing. Not my body, not where I slept. I couldn't even go to the bathroom alone or take a walk. It was too much. Too much.

"You can't make me stay here. I can leave when I want."

"You're right. You can leave when you want, but...I want you to stay. The second you're aboveground, Nina, you'll regret your choice. Just...trust me? Please? Just a little bit longer. Can you stay with me a little bit longer?"

Tiny twin rivers dripped from my jaw onto my dirty shirt. I closed my eyes, but all I could hear was the dripping. The damn dripping. It wouldn't stop.

"No," I whispered. I ran for the door, and Claire and Jared grabbed my arms. With my full strength, I took one step after another, slowly but surely making my way to the doorway.

Claire grunted against my strength. "Nina, stop!"

Bex joined his siblings, grabbing both of my ankles and wrapping his feet around them. I could have broken free, but I didn't want to hurt him. I didn't want to hurt any of them, I just needed to be aboveground, to breathe fresh air and feel the sun on my skin. To hear my voice—just one time—without an echo behind it.

"Nina, look at me! Look at me!" Jared said, positioning his face in front of mine. "You have to stop. You're going to get yourself killed, and the baby will die. Do you hear me? We'll all die!"

I stopped struggling, and my body went limp as I sobbed on the ground against my husband. My focus on survival, irrational or not, had become a monster.

Claire and Bex took a step back with labored breath. I'd given all three of them a run for their money.

Jared stood and pulled me with him. "Okay?"

I nodded, watching him walk into the tomb. "I'm sorry."

Chapter Twenty
Legion

I bolted for the top of the stairs, shoving the altar out of the way. I crawled out of the hole, squinting against the bright sun filtering in through the rotunda.

I took a deep breath, letting the warm, fresh air fill my lungs. I bathed in it, taking in every bit before Jared dragged me back underground. After a few seconds, the warm air went away, and the cold, dark feeling of the tomb surrounded me. Jared had barely let me take an entire breath before he'd forced me to return.

I opened my eyes and realized I was still in the Sepulchre. The room was full of shells, poised to pounce. I could hear Jared crawling up the stairs, yelling my name, but immediately I was attacked. I fought off one, and then two and three at a time. By the time Jared reached the top, I had already taken out half the shells in a fury of moves I didn't even have to think about. A small woman threw herself at me, her arms flailing about. Jared incapacitated her with a single blow. Claire and Ryan reached the top, quickly followed by Bex, and the mob inside the Sepulchre quickly thinned. More filed in, though, and we were running out of room.

"Back up!" Jared commanded. "Back downstairs!"

The walls shook, and two large, dark forms squeezed their misshapen bodies into the entrance of the Sepulchre. They weren't shells, but demons, large demons with gray skin and mouths full of teeth under moist snouts.

The one on the right grabbed Jared while the other took my shirt in one hand, and slammed my back against the opposite wall.

“Hey!” Kim yelled from the mouth of the stairway. “Get the hell out of here!” Even though the monsters stood two heads taller than her, she didn’t seem nervous in the slightest. The demons wailed at her, shielding themselves with their shoulders, but they didn’t retreat.

The demon that Jared fought barked at the black-eyed minions filing into the room, and before anyone could react, a half-dozen of the shells dove at Kim, pushing her down the stairway. Her scream faded as she rolled further underground.

Bex leapt in after her, and Claire and Ryan went to work on Jared’s demon.

I tried to rip my shirt to escape the grip of the brute, but his hands were gigantic, and I couldn’t break free. A shell in military fatigues slipped into the room, walked to me without hesitation, and held a pistol to my temple.

The demon holding me signaled his partner, capturing Jared, Claire and Ryan’s attention as well. In a move so fast I could barely follow, Jared pulled his sidearm from his belt and held it on the shell. The entire room froze.

“Don’t. Move,” Jared said.

I nodded. I was sure he was furious with me. His eyes glossed over, and his teeth clenched.

The shell spoke. “We’re taking her out of this place. Do not follow, or we’ll cut the child from her in the street.”

Jared held his gun on the shell, his entire body shaking with rage. Finally he lowered his weapon a little. “I love you,” he said, immediately tensing his arms again.

I smiled. “It’s okay. You’ll just save me like you always do, right?”

“Right. Just wait for me.”

“I’ll wait for you,” I said.

Hesitant, and clearly conflicted, Jared lowered his weapon. In the next moment, I was dragged backward with such force that I felt I was flying. The rooms of the Sepulchre flew past, and then I was in the sunlight. The streets blurred as the demon raced me through the old city. A few minutes later, I was dragged into an old building.

The fiend tossed me, and I skidded to the middle of a concrete slab. At first glance, the room was a filthy mess, and then I realized the pile of sheets was a provisional bed. No medical supplies or baby blankets.

"What will you do to him?" I asked, hesitant to make eye contact with the rotting pile of flesh standing at the door.

"He waits to devour him."

I groaned. Pain seared through my body, and I knew I would have to calm down if I were to slow down the contractions. The more time I gave Jared to reach us, the better chance we had. I climbed onto the tufts of sheets, and leaned back on the heels of my hands.

A shell, a large woman, was allowed entry. I braced myself to be attacked, but she grabbed a fistful of my sweat-drenched hair, lifted me to my feet, and then ripped off my clothes with her free hand. She pulled an oversized nightgown over my head, pushing me to the floor. I raised my hands to defend myself, but she only grabbed my wrists and tied them with cloth restraints attached to wires. Those thick wires were fastened to the cement floor with bolts. Once she completed her task, the woman left me alone with the demon.

Dirty windows lined the wall to my left. The outlines of dozens of shells cast shadows against the muddy glass. I wondered if I could take the giant standing guard at the door, but I knew that Jared and Claire had trouble with him, and I hadn't exactly trained how to ignore labor pains while on the offensive. I subtly tested the bolts. They seemed fairly secure, but I was sure I could break free when the time came. The one exit would pose a problem; I didn't know what else waited on the other side. I could probably break through the window, but once again, the contractions…

I tensed, trying to breath through the pain. "Oh...my God!" I grunted. Deep breaths turned into panting. Sweat dripped from my hairline into my eyes. Just when I thought I might break in half, the contraction subsided. I let my body relax against an old cushion propped against the wall.

"Can I have some water?" I asked.

The demon's beady eyes shifted toward me. He snarled, and then looked ahead.

The cramping grew more intense with the next few contractions, and then I felt a warm gush between my legs. When I looked down at the clear liquid that had drenched the sheets, I realized my water had broke. A short relief of pressure came, quickly followed by a spasm so intense that I nearly passed out.

I wailed, and moved back against the wall. Nothing I did escaped the agony. "Please," I whimpered between breaths, "help me." Another wave washed over me; my blood-curdling screams echoed throughout the building. The panting didn't help, nothing helped. My hands balled into fists, shaking and white-knuckled.

When the agony paused for a minute or two, I would let my body fall limp against the cushion. Already exhausted, I knew unless Jared saved us, my abilities would be worthless.

The intensity of the next contraction took me by surprise. I sat up straight, my knees bent and widely spread, and I strained against my restraints. Unsure of what I was even saying, my mouth formed every obscenity I'd ever heard in my life. When it was over, I collapsed against the cushion, bawling, whimpering for my husband. Pressure between my thighs provoked me to reach down. Something soft and wet, covered in hair was barely peeking out from inside me. The baby was beginning to crown. I looked to the demon. He didn't even seem to be on alert. Jared wasn't even close.

I closed my eyes, making a concentrated effort to relax all of my muscles. Even when the pain came again, I refused to give into it. I refused to push. When the agony became too much, I held my screams inside. Any tensing on my part could push out the baby, and that was something I refused to do until I saw my husband. The waves crashed into me, and I lowered my chin to my chest, bit my lip, and stared intently at the wall across the room. I would. Not. Push.

My body shook uncontrollably. Just as the pain subsided, movement outside the windows caught my attention. The guard at the door made a noise and shifted. He was nervous. Jared was here.

The shadows of the shells weaved back and forth. There was a large explosion, then a blotch of crimson sprayed against the mud on the glass, highlighted by a ball of fire. The glass broke, and my husband pushed through, his eyes wild but focused. He immediately attacked the guard at the door, filling the creature's head with an entire clip of bullets. Once he fell to the ground, Kim ran into the glass opening. She made her way to the door, and closed it, holding her palms flat against the metal.

"I got it!" she said. She was covered in blood, and noticeably injured.

"Are you okay?" I called to her.

She smiled. "Never been better. You just worry about delivering that ba—"

Before she could finish her sentence, a shell burst through the broken glass and pointed his gun at Kim. She turned, her eyes wide.

"No!" I screamed.

Jared charged the shell, but was too late. The bullet burst through Kim's chest, blowing her back against the door.

"Kim!" I cried, watching her limp body slide down the door to the ground. Her eyes were open, but she was dead before she hit the floor. "Kim!"

"Nina!" Jared yelled, running to me. He slid on his knees and released me from the restraints, and then slipped his backpack from his shoulders, opening it and pulling out supplies.

Before I could speak, the overwhelming spasms engulfed me. I wailed, but I wouldn't push.

Jared checked between my legs, and his eyes grew wide. "He's crowning, sweetheart. Push."

I shook my head. "She's dead."

"I know, but you have to push."

"I can't."

Jared smiled. "Yes, you can. You've done so well."

I peeked at Kim. "They're out there. Waiting for him."

Jared touched my cheek. "I'm here. I won't let anything happen to him."

"They abandoned us," I cried.

"Who?" Jared said, laying out sterile cloths.

"Heaven! Where are they? Where is Samuel?" The pain came again.

"Nina, push!" Jared said.

"They'll kill him!"

Jared grabbed my hand and squeezed. "Look at me," he said, watching me as I panted. "I won't let that happen. We will protect him. Together."

Tears welled up in my eyes. "I don't know if I can."

"You can, and you will. Now, push!"

I nodded and pushed myself up on the heels of my hands. When the contraction came, I pushed through it. My voice was low and gruff and I grunted, using all of my remaining strength.

Claire and Bex jumped through the glass opening, and paused, seeing Kim's body sitting still against the door. They walked over to her. Claire gently shut her eyes, and then she rushed over to me. She got on her knees behind me, and hooked her elbows under my arms.

I stared at Kim, but Claire used her cheek to bar my line of sight. "Don't look, honey."

I wailed, mourning for my friend. Claire hugged me tight. "I'm so sorry. I'm so sorry," she repeated, over and over.

Ryan leaned against the opposite wall, his rifle in hand, tears drawing clean lines down his dirty face.

"Could you grab a cloth and wipe her forehead?" Claire said. Ryan didn't hesitate, digging through the pack and then patting down my brow. He combed back my wet hair with his fingers and then kissed my cheek. "Doing good, Nigh. Hang in there."

I began to speak, but the urge to push came again, so I heaved. I pushed so hard that my body trembled. Yelling seemed to help, so I did. I yelled, and screamed, and cried out. I cried for Kim, and for the pain, and for fear of what would happen once Bean was vulnerable.

Jared held open my shaking knees. "You're almost there, Nina."

Just as he said the words, the baby seemed to spill out of me and into Jared's arms.

He laughed out loud, in shock, holding his blood-covered child in his arms.

Claire helped me to relax back against the cushion, and then she assisted Jared in cleaning off the infant and cutting the cord.

Bex pushed his back against the door. "We've got some nasty ones on the way! They're boiling up straight from Hell!"

Ryan gripped his rifle, and Claire stood. "Oh my God," she whispered. "They've sent an entire Legion."

Chapter Twenty-One
Mother

There is a distinct difference between the ability to create life and the innate need to protect it; to cherish it. The life you've created is the one being you love most in the universe, and that intense love evolves into something that goes far beyond a sense of duty. It is instinct; pure and undeniable. As a direct result, one must neglect all else to preserve it. Even those we have claimed to love before.

The mother that throws herself in front of an oncoming car, the mother that eats a can of generic peaches when the last bit of food isn't enough to share, the mother that wears a ratty dress to work so that she can keep much-needed shoes on those tiny, precious feet…that is the distinction of a mother's love: self-sacrifice.

In the second it took for those tiny lungs to fill with enough air to belt out that first glorious cry, nothing else mattered. Not even me.

"Is he okay?" I asked.

Jared in awe at the gooey, glistening child in his arms. "Uh...yeah. She's okay."

"She?" I said, stunned. I had prepared myself for almost everything that could happen when I delivered. A girl was not one of them.

"It's a girl?" Claire squealed.

"It's a girl?" Bex groaned.

Jared wrapped her in a clean blanket, and carefully lifted the tiny bundle to look into her eyes. He had no expression except for the smallest hint of a smile. His eyes focused on me, and then put her in my arms as if he were passing on the most fragile, priceless, precious treasure in existence.

I nestled her in the crook of my arm, and until that moment the times I thought I had sacrificed seemed trivial. Everything and everyone in my life was less important, less urgent. My life was simply an extension of the tiny, soft, innocent wonderment before me. I knew how millions of other women before me could behave so erratically, be so forgiving, and so courageous. My heart was no longer on the inside of my body. It was in my arms.

"Jared?" Bex said. With one hand he held the door closed, with other, he gently slid Kim's lifeless body away from the door and against the wall.

A loud bang vibrated the wall, and Bex flew back, skidding across the floor. The door blew open, and creatures filed into the room, immediately attacking. A foul odor filled the room, and I held my baby close to me. Jared stayed close, violently fending off any demons that dared get close enough to his family.

Every window on the opposite wall from the door exploded. Jared covered us with his body to shield us from flying glass. When the dust cleared, Samuel stepped into the room, standing next to a familiar face in full armor.

"Michael," Jared breathed, stunned. It was Isaac's father, his entire army of warrior angels behind him.

The demons snarled and shrieked.

"You shall not touch this child," Michael said, drawing a long sword.

"Come!" Samuel challenged, raising his arms. "We welcome Hell's most terrible wrath!"

The demon that had taken me from the Sepulchre lifted his head and bleated, and then led a charge into the street.

Bex and Claire stood to the side, watching hundreds of demons surge past them, casting off wind like a freight train barreling through the room. The clash outside between

Heaven and Hell was audible, like nothing I'd ever heard before, and then at once, it was silent, crossing planes.

Jared grabbed each side of my face with a broad smile. "We did it, Nina! Heaven will protect her!"

I sighed with relief and hugged my daughter to my chest. The quiet we shared was frozen in time. The end of the war around us was instantaneous. Bex, Ryan, Claire and Jared all looked in wonder at my little girl. She lay still, peering around with her big, round, cloudy eyes, blinking at the bright light.

Jared kneeled before me, still breathing hard, his face red and marked with shades of blood and dirt from his fight to reach us. Ryan and Claire crowded around us, their worried expressions softened by the sight of the child wrapped in my arms.

"You're amazing," Jared said. His voice cracked an infinitesimal amount as he spoke, but I couldn't look away to see his expression. The little girl in my arms was breathtaking.

Claire took a few silent steps until she was next to me. She rubbed her palm on her jeans and then reached out her small hand, extending her index finger to touch the baby's pinky. "She's…here," she whispered, in awe.

"You did it," Ryan said with a half-smile.

Jared crawled to the opposite side of Claire, tenderly putting one arm behind my neck, the other touching his daughter's cheek with his thumb. He kissed my hair and leaned in to whisper in my ear. "I didn't think I could love you more than I already did."

I looked into his eyes and smiled. "You did it, Jared. You saved us."

Jared's blue-gray eyes glossed over, and he pulled me closer, the three of us in a tender embrace.

After a few quiet moments, Jared's arms tensed, and he looked to the doorway. Claire flipped around, her hands balled into fists at her side. Bex stood in front of my makeshift bed, crouched in a defensive stance.

Ryan quickly cocked his gun and aimed at the door, ready for whatever the Hybrids were bracing for. "What now?" he said, his eyes focused at the same point as the others.

Claire shoved Ryan against the wall and then pointed at him. "Stay there," she said firmly. "Don't. Move."

Ryan lowered his weapon, and waited.

The door opened slowly, and a man in a white suit walked, slow and lithe, through the threshold. His hair was shiny and black, his eyes deep-set and calm. He was beautiful and grotesque at the same time; a baby-faced supermodel with eons of hate and bitterness flowing through his veins.

Bex took a step, but Claire held out her hand and flattened it against his chest, restraining him. "Stand next to Ryan."

"But…" Bex protested.

"Do it!" she growled. I'd never heard her take that tone with her little brother.

The man's eyes darted to the youngest Ryel, his head unmoving. It was unnatural, frightening. Bex slowly walked to the wall, wary of the pair of eyes that studied his every move.

I pulled my infant daughter closer to me, turning slightly so that my shoulder was in a position to protect her. I didn't notice the movement until I realized it had drawn the man's attention back to us.

"Desecration," the man breathed. His was more of a hiss than a voice. "Even more than your father."

"Do not speak to her," Jared said, his tone low and terrifying.

Ryan looked to Claire. He was confused and worried, but he didn't move.

The man took another step.

Jared stood, and lifted his hand, pointing at the black-haired man. "She belongs to Him. You can't touch her. You may kill us all, but He's commanded that she live."

The man took in a deep breath through his nose, his eyes rolling back into his head. His lids shuttered, and then popped open, focusing on the baby. When he spoke, his voice was many; distant and loud simultaneously. "If you've noticed, I quite enjoy doing things He forbids."

"Should I shoot?" Ryan whispered out of the corner of his mouth.

"No," Claire said, her voice strained. "Don't move."

Ryan frowned, clearly unsettled. "What is it?"

"The Devil," Bex said.

The man's pupils bled into the whites of his eyes, the darkness inside them glistening from the light of the fire outside. He took another step.

A large vein bulged from his pasty forehead as his calculating eyes targeted my daughter.

Jared didn't wait for him to take another step. He charged, stopping abruptly when the Devil grabbed him by the throat. Claire immediately reacted, attacking him with astounding speed. Her small body flew against the wall, and Ryan reacted.

She held up a hand. "Don't," she said, standing.

Jared managed to pull free, and then he attacked him again with a series of punches. They traded blows, and suddenly Jared was struck to the ground. Claire rushed Satan again, but she was blown back, this time held by an unseen force high against the wall. She screamed in agony as dozens of deep, bloody gashes formed across her face, neck and body. Blood oozed from her wounds and down the front of her clothes, dripping from her shoes onto the floor beneath her.

"No!" Ryan yelled, raising his weapon.

Bex reluctantly stopped him.

Ryan grabbed Bex's collar. "Help her!"

Jared crawled to all fours, and then attacked the King of Hell again. He groaned and grunted with each heavy blow Satan dealt him, and soon he was overpowered, and thrown to the floor. The man in white jerked his hand, commanding Jared's body against the wall under Claire. Her blood flowed from her wounds and dripped in a steady stream onto her brother's shoulder.

Claire closed her eyes, her lids fluttering. "Help us," she whispered. "Don't you see? Help us," she begged.

The Devil took another step. He was just a few feet from my makeshift bed. I held my daughter's tiny head in the crook of my neck and touched my lips to her white, wispy hair. She smelled like her father, but softer, more pure. I looked up at her assassin from under my brow, terrified and hopeless, cowering in his presence.

Jared took off once again, his form obscured by the speed. They crashed together, and with barely visible movements, they blurred from one space in the room to the other, stopping momentarily, and then moving again. Soon they were back where they started, and Jared was on the floor, his blood spilling from his wounds.

Satan leaned in slowly, relishing my terror.

"Help her," Claire begged in a tiny whisper.

Ryan moved toward me with desperation on his face, but Bex grabbed his shoulder. "Let me go!" he said, struggling. Bex wrapped both of his arms around my friend, forbidding him to step in.

Bex and Ryan were going to watch us all die. If Bex could somehow escape with Ryan, Claire could be saved, but that would leave my child vulnerable. A million thoughts ran through my head, hopes that even if I were killed, Jared would survive long enough to get our baby to safety.

In that moment, anger replaced my fear. I remembered Eli's words, and courage I never knew I owned swelled inside of me. "You can't have her," I seethed, lifting my chin in defiance. "I am not afraid of you." My eyes filled with angry tears.

He smiled. "And what will you do?" he said, looking over to Kim's lifeless body. In one blurry moment she was in his arms. He cradled her, looking almost paternal as he brushed her cheek with his blackened fingers. He scanned her face with a somber expression, and then leaned down to smell her hair. "She had a heartbeat not an hour ago. Dreams. Aspirations. And now," he said, tossing her limp body across the room with one hand, "nothing."

I closed my eyes, unwilling to let fear rob me of rational thinking. Before I was a mother, I might have run from the room, but I had carried her inside of me for the better part of a year, and I had survived Hell before. Something inside of me whispered that my child was safe in my arms. I would have faith in what Eli had told me, and I would stand my ground. Nothing was stronger than a mother's love for her child…not even Satan.

Claire dropped to the floor, and Ryan rushed over to her. Jared attempted to get to his feet, but instead resorted to crawling toward me. Jared made his way to his family, and then slowly stood on his knees, weaving with exhaustion. Once again, he was all that stood between us and death.

Satan took Jared's throat in his hand and lifted him off the ground. Jared gripped the man's arm with both hands as his feet dangled above the floor. Moving his arm to the side, Satan held Jared in the best position to watch the end.

Long, blackened fingers reached for the child. Without thinking, I pulled her to the other side of my body, and with my free hand, gripped the Devil's wrist. It was cold and thin. My skin blazed against it.

"Don't. Touch. Her," I breathed.

He frowned, noticeably confused. He tried to advance his hand to my child, but he was unable to move.

"That's far enough, Lucifer," Samuel said. As usual, he had blinked into our plane without detection, but time Eli was with him.

"What is this?" Lucifer said, struggling to reach the child. He was clearly straining, but he was powerless in my grasp.

Eli smiled. "Daddy says no."

Lucifer wrenched his hand back, his eyes wild with anger. "He's allowing this…this human to defy me?" he howled, dropping Jared to the ground. "Do you know what this means?"

"War?" Samuel grinned. "Too late."

Satan began to speak, but Eli held up his hand. "Enough, Lucifer. It's over. He has chosen to spare the child."

Lucifer charged at us, his arms extended, his fingers curled, preparing to kill the baby angel in my arms. Just before he reached us, he was blown back and held against the wall. Large, long fingers curled around his neck. Lucifer's eyes widened. The Prince of Darkness was afraid.

"Gabriel?" Lucifer said, surprised.

"He said enough," Gabriel snarled. "Go back to your pits, Satan. He will not ask it of you again."

"Dad!" Bex said, his hopeful and excited expression matching Claire's.

A figure stepped into the room from outside, through the broken remains of the windows. It was Michael, battle worn but victorious. “Enough.”

Samuel stood beside Michael, crossing his arms; Eli stood before the warriors. His immaculate white shirt was a stark contrast to their heavy armor. Another form stepped over the broken glass and into the room, and then another. Soon, twenty members of Michael’s army were in the room.

“The time of great suffering has come,” Lucifer seethed. He stepped to the side, away from Gabriel’s grip.

Eli lowered his chin. “You will leave this family alone. Hell will leave Gabriel’s children, and their children’s children, alone. He has commanded it,” he said firmly. “The child has found favor with God.”

“It is not human!” Lucifer hissed.

Gabriel took a step, his hands balled into fists at his sides. “She is my granddaughter.” His voice boomed, but he did not yell. “I swear to the Most High, your punishment will have you wishing for the pits of Hell if you threaten her again.”

“Vile!” the Devil screamed. “Vulgar! Iniquitous! Despicable!” After his tantrum, he smiled. “Well. He’s finally stooped to my level. How delicious.”

“Blasphemy!” Samuel said, taking a step. Eli stopped him.

Before Eli could utter a command, Satan disappeared.

I took a deep breath, letting out a sob. Jared crawled back to us, wrapping his bloody, sweaty arms around our daughter and me. I shook as I cried, kissing my baby’s soft, delicate forehead as Jared kissed mine.

“Claire?” Ryan said, holding her in his arms.

Eli calmly walked across the room, kneeling beside them. “You look a fright.”

Claire managed one weak laugh. "Really? I thought for a brush with the Devil I look pretty fly."

Gabe joined them, evaluating her wounds. "Pretty ugly, kiddo." He looked to Eli.

Eli motioned to Samuel, and Samuel was suddenly kneeling next to Eli, lifting Claire from Ryan's grasp.

"Wait," Ryan said.

Samuel ignored him, setting Claire on her feet. Her clothes were still ripped, but the gashes from her face and body had disappeared.

Gabe helped Ryan to his feet with one hand, and hooked his arm around Bex's neck with the other. "Thank you," Gabe said, seemingly to himself. I knew it was God he spoke to.

Ryan pulled Claire into his arms and smashed his lips onto hers, kissing her over and over. "You okay?" he said, visibly upset.

She smiled. "Just another day at work."

He hugged her tightly, a single tear running down his dirty cheek. He breathed in quickly, and then exhaled a faltering breath.

"In case I forget to tell you later," she said, pulling back. "I kinda love you."

Ryan laughed once. "Just remember who said it, first."

She nudged him, and they turned to watch Bex slowly return to Kim's body. He frowned, trying to hold back the overwhelming sadness that we all felt.

Ryan fetched a sheet from the corner of the room, and Claire helped him to spread it on the floor. Bex lifted Kim's body from the floor, laying her gently on the sheet. He straightened her bent legs, and crossed her hands against her chest.

Eli stood next to Ryan. "We offer Kim's soul to you, Father. Please welcome her into your kingdom, and your arms. Extend comfort to her father and to her friends, and remind them daily that the sacrifice she made, was made in love."

"I'm sorry," Bex said, covering her face with the sheet.

Ryan choked, and he and Claire wrapped their arms around each other.

My emotions were so tapped that I couldn't find the tears to cry. I just stared at her outline under the sheet in disbelief. She was really gone. I imagined the horrible task of informing her father, and Beth. How we could possibly explain how she died?

"We'll take care of it," Jared said. "She'll receive the burial and respect she deserves."

"I just want her back," I said quietly. "This is my fault. I shouldn't have left. We would have all been safe if I'd just stayed in the Sepulchre."

Jared touched my cheek. "Anxiety is a struggle for anyone. You did what you believed you had to do in the moment, and the survival instinct is nearly impossible to ignore as a Hybrid. You didn't want this. Kim knew that."

I nodded, but knew the guilt would haunt me for a lifetime. The threat I felt in the tomb was very real at the time, but looking back, I let my fear get the best of me, and it cost Kim her life. I would carry that for the rest of mine.

Gabe kneeled beside me to better see his grandchild. "She's absolutely beautiful," he said, touching her tiny hand.

"Thank you," I said, my eyes finally filling with tears.

"You don't understand what you've done here," he said, wiping the tender skin under my eye. "You saved her, and she will save us all."

“That’s a big job for a little girl,” Jared said, looking down to the precious bundle in my arms. “Good thing she’s strong like her mom.”

I lifted my chin, and touched Jared’s lips to mine. His lips were warmer than mine for the first time in months. His scent mixed with our baby’s, and I felt lightness from relief that was vaguely familiar. Feeling safe was like a distant memory, and it came to me in such a surreal way, as if I couldn’t trust it. But, our family was safe. We earned a new beginning for us, for all of us, that Heaven had created. With that thought, I looked on the precious beauty in my arms. “Eden,” I whispered.

“What was that?” Jared said, nearly euphoric.

“Her name is Eden.”

Epilogue

My hands were soaking wet. I wiped them on my gown, but they immediately became moist again. You can do this, I thought. This is nothing. Definitely been through worse. I had, but there were hundreds of people watching. Waiting.

I turned to look for my husband. My eyes weren't what they were when I was pregnant, and it was very frustrating to return to being a normal human after experiencing life with abilities. An arm waving above the crowd caught my attention, and I saw Lillian smiling from ear to ear. Next to her sat Cynthia. Bex, Claire, and Ryan sat on the other side of my mother, with Jared on the end, trying to keep hold on an excited and wiggly Eden. She was ten months old, with rolls on rolls, and wavy blonde hair. Her cheeks were so chubby that they hung down like a basset hound's. I could see her big blue eyes all the way from my seat. She stood on Jared's lap, bouncing and waving, flashing her two gapped front teeth. It seemed to be all Jared could do to see around her, but it was her big brown bow that obstructed his view. I couldn't help but laugh watching him try to see around it.

We had spent the last ten months in utter bliss. I finished my senior year at Brown as any other student, sans husband and child. No more looking over my shoulder. No more fear. Life was normal. Better than normal. We were living our happily ever after, and our daughter watched our absolute joy in our new freedom.

"Nina Grey Ryel," the announcer called.

I walked up the stairs and across the stage, taking my diploma from the president. She greeted me, and I made my way across, shaking the hands of people I'd never met, but were obviously important at Brown University.

Beth and Jared, Tucker, Josh and Lisa were among my classmates, and we were sad and excited that we had finally made it to graduation.

After the ceremony, we made our way to the famed Van Winkle gates, and danced through with the band and Bruno, Brown's mascot. Beth and I laughed and skipped all the way down the street, meeting my family at the end.

I was surrounded with hugs and kisses from my in-laws, and even from my mother. Eden reached for me, and Jared handed her to me, trading her for a kiss. Eden wrapped her chubby arms around my neck, tangling her fingers in my hair, and opening her mouth to give me a big, wet baby kiss on the cheek.

"Oh, thank you!" I said with a smile.

"I thought we could meet for dinner," Lillian chirped.

"Yeah," I nodded. "Do we need to bring anything?"

"Nope," she winked. "I've been at it all morning." She kissed me again, and then nuzzled Eden's cheek before kissing her children goodbye. "See you at six!"

Jared stuffed his hands in his pockets. "We might be a little late, Mom. We've got to make a stop."

"Oh?" I said.

"It's your graduation present."

"What is it?" I said, lighting up.

Jared laughed. "You know I won't tell you!"

I feigned disappointment. "I loathe surprises!"

"No, you don't," he said, hugging me to his side.

Claire winked at Jared. "We'll see you guys at dinner. Congratulations! Bye, Edie!" She kissed Eden's fat fingers, and then she and Ryan walked to her Exige, wrapped in each other's arms. Bex rolled his eyes and reluctantly followed.

"I need to change," I said.

"Okay. We can do that, too."

Jared drove to the outskirts of town. We were on the same road as the warehouse, so I squirmed in my seat with excitement, believing Jared was taking me to see Eli. But we stopped several hundred yards from the warehouse. I could barely see it.

Jared pulled into the driveway of a two-story house.

"Where are we?"

"Home," he smiled.

"Huh?" I said, taken aback. I looked at the house again. It was white with green shutters, and had a porch with a swing. Very Norman Rockwell.

"Let's go," Jared said. As soon as his door shut, mine opened, and then he opened the back door to unfasten Eden from her car seat. "Come on!" he said, barely able to contain his enthusiasm.

I held his hand, and we walked to the front door. Jared used the key, and then pushed the door open. I couldn't believe my eyes. The inside was identical to the loft. The same pictures on the walls, the same decorations, even the same layout. The only difference was that the upstairs wasn't visible.

"It's ours?" I said, overwhelmed.

"It is. Our bedroom is upstairs, down the hall from Eden's, and there's a guest bedroom, too."

I hugged him tight, burying my face in his chest. "Jared! I love it! I can't believe you did this."

He suppressed a smile. "Cynthia isn't happy."

"She'll get over it!" I said, looking around in awe.

We trotted up the stairs, and I gasped at our bedroom. It was as if nothing had ever happened to our loft. It was the same. Excited to see the new additions, I rushed to Eden's room. Jared had made sure to decorate it exactly as it had been at Cynthia's. He sat Eden down in her crib with some toys, and then led me to the guest room by the hand. It was empty, and the walls were white and bare.

"You left this one for me, didn't you?" I said, squeezing his hand.

"I didn't know how you'd want it, so I thought I'd just leave it alone. A blank canvas."

"I love it. I love all of it. I will sleep better tonight than I have since we lost the loft." I looked at him. "You gave me back our home. I can't tell you what this means to me."

His eyebrows pulled together. "Not even a fraction of what you mean to me."

I leaned up on the balls of my feet and wrapped my arms around his neck. My lips pressed against his, and I smiled at the warmth he emanated. I'd missed how hot he felt against my human skin. His strong hands pressed against my back, and he pulled me closer, every emotion he'd ever felt coming through in that kiss.

"I'm happy," I whispered. "I'm so happy…," I said against his mouth, "and it's all because of you."

The End.

Acknowledgments

I must thank the person who pushed me to begin Providence. The same person who swung her pom-poms every step of the way, through every book, and in between. My dearest friend Beth, I thank you so much. Your support, encouragement and insistence has brought Providence -and me-to the end of this series. Every good thing that has happened to me in the last three years stemmed from your insistence that I could.

I would also like to thank my mother Brenda for her assistance in any way I asked, or that she could.

Many thanks to authors Jessica Park, Tammara Webber, Abbi Glines, Liz Reinhardt, and EL James for your advice, your encouragement, and direction. I adore each and every one of you, and I am so very glad that we crossed paths;

To Jim Thomsen for his patience and expertise;

To Dr. Ross Vanhooser for believing in me and putting action and risk behind that belief;

To Harmony Hempfling, who is the best listener, and a fantastic beta reader.

To Maryse at Maryse.net and reader Nikki Estep for their enthusiasm and being instrumental in my success as an author;

And to my amazing husband, Jeff. You are infinitely supportive, patient, and love me even when I'm ignoring you for fictional people. You are my partner in life; my everything, and I wouldn't think of doing any of this without you. I wouldn't want to. Thank you so much for being everything that you are.

Jamie McGuire

Born in Tulsa, OK, Jamie now resides in Enid, OK with her husband and three children. Jamie is a registered radiographer, as well as independent author. Jamie has also written books one and two in the Providence series, *Providence* and *Requiem*, and New York Times best selling contemporary romance, *Beautiful Disaster.* Visit JamieMcGuire.com for information on upcoming novels.

19925668R00159

Made in the USA
Lexington, KY
14 January 2013